Mike Mason's

Twenty-one Candles

Stories for Christmas

"It has been my delight to listen as Mike Mason read aloud many
of these stories—a score and one more of narratives that circle like
candlelight around a season when light is scarce. Now, reading them,
they bring a unique brightness, because in one way or another they
illuminate more than just snow scenes and families around hearth
fires. With a light and often whimsical touch, Mason's tales speak of the
way 'people dwelling in darkness have seen a great light' (Mt 12:16)."

> Luci Shaw
> *author of* **Breath for the Bones: Art, Imagination and Spirit**

"The best moments of Christmas are spent in the evening by the
fire, telling stories... stories of courage and conviction, of discovering anew 'peace on earth; goodwill toward men.' My friend, Mike
Mason, has penned a collection of heartwarming stories to be told
time and again, every Advent. May *Twenty-one Candles* become a
Christmas classic for years to come!"

> Joni Eareckson Tada
> *Joni and Friends International Disability Center*

"In the tradition of our favorite Christmas tales, passed down from
such masters as Charles Dickens and O. Henry, Mike Mason has
lit *Twenty-one Candles* to shine fresh light into our darkness. Some
shine with a mythopoeic ambiance, while others glow like mirrors
from day to day life. They celebrate Christmas in ways you'll want to

share. Gather around the Christmas tree; put another log on the fire. Mike Mason's stories want to be read aloud—read to families, to friends, to church groups—and you'll delight in sharing them."

D.S. Martin
author of Conspiracy of Light: Poems Inspired by the Legacy of C.S. Lewis

"If you haven't read Mike Mason you live an impoverished life. Here is a book of frosty magic, wings of light, and the enchanting music of wisdom. With characteristically honest and beautiful prose, Mason has given us a gift that will warm hearts and kindle contemplation. These are stories that both refresh and rebuke. Read them and be awakened to joy."

Andrew Case
author of Water of the Word

"These short stories are filled with charming, relatable characters discovering the spiritual origin and inspiration behind Christmas: Jesus Christ. *Twenty-one Candles* skillfully draws readers into its stories, inviting us to look beyond the veneer of a commercialized holiday season. Scratching the surface of our Christmas tradition, Mason captures glimpses of a loving God yearning to restore relationship with His children."

Leonard Buhler
President of Power to Change

"As a young Christian and a young writer, the fiction of Mike Mason always encouraged and inspired me. This collection of his Christmas stories does the same. Strong stories, bright stories, heart, and soul, and life stories that can be read anytime of year, but especially during Advent and Christmas. Pick up this little book and let Mike's imagination and the spirit of God fill you with light."

Murray Pura
*Author of **The White Birds of Morning***

"In *Twenty-one Candles* master storyteller Mike Mason has carved out another classic. Truly a book for everyone that will captivate and inspire with its humor and unique way of spreading the true spirit of Christmas."

Wally Armstrong
*author of **The Mulligan***

"*Twenty-one Candles* should be as mandatory as mistletoe and manger scenes. Mike Mason's collection of funny, poignant, and inspired stories is a rare gift. The Christmas Spirit is alive and well, my friends—read all about it!"

Carolyn Arends
*Recording artist and author of **Living the Questions***

"*Twenty-one Candles* captures the spirit of Christmas in a way all the commercial glitter never will. Mike shows the love and delight of the Messiah resonating in the hearts of those who need love and joy, and find them."

David Gregory
*author of **Dinner With a Perfect Stranger***

Also by Mike Mason

Fiction

The Furniture of Heaven
The Blue Umbrella
The Violet Flash
The Mystery of the Word: *Parables of Everyday Faith*

Non-Fiction

The Mystery of Marriage: *As Iron Sharpens Iron*
The Gospel According to Job
Practicing the Presence of People: *How We Learn to Love*
The Mystery of Children: *What Our Kids Teach Us About Childlike Faith*
Champagne for the Soul: *Celebrating God's Gift of Joy*
Adventures in Heaven

www.mikemasonbooks.com

Twenty-one Candles

Stories for Christmas

MIKE MASON

TWENTY-ONE CANDLES

Published by

Alphabet Imprints
4618 217A Street
Langley, BC Canada V3A 2N7

www.mikemasonbooks.com

ISBN 978-0-9936187-0-3

Alphabet Imprints is a division of Alphabet Communications Ltd.
www.alphabetimprints.com

Printed in USA

14 15 16 17 18   5 4 3 2 1

for Chris

Yabbakadoodles!

Contents

Foreword

Reading through this book, after almost three decades of friendship with Mike and his stories, I am crowded with feelings, memories, insights.

Loren Wilkinson introduced us, and I felt a kind of awe in meeting a man who made his living doing nothing but writing. I was early down the road of living as a professional artist—in my case, the art form was theatre—but already it was clear that my road would be cluttered with the many distractions that come in the business of running a theatre company. To the point where not much time gets spent actually creating the work.

Not so for Mike. Thirty years later, this is still what he does. Mike writes. He keeps the distractions of life, the machinery of "having a career," to a minimum—so that he can write. Think deeply, feel vividly, and write.

If you know Mike's masterful book *The Mystery Of Marriage*, you know that he has always been drawn to the monastic life. And while marriage and fatherhood and friendships and church and other enthusiasms have pulled and pushed, Mike has pursued his art with a simplicity and a singleness of purpose that is clearly vocational, in very nearly the same sense as a monk or priest.

These stories grow out of simplicity, silence, solitude. Informed by enough everyday, in-the-world experiences, interactions, struggles to keep them real. Yet nurtured in a life with enough space for thought, contemplation and fancy to let them go deep.

This lends his stories a peculiarity, a distinctiveness, that makes them arresting. Reading—or, even better, hearing—a new Mike Mason story will never feed me food I've already tasted. Mike straddles two worlds, the quotidian and the eternal. The same two worlds we all of us straddle, of course. It's just that Mike gives so much more time and attention to that latter world than most of us do, and it permeates his writing, marking it as something that comes almost from another culture, or another era. And of course those two worlds aren't separate worlds at all—and the reality of that intermingling, that co-existence of the mundane and the mystical is perhaps the recurrent theme of Mason's writing.

And when is that elusive truth more at the centre of things than at Christmas? When Eternity dons flesh, when "the Father of all mercies puts Himself at our mercy," the

Emmanuel moment when God becomes human, "the high and lifted up becomes low and helpless," and the earthy realities of birth and death and taxes get all caught up in momentous heavenly events that defy understanding—or even belief, at times.

So it's no wonder that Mike is drawn to Christmas. For him, it's the best of times and the worst of times, with "sensitive souls caught in the machinery of a fraught festival," as he so perfectly puts it—his own sensibility as sensitive as you will find. It's almost as though he lays himself bare to both the terror and the comfort of the occasion, and these stories are the raw reports back from those front line encounters.

The range is marvelous. "Three Fools" reads so well aloud, is so terrifically funny in front of an audience, we use it year after year in Pacific Theatre's "Christmas Presence" show—an exquisite contrast to Eliot's "Journey Of The Magi," say, or Frederick Buechner's "The Magnificent Defeat." And the remarkable thing is, his brash and silly (from "selig," which means "holy") piece absolutely holds its own next to the work of those masters—and brings wisdom and poetry of its own. "Sometimes I Tremble" matches it step for step with its vivid opening paragraph, the economical story-telling of a good Christmas-table anecdote, and a zinger of a last line.

"The Ghost Of Christmas" achieves a truthfulness of characterization and a beauty of narrative arc that places it among my favourite literary short stories by any author.

W.R. Wheeler is the sort of character who is routinely caricatured in literature, or at least condescended to. Mike strikes an extraordinary balance between observation and empathy: he knows W.R. (or people like him), he loves W.R., perhaps in ways he identifies with W.R. (for how can we love without seeing at least something of ourselves in the other?), and yet when he weighs W.R. in the balance, he finds him wanting. And yet... This is one of my three favourite Christmas stories—right alongside Dickens and Capra (but not counting Matthew and Luke). And believe me, I read a lot of Christmas stories.

"Festival Of Lights" is an exemplar of the author's sensitivity to those inner realities that marks all his writing—with the sort of dramatic reversal, rooted in the mutability of the human heart, that somehow seems particularly apt at this season.

The darkness Christmas holds for many of us is evinced by "Crack," grounded in the actual experience of a mutual friend, but shaped by Mike's story-telling vision. "Miles" has a reckless inventiveness suited to a season that's all about whimsy and outrageous generosity. But mostly the story gets at what it is to be a brother, or a friend, at this Christian festival which celebrates our closest relationships and shared childhood. One might observe a meaningful Easter in solitude, on a spiritual retreat, but "Christmas alone" conjures mostly pity, or self-pity, and this crazy (and crazily touching) little story takes us to the centre of what it is to be family.

"The Christmas Letter" has all the friendly, yarn-spinning cadence of Canada's national story-teller, Stuart McLean—indeed, it reads particularly well aloud, and I'd love to hear Mr. CBC take a crack at it. But then the story veers off in a direction that's distinctly Mike Mason. And "Bound For Glory" is almost a vision out of Kafka, or Tolstoy, or any of the Eastern European writers who know the darkness of life in times of real oppression—a dream-like dark fantasy that draws the reader in with an inescapable gravity. At a certain point one may sense where the story is headed—but one may also be wrong. And whether we guess right or we guess wrong, this is a vision conveyed with such force and artistry it achieves a mythic power that stays with us for a very long time indeed. A fitting conclusion to a book of such invention and mystery; a fitting culmination of a season with such eternal resonance.

I've been present at the birth of many of these stories, and over the years have seen several grow into dear, lifelong friends. I'm a little envious of those of you who are about to encounter this trove of riches for the first time, and confident that you, too, will find stories here that will become part of your Christmas, and part of your own life story, for years to come.

Ron Reed
Artistic Director, Pacific Theatre
Vancouver

Preface

I'm leafing through a file of old Christmas stories with a view to gathering them into a collection. For three decades I've written a new Christmas story every year to give out to friends as a greeting card. A tradition that pre-dates the internet, it's been one way to get instantly published. We also host an annual party on Christmas Adam (if you're not familiar with that term, read "Yabba-ka-doodles!") at which I read my latest story aloud. So I've not only had my own publishing house but a radio station as well.

All at once, as I look through the file, my eye falls on an unfamiliar title: "Honorable Pigeon." *Hm*. I don't remember writing this one. It consists of five pages of yellow newsprint, the kind I used in my early days as a writer. Moreover, it's a typescript. Let me repeat that word: *typescript*. Composed on a typewriter. One of those ancient clackety contraptions that's like a can of dry alphabet soup jury-rigged to a keyboard. That's how old this story is.

I can hardly wait to read it—and lo and behold, it's pretty good! By the second page I'm really hooked. It's a few days before Christmas and a tense dialogue is taking place between a fervent Muslim and a nominal Christian. The Christian is getting his clock cleaned. He's left speechless, shaken, deeply perplexed.

The dialogue ends; there's one more paragraph; and then ...

Nothing.

That's it. After five pages the story drops off a cliff. I never completed it, nor did I make any notes about possible endings. How could I have left this thing hanging? It cries out to be finished.

For the rest of that day I'm a man in another world: the world of Nat and Midge and Bashir and their unfolding story. The world of fiction. And the next day I sit down and write the ending.

That's how my 2011 Christmas story happened. Now that I've told you, you may be able to detect a difference in the writing styles of the two halves. But I'm also impressed by how the new ending grew almost seamlessly out of the old beginning, as though some three decades had not passed, as though the solution to the story's mystery were all that time sleeping in my subconscious.

Like "Honorable Pigeon," each of these stories has a story behind it. In the case of "The Changeling" I happened to read an account in a medical journal of a man whose face was horribly disfigured—so much so that he lived entirely alone, never wanting to be seen by anyone and going out only at night. I wanted to tell his story.

"Sometimes I Tremble" had an obvious trigger: a man who dragged a large wooden cross through our town. As for "Miles," a friend told me of an intriguing custom he shared with his brother, of encasing each other's Christmas presents in elaborate and increasingly impenetrable wrappings. My imagination took off from there.

"Born With Wings" is a true story. Though I've changed names and shaped the events into fiction, it's essentially as it happened in reality. As the husband of a doctor, I hear a lot of stories, both happy and sad. This one is both. My great thanks to the parents of this story's small hero for letting me tell it.

A few of the other stories are also based on real events. I'm grateful to the postmaster who gave me "The Festival of Lights," and to my wife Karen for the story behind "Christmas in July"—although she wants me to stress that the part about her first crush is not true! As for "The Giver," thanks to my daughter Heather I didn't have to alter even one detail. And "A Subtle Change," though fictionalized, is based on an actual game we played in a group I belonged to. I'll let you guess who inspired the Stewart character.

At the other end of the spectrum, "The People Upstairs" is entirely fictional, although it does truly reflect my feelings about an apartment building I lived in years ago. For me it illustrates the maxim that *setting is character.*

"The Ghost of Christmas," on the other hand, is frankly character-driven, based on my wife's unforgettable grandfather (though the related events are made up). And while "Bound for Glory" has not a shred of literal truth, at a deeper level I feel it may be the truest story in the book. How it came to me I have no idea; it arrived fully formed, clear out of the blue.

My very first seasonal story was "Christmas Rocks," and I love its youthful naiveté. As for "Yes, Mr. Church, There Is a Jesus," I confess that I wrote it mostly for the title. As fond as I am of Santa Claus, I like how this tale puts him in his place.

My overall title for this collection plays off the story "Seven Candles." This is the one piece for which I cannot claim full authorship. It was first told as a bedtime story to a little girl named Emily by her father. That father, Bob Gemmell, my friend and neighbor and a fabulous storyteller, was kind enough to make an audio recording so that I could write it down. In the process I added a few literary flourishes, but the story is really Bob's and I thank him very much, and Emily too, for allowing me to include it here.

Last year's story, "The Christmas Letter," illustrates well the subtle balance I've hoped for in all these stories: to produce a work of good literature, well-written and entertaining, that reveals something of the gospel. This is not easy to do. Good literature eschews preaching, but esteems truth. Why the two don't mix well is, I suppose, attributable to the different provinces of the right and left brain.

But people do, after all, possess a whole brain (or most do) and it is the whole person I write for.

Do I have a favorite story? If I had to choose, it might be the newest one, "In the Stillness of the Night." This began with a Christmas card from a friend in which he related his experience of playing his penny whistle in an old railway tunnel. Reading this short anecdote left me in a state of profound, glowing stillness. Over the next fifteen minutes the whole story came to me—one of the rare instances in which I haven't so much composed a story as simply written down a kind of vision.

This collection comprises a wide variety of tones, from lighthearted to serious, and of genres, from realistic fiction to parable to children's fantasy. But all are suitable for reading aloud around the fireside on Christmas Eve, or perhaps in the mellow lull after the big dinner. About half of the selections have been previously published in other books and magazines, but all have been extensively rewritten. And many pieces have had another kind of public airing that deserves special mention. Each year in my home city of Vancouver, our local Pacific Theatre puts on a show called *Christmas Presence*. A spontaneous evening of live music and storytelling hosted by artistic director Ron Reed, it's my favorite night out of the year. And the chance of maybe, just maybe, hearing Ron present a story hot off the press from Mike Mason—well, I can't deny what a thrill this is.

I should mention that the dates of composition are noted at the end of each story. If you notice a hiatus of several years, it's because I stopped producing Christmas stories during this period and turned to writing a Christmas novel. It's a children's fantasy entitled *The Blue Umbrella*, and its sequel, *The Violet Flash*, is set at Easter.

Christmas, I confess, is my favorite time of year. And I say this in spite of the fact that it is also the most painful. Always in early December I begin the Advent journey with great hope and joy and wonder, and always by the third week or so I get thrown from my horse—or my donkey. Nothing like a donkey for a bumpy ride, and somehow this season always gives me the bumps, embroiling me in strife, struggle, moodiness, disillusionment. If this is true for many people, it's partly because we are sensitive souls caught in the machinery of a fraught festival. Christmas is a collision of heavenly grace with worldly crassness, the occasion for a thousand darknesses—family tensions, greed, grief, loss, depression—to be hauled for inspection into the presence of light. T.S. Eliot said it so well in his poem "Journey of the Magi": *"This Birth was / Hard and bitter agony for us, like Death, our death."*

Death, however, is not the final word of Christmas, any more than of Easter. Despite the difficulty of this season, there always comes for me a point when Christmas happens, when God comes through and pulls me out of the pit.

Consider my journal entry for December 25, 2007:

A ragged ride through Christmas Eve. To bed

very late, feeling confused and cut off from everyone, a troubled night. Awoke suddenly, dreading the day, swamped with nameless anxiety.

After breakfast we had a brief prayer time, which Karen began with, "Lord, I just want to say a little prayer...." Something about that line struck my funny bone and I burst into laughter. Astonishingly, what came out when I opened my mouth was a very distinct "Ho, ho, ho!" And then a long string of ho-ho-ho's. (I never laugh like that.) Karen even commented, "Sounds like Santa Claus has arrived." And then I laughed and laughed uncontrollably: a gift of holy laughter! Just what I needed to free me up to rejoice in the day.

Another year when I'd been through the seasonal wringer, I found myself meditating on Isaiah 9:2: "The people who walked in darkness have seen a great light." And on Christmas Day I saw that light. I saw it in our nativity scene, which we always set up by the fireplace. I don't know quite how it happened, but as I peered at the figure of the babe in the manger, the Great Light of Christmas shone out and flooded my heart.

Yet another time, when I'd been struggling a great deal with church-related problems, on Christmas Eve I was impressed with how beautiful our church was. There were a couple of dozen decorated evergreens, a multitude of wreaths and boughs, and a large, gorgeous red sash draped behind the altar. I felt I was inside an enormous Christmas present! And the Lord said to me, "Yes, My church *is* a gift. Will you receive it?" I did, and my problems resolved.

The next day I stood outside watching the sunset. There was just one cloud in the sky—a long reddish ribbon draped across the horizon—and I heard the Lord whisper, "You see? This whole world is a gift."

These are just three examples of the kind of thing that happens to me at Christmas. It's why I write Christmas stories. Like a comet returning annually to the earth, heaven draws near in December, just as it did for the magi and the shepherds who both witnessed celestial prodigies. As Shakespeare wrote in the only significant reference to Christmas in all of his plays—

> *Some say that ever 'gainst that season comes*
> *Wherein our Saviour's birth is celebrated,*
> *The bird of dawning singeth all night long;*
> *And then, they say, no spirit can walk abroad;*
> *The nights are wholesome; then no planets strike,*
> *No fairy takes, nor witch hath power to charm,*
> *so hallowed and so gracious is the time.*
>   *(Hamlet, Act I, Scene i)*

At Christmas we celebrate the central truth of Christianity: that God has deigned and dared to descend and dwell among us, even as a baby. The Incarnation: this is the great unthinkable thing. It is the one belief that most clearly defines our faith, the thing unbelievers cannot accept, that boggles and outrages the secular mind. The idea of worshipping a human being!

My goal in writing is to incarnate something of this gospel in fiction. My hope is that through these stories a ray or two of the Great Light may somehow pierce the world's darkness, just as it does my own heart year after year.

So here they are, my twenty-one small lights.

Advent 2013

The Three Fools

It's easy to forget that the wise men did not visit Jesus in the manger as a baby. No, they found him some two years later living in a house on the outskirts of Bethlehem. This is important.

They knew they were looking for a child, not an infant, and this was a matter of some awkwardness for them. They wondered what sort of behavior would be appropriate in the presence of a child-king. They pictured themselves kneeling, presenting their gifts, and then perhaps sitting stiffly on the edge of wooden chairs and sipping tea. Their conversation would be mainly with the parents, of course, while the child looked on serenely, wonderingly. With careful humility they would avoid His large, omniscient eyes.

This is not how things turned out.

These men were bachelors, remember. Monkish types,

apprenticed from birth to a serious pursuit. Contemplatives used to sitting on their duffs and reaching after the ineffable with their noggins.

What could they possibly know about the terrible twos?

How surprised the magi were to find their little king blazing around the house naked, chattering up a storm, and leaping onto their laps to tweak their beards! Even more surprising, they found they did not react to these improprieties with horror. Instead they felt all the stiffness draining out of them, lifetimes of reverent caution melting like marshmallows in hot chocolate. They were charmed, delighted, won. Truly and deeply.

In no time they found themselves regressing into the childhoods they had never had. They got down on their knees, alright, but it wasn't to worship—it was to give the kid camel rides on their backs, and then to roll over like great fat bears while the boy who had made the universe used their bellies for trampolines. Yes, they fell down before their king, yet not in some formal act of prostration, but bowled over like ninepins by the thunder of a child's chortle.

People who have had no childhoods are old at forty. They have lived their lives, they can see no way forward. There is nothing left for them but to go back, back where they have never been. This prospect is terribly frightening. Imagine being frightened of becoming a child! It's like being afraid of ice cream.

But just so did things stand with the magi. Even the stars—which to the Boy King were like so many marbles, so many toy jewels for scattering and gathering—were to these men objects of utmost seriousness. Had they not given themselves to following a star, believing this to be the great high purpose of their lives? And where had it gotten them?

Rolling around in their sumptuous robes on the dirt floor of a hovel, that's where. Snotty-faced, squealing like pigs, hooting till their sides fairly split, squirting out buckets of tears. Ripping open their fine silks and brocades so that the holy little hoodlum could blow trumpet kisses into their bare tums. Years later they would still feel the amazing soft violence of his kiss in their navels, as if he really had found an aperture there and played them like an instrument, blown them full of brassy jubilance.

"Say, little fellow, you're full of beans, aren't you?"

"You better believe I am!" said his laughing eyes. "Now you open wide your mouths, your ears, your hands, and your hearts, because I'm going to fill you up with beans too."

And he did. They gave him their tawdry treasures; he gave them beans. A bean for rib-tickling; a bean for wrestling; a bean for giggling and guffawing; a bean for indignity; a bean for innocence, and one for dance.

Did the magi know beyond doubt that they had found their king? Oh yes, they knew! They knew it when the little guy sat astride their backs, smacked them on the rumps and cried, "Giddyup, Frankincense! Mush, Myrrh! Hi ho, Gold—away!"

"Jesus, hon," his mother kept saying, "don't embarrass the nice men."

But he was born to embarrass nice men, to embarrass them with riches. All day long the great sages lay in the dirt, collapsed in ecstasy, slain by the spirit of an urchin. And all night they lay there babbling in tongues, humming snatches of psalms and Mother Goose rhymes, burbling musically like babes. That night the greatest astrologers of the ancient world finally saw stars—saw them for the first time as they are, rolling 'round heaven to a toddler's tune.

These men who had come to pray, ended in play. They came to give gifts, but ended by leaving what they had long ached to be rid of: starched collars, tinsel crowns, jaded adult wisdom. That first Epiphany, wise men turned into wise guys, jokers, fools for Christ.

(1994)

The Changeling

J oe Szloboda finished his bacon and eggs and coffee and put on his duffle coat to walk to work. It was Christmas Eve and huge snowflakes drifted down like petals out of the black, serene night. Joe stopped to look at them in wonder. He tilted back his head, opened his mouth wide, and stood waiting for one of the cold, wet flakes to land on his tongue. Tasting the little cold fallen star, he whispered, "H-H-Holy J-Jesus, m-m-m-may all cr-r-r-eation b-b-bless you this n-n-night!"

Most people couldn't understand a word Joe Szloboda said. Besides stuttering horrendously, whenever he spoke to anyone he had a habit of looking down at his feet and mumbling so softly as to be almost inaudible. For years he had been unemployable, but for the past decade he'd held a job as a night janitor at a small department store. He slept most of the day, ate breakfast just as the rest of the world was sitting down to supper, and then worked in the store from closing time until the wee hours of the morning. The schedule had been hard to adjust to at first, but the strange new rhythm had gradually introduced a marvelous order and calm into Joe's existence, so that at forty-five he now enjoyed a greater well-being than ever before. Indeed Joe Szloboda, without having planned it, had somehow stuttered his way into a life of extraordinary peace and interior joy.

In recent years he had developed a habit of arriving at the store about an hour before work. During this time he liked to sit down in the furnace room, where he was sure of not being disturbed, and read his bible. This was the place where he had learned how to pray, in the middle of many a long night when he felt so lonely that he could not find the strength or heart to sweep one more square foot of floor. At such times he would come down here, sit on a three-legged stool, and talk to the warm, humming darkness. Here he could hold up his head and speak eye to eye. There was a faint dancing glow from within the furnace. Though he stuttered as thickly as ever, he knew his prayers were comprehended. There was One who came to meet him in the night. Even ten minutes of prayer, he discovered, could not only restore his physical strength but give him peace and a light heart.

Gradually devotions took the place of his coffee breaks. He thought of it as having coffee with 'the boys': Father, Son, Holy Spirit. And so he would read and pray; work; pray again; return to work; then read and pray some more. The work itself took on an attitude of prayer, and in time his entire shift at the store became infused with the deep life of contemplation normally associated with a monastery.

It was still snowing when he arrived at the store. Standing for a moment in the back laneway, he watched the big flakes floating out of the vast night and making the most perfect landings on hydro wires, on fence posts, on window sills, and on one black cat huddled among the garbage cans. The singing of a group of carolers floated over from the next block. Joe caught another snowflake on his tongue and thanked Jesus for it. It was better to him than any present that could be bought in the store that he would spend his Christmas Eve cleaning.

Inside the building, he paused again and said, or rather thought, another short prayer. He wanted everything he did in the store to be a sacrifice to Christ. Often as he went down the stairs into the furnace room he experienced a palpable wave of relief, of homecoming. In his small apartment he slept and ate and it was always noisy. But here he worked and he prayed. The store at night was as still as any church. The basement room was warm and plain and dark with an aura that welcomed and embraced his loneliness like a presence, a friend, even a family.

His bible he kept in an orange crate under the stairs, wrapped in a velvet cloth. Also in the box were a wooden cross that he had carved himself, and a candle. He always read very slowly, looking through and beyond the page more than at it, and he liked to read by candlelight. To-night this seemed especially appropriate, and spreading the velvet cloth over the crate, he set the cross on it, lit the candle, and opened his bible to the Christmas story in Luke. When he came to the account of the shepherds with the words, "And the glory of the Lord shone round about them," Joe paused and said the verse out loud, over and over, stuttering as usual. The words of the Lord were quiet and calming, like snowflakes that had been falling and falling forever through supernal space and were finally coming to settle with exquisite gentleness in the pit of one human heart.

Eventually, kneeling on a small square of carpet on the cement floor beside the orange-crate altar, Joe prayed, his one candle burning almost audibly and the furnace glowing, as outside the great night filled up with the infinite white of Christmas.

By the time Joe made his appearance upstairs, the rest of the staff would normally have left and he would have the building all to himself. Again, he found an extraordinary sense of Presence here, inhabiting the deserted aisles and ascending and descending the great empty stairway in the middle of the store. During the Christmas season the first thing he liked to do was to inspect the nativity scene. It was just inside the big set of revolving doors that opened onto the street, and sometimes careless shoppers would have tossed litter among the figures of Mary and Joseph, the animals, the wise men and shepherds. Once Joe had found a pop can in the cradle with its straw leading to the infant's mouth. So he liked to clean out the debris and straighten and dust the figures.

This night in particular, as he stood before the crèche meditating on the Lord's first earthly home, the life-sized figures seemed so vivid that he might have been there in Bethlehem himself, just one more of the adoring souls. To leap back over two thousand years, yet to be in the eternal present, in the presence of Eternity Himself—it was an awesome sensation, passing understanding. But all at once Joe experienced a stranger sensation. Something appeared different about the crèche, something he couldn't put a finger on. His entire body tingled like the plucked strings of an instrument. And then his mouth fell open in astonishment.

"O, Jesus!" he whispered.

And then, "My precious Lord!"

And just as if his own name had been called, Joe Szloboda stepped up to the cradle and knelt down beside it. Joy leapt within him, a gush of joy like a great fish bursting out of water into sunlight. For what Joe saw was not the painted plaster infant with the golden halo that he had lovingly dusted so many times. No. What he saw was a *live baby*, a tiny breath of pink flesh who couldn't have been more than a day old. While the plaster Christ had sat up boldly and fixed the world with a thoroughly adult gaze from amid its straightjacket of swaddling bands, this living infant, this little human rosebud of ineffable wonder, was bare naked and sound asleep.

Joe Szloboda did not know the first thing about babies. But that did not stop him from casting aside all reservations regarding his own clumsiness and all questions of religious protocol to reach out and gather up the helpless infant into his arms. This baby needed mothering and Joe was there to give it. None of the other figures had come alive; even Mary looked on cold and unmoved, statue that she was. And so, removing his own flannel shirt and wrapping the live child in it, Joe knelt down in the straw amid the staring crowd of plaster witnesses and was perfectly enraptured with the holy infant warm and still asleep and astoundingly light in his arms.

Just then, hearing a sound, Joe looked up to see Mr. Frank Thomas, the store manager, jangling a bunch of keys as he came in through a side door. The first thing this man saw was his janitor in a white undershirt kneeling beside the manger in the nativity scene with bowed head. What— was the fellow *praying*?

Naturally Thomas wondered what to say, whether to say anything at all. He knew Szloboda was a strange character. When the manager had first come to the store he had made a heroic effort to engage the stutterer in conversation. But with Joe this was impossible, and Thomas, like the rest of the staff, soon abandoned all attempts to get to know him. What with Joe's odd hours, his incomprehensible speech, and his excruciating shyness, it had been years since any human being had exchanged more than a few words with him. Everyone, and especially Joe himself, had simply given up. And as tends to happen in such cases, people assumed there was more wrong with Joe Szloboda than just a speech impediment.

Accordingly, Frank Thomas stared uncomfortably at Joe, while Joe, still overcome with awe, cradled the baby in his arms and gazed back. Finally, breaking into nervous laughter, Thomas burst out, "Hello there, Joe. A merry Christmas to you!" But the janitor's mysterious expression did not change, nor did he make any reply, and Thomas, following another awkward pause, went on to explain that he had a couple of last-minute presents to pick up. "You know how men are when it comes to shopping," he quipped.

Drawing closer to the kneeling janitor, he grew more curious.

"Say, Joe, what have you got there? Is something wrong?"

Staring up at Thomas with probably the biggest eyes and the steadiest gaze the manager had ever seen, Joe replied in a tone both bright and dark with wonder, "Mr. Thomas—Jesus is alive!"

Thomas gawked. Jesus? Alive? The words did not register. What did register was the startling fact that the imbecilic Joe Szloboda had looked him straight in the eye and spoken to him perfectly clearly and intelligibly.

Once again the manager was at a loss for words. But the thought that occurred to him was that all these years this man had made a fool of him and of everyone in the store. For it turned out that he could speak as plainly as anybody! What sort of game was he playing? Thomas's attitude hardened into suspicion.

Still, he remained curious.

"Come on, Joe, what's going on here? What have you got there?"

Again Joe fixed him with a gaze of unnerving beatitude, and in sentences of clear, unbroken English he repeated that Jesus Christ, our Lord and Savior, was alive.

"He's as real as you or me, Mr. Thomas. It's a sign."

This time the janitor's words registered with Thomas. The thought struck him that maybe this guy was a real nut case and had finally gone right around the bend. The manager hesitated. Propriety dictated that he say something pleasant. But how polite it was necessary to be to a lunatic?

Joe spoke again. "Come and see, Mr. Thomas. Behold the Christmas child!"

Instinctively Thomas stepped forward. And looked. He noted the empty cradle. And then he peered into the nest of flannel shirt in Joe's arms.

And he saw just the face of a tiny, live baby.

"Hey! Wh-what's going on here?" he stammered, taking a step back. "Joe, where did that baby come from? What's it doing here?"

But Joe just shook his head in wonder.

The manager stood up straight and looked all around the store. He wanted to pick up his few gifts and return home to his family. But the sight of a live baby raised a thousand questions. And he could hardly leave this help-less infant in the hands of a madman.

"Joe," he said earnestly, "where did you get that baby? Who is its mother?"

Smiling, Joe pointed to the painted plaster figure of the Virgin Mary.

Thomas folded his arms. The man in the straw had a one-track mind. Was he deliberately playing dumb? Flus-tered, impatient, the manager peppered the janitor with questions. The answers came back clear, calm, grave. To hear such a voice emerging from the lips of a man who had always let on to be totally inarticulate—it seemed mon-strous.

Eventually Thomas satisfied himself that he had pried out as much of the plain facts as he was going to get: that in stopping to clean the nativity scene, Joe had discovered this real baby in place of the plaster doll. It was as simple as that.

Summoning every ounce of his forbearance, Thomas got down on his knees before Joe and the little bundle, and placing his two hands squarely on the janitor's shoulders, he spoke to him as coolly and seriously as he knew how.

"Joe, listen to me. This is very important. That baby is *not* Jesus. You've made a mistake. It belongs to somebody and we've got to find out who."

With eyes as big as the night, Joe regarded his man-ager sadly and said, "Mr. Thomas, don't you know? Jesus belongs to you."

At that Thomas flew off the handle. "You stupid

numbskull! That baby is no more Jesus than I am! Some teenager had that kid in a back alley and she's left it here to get rid of it. That's all there is to it. And we have to figure out what to do with the thing."

Rising, the manager re-folded his arms, vaguely satisfied with his little explosion. Then he noticed, lying in the straw behind a sheep, the real Jesus, the original plaster doll. Striding over to the thing, he gave it a kick, then turned and glared at Joe.

"There's your baby Jesus!"

Motioning, he commanded Joe to bring the kid and follow him up to his office. Joe obeyed, and the two men mounted the great flight of stairs in the center of the store, the janitor slightly behind and still cradling the strange, warm bundle who, through it all, had remained fast asleep in his arms.

In the manager's office Frank Thomas sat in his black leather chair behind the oak desk and waved his employee into a straight chair in the corner. Reaching for the phone book, he thumbed brusquely through various listings. Who to call? The cops? Social services? Surveying the array of government departments, he grew confused—though long managerial practice had taught him to appear, even to himself, to know exactly what he was doing.

Finally he called the police, gave a curt explanation, and sat back to await their arrival. It had been good, for a moment, just to talk to a sane human being. His inability to communicate with Joe, and the eerie transformation in the latter's speech and manner, was telling on his nerves. And now there was more time to be passed alone with this man.

Beyond the window snow sifted down in white, otherworldly silence. Absentmindedly Thomas studied it, and for a long minute the dark glass revealed a deep skyful of stars dancing in wild, incomprehensible celebration....

"Mr. Thomas, would you like to hold the holy child?"

Joe's voice seemed to come from the other side of the universe. Turning to the man and the baby in the corner of his office, Thomas saw them as if for the first time: the sleeping newborn wrapped in plaid flannel, and lowly Joe Szloboda in his undershirt with his eyes shining and his big red hands buried in the warm bundle. They did look, the two of them, a holy sight. And on Christmas Eve!

There would be a few minutes yet before the police arrived. Perhaps, mused Thomas, he had been too hasty with Joe. He considered asking the man directly about his stutter.

At that point, however, the buzzer rang at the front of the store, and Frank Thomas hurried downstairs to usher in the authorities. There were two of them, a man and a woman, and as the four adults gathered in the small office it seemed very crowded. Thomas prattled away as though he were the one most knowledgeable about the case. As best he could determine, the baby had been left in the manger—exchanged for the plaster doll—just before closing time. The janitor was a bit slow, Thomas added, and seemed to be under the delusion—he lowered his voice decorously—that the abandoned infant was Jesus Christ. At this the officers raised their eyebrows and studied Joe.

Joe, for his part, said nothing. Even after his boss had run out of words the janitor sat perfectly still, gazing down at the baby and making no reply to any question. During these cavernous silences the sound of the snow could be heard splatting against the window pane. After a while the policewoman stepped forward and gently asked Joe to hand over the child to her. Reluctantly, but still without a word, he surrendered his precious bundle.

Just then the baby woke up and began to cry. The manager and the male officer, out of their depth, glanced awkwardly about the room, while the woman rocked the child, cooed, walked him up and down, nestled him against her blue uniform and spoke ever so soothingly, all without being able to comfort him. At length the janitor broke his silence to say, "Try holding him close to your heart."

At this the policewoman, accompanied by her colleague, took the child from the room, leaving Frank Thomas and Joe Szloboda alone to listen to the plaintive crying as it receded, floating back up the stairway haltingly, chokingly.

When the sound had died away completely, all they heard was the snowflakes batting like tiny fists against the dark pane.

(1982)

Crack

When I was a little boy, my dad used to punish me by locking me in the cellar. He'd slap me around and then drag me downstairs and leave me. I never knew how long I'd be there. The cellar had no windows, so there was no time. But I think it was often for a night or two, because I'd try to sleep but couldn't much because it was too cold, even in summer. Strangely enough, I don't remember being frightened down there. It felt almost safe. At least safer than being upstairs.

The place was a fruit cellar, a tiny room with walls of cinder block and long shelves for my mother's preserves. Just enough light came from the crack under the door to play my games. I played store with the Mason jars or I made little towns out of potatoes with carrots for people. I even played with the cobwebs. I was good at keeping busy.

This went on until I was seven. Then my mother died and my father abandoned me, and I went to live with an aunt who treated me well. But by then I was old enough to make my aunt suffer.

Years later I went to see a play called *Remnant*. It was one of those modern, way-out things and it made me mad that I couldn't understand it. But one character intrigued me. He was named Loner and he was a wild, dark, criminal type. Almost an animal. He wore leather and studs and also a big, ugly, metal appendage attached to one of his arms like a mechanical claw. If anyone came near him he brandished his claw. It was like a weapon that was part of himself.

The one thing I understood in the play was this: There was a Christmas tree on the stage, and at the very end something happened, some kind of breakthrough, that made Loner go up to the tree and take off his big claw and hang it there like a grisly ornament.

Afterwards I thought about this, off and on, for years, about Loner standing there disarmed, stripped, before the Christmas tree, with that thing hanging on it. And how when Loner walked away from that tree, he was free. He was, finally, merely human.

Last year, two weeks before Christmas, I was decorating my own tree in my little apartment. And suddenly it hit me. I felt these weights all over me, these heavy, ugly things. I could actually sense their horrid shapes. And I began to take them off. First the long, twisted claws, from both arms. Then some kind of chain from around my waist. And finally a big, black headpiece. As I removed these, I placed each one carefully on the tree, just as if they were the most delicate and beautiful of ornaments. Then I knelt down, and stayed that way for a long time.

When I got up, I went straight to the bathroom to look at my face in the mirror.

Oh—I was shining! I was radiant!

I was in a river, just floating along in the current and doing whatever came next. And the next thing was that I sat down and wrote a letter to my father, which I mailed that very night. I forget the words I used, but it was all about how I forgave him and asked him to forgive me. I wanted to let everything go, every last scrap of it. I wanted to be free.

As it turned out, my father never received this letter. We'd had no contact for twenty years and the last address I had for him was defunct.

But here's the strange thing. Two weeks later, on Christmas Eve, my dad phones me, clear out of the blue. He says he's in town and wants to visit. He knows nothing about any letter. But it's almost like, at some deeper level, he does know. He knows something is different and he's being drawn like a moth to the light.

When he comes to the door I throw it open, and for a moment we just stand there, looking at each other. I'm not wearing my claws, chain, mask. As for him, one sleeve is pinned; he's lost an arm. What have I got to lose? So I throw my two arms around him and whisper in his ear, "Dad, I love you."

And what does he do? He pushes me away. Violently.

"Whaddya think yer doin'?" he hisses. "Cut that out and don't ever try it again."

Okay, I think. Okay. Give him space.

Now this man is in my living room, large as life. He asks for a drink, I fumble around for it, then we sit and talk. The first thing he tells me is all about the machine shop accident. With the compensation, he hasn't had to work. He goes on to other stories, the crazy adventures of a boozer, con man, crackhead—and I grow bored. The feeling of loving him is gone. Wasted as he is, he's still a big man, and gruff, and I'm feeling small, like I'm shrinking. But I can't take my eyes off him.

That afternoon we go for a walk along the beach. At one point he stumbles on a bit of driftwood, and as he goes down I catch his one arm and for a moment we lock eyes. All at once I notice how really old he is, elderly and feeble.

Back at the apartment, he announces he'll stay for the night. I know he just wants a warm place to sleep. Neither of us is tired and there's nothing more to talk about, so till long after midnight we sit up in the living room watching Christmas shows on TV. And once again I feel I'm in the current, just flowing along, doing the next thing and the next. And when at last it seems time to say good night, I decide to try again.

We're standing now, beside the tree, and I look into his eyes and say, "Dad, I love you." No hug this time, just the words. But I hold his eyes, and I'm really feeling it.

This time it grabs him. He shivers, sort of, as if a hand has reached out and shaken him. He has to steady himself on the arm of the couch as he sinks down. Something seems to lift off him, a layer of something, like a dark smudge. He's like a man waking up, just coming to. I sit beside him and put one hand on his shoulder. He doesn't push me away, he lets it stay. I can feel him trembling. Tears are making little creases in his cheeks, as if his flesh is melting. I'm crying too. Finally I put my arms all around him and give him the hug we both need. He hugs me back, and even when we let go we still keep our arms there, draped around each other's shoulders.

And there we stay the whole night through. Pressed close, with the Christmas tree winking on and off like a heartbeat of light. We don't say a whole lot. But I say what I need to. All of it. And he says a few things too.

Finally I drift off to sleep. Imagine—me resting there like a child in the embrace of my former jailer and tormentor. What a night!

I don't know, but I like to think my dad stayed awake long after, just watching me and pondering. By the time I awoke, he was asleep. Curled up there, on Christmas morning, he looked like a little boy. And I—I felt like a man! Oh, the whole world was turned upside down!

Drifting into my bedroom, I fell asleep again, and when I got up it was late afternoon and my dad was gone.

That was a year ago. I waited—one month, two, six. No word at all, and when I tried to contact him I found he'd moved on with no forwarding address.

Soon it will be Christmas again and I wonder if he'll call. Maybe it doesn't matter. We had our night. When a door opens a crack, it doesn't take much to blow it wide.

(1995)

Yabbakadoodles!

While studying theology at Regent College, I knew an Old Testament professor, Dr. Bruce Waltke, who had worked on the translation committee for the New International Version of the Bible. In his lectures Dr. Waltke loved to linger over the subtleties of ancient Hebrew, expounding vastly different interpretations of a single word or phrase, and building a strong case for his own favored translation. But he also pointed out that translation is not salvation. As he was fond of saying, "I've known people who were saved through a verse of scripture that I know is mistranslated."

I thought of this on Christmas Adam in 1999. In our family we traditionally refer to the day before Christmas Eve as *Christmas Adam*. Similarly, Boxing day is *Christmas Cain* (or sometimes *Christmas Candy Cane*), and the day after is *Christmas Abel*, and so on. For years we have celebrated Christmas Adam with a story party, a gathering of friends and neighbors who are invited to bring a story or a poem to read aloud. I usually write a new story, and someone else brings a guitar, and everyone donates a plate of goodies, and we read and sing and chew and chat the evening away, and no finer entertainment can be found anywhere.

In 1999, two months before Christmas, I had begun a ninety-day experiment in joy. I made up my mind to be joyful for the next ninety days, and the results were eventually published in a book called *Champagne for the Soul*. Since this was an "experiment," there was room for failure. If at times I felt gloomy, short-tempered, or just plain blah, I wouldn't beat myself up for it. Rather, recognizing that self-condemnation is a chief enemy of joy, I would simply return as best I could to my quiet resolve to rise above all circumstances and to do whatever it took to lay hold of joy. In this way I hoped to learn some of joy's secrets and to emerge a more joyful person. I pictured joy as being like a flabby muscle that, if exercised every day, would gradually grow stronger.

The first month of my experiment was amazing. A moody person by nature, never in my life had I experienced such a steady flow of pure happiness. By the second month, however, difficulties set in. As Christmas approached, it would be fair to say that my days were more characterized by struggle than by joy. Still, every day in surprising ways a measure of joy kept coming to me. I was learning not to focus on the darkness, but to be always on the lookout for light.

Christmas tends to be a hard time for me, as it is for many. As the angels gather to announce their glad tidings, there is a parallel gathering of the demons of materialism, busyness, unrealistic expectations, old sadnesses, family strife. In order to be touched by the true joy of Christmas, it seems we must first encounter our own joylessness and our clumsiness at celebration.

By December 23, Christmas Adam, I was wound up tighter than a drum. I'd hardly slept the night before and I woke up feeling embroiled in problems. I'm not normally a party person, and the thought of having to get into the holiday spirit with a roomful of people that evening was overwhelming. Worst of all, here I was in the middle of this wretched experiment in joy! The happy honeymoon was over and I'd begun to think of joy as a hard taskmistress. And of Christmas as her nasty elder sister.

Fortunately, there was one thing on Christmas Adam I looked forward to: breakfast with Chris Walton. Chris is that rarest of people in my life, someone who always blesses me. No matter what he's going through, what mood he's in, or what we do together, somehow I always leave his company feeling brushed by heavenly light. As we aren't able to see each other often, our times together are all the more precious.

So, nursing the kind of hangover that comes from imbibing too much gloom, I set off for Ricky's All Day

Grill to meet Chris for bacon and eggs. In my friend's presence I gradually relaxed as we talked of favorite books and music, Christmas plans, our families, and Jesus. I particularly recall our discussing a new book called *The Bible Jesus Read*, and speculating on what it might be like to read the Old Testament through Jewish eyes.

The more we talked, the more I sensed a quiet joy tugging at my sleeve like a little child. By the time we rose to leave, though I cannot say I felt entirely happy, a change was stealing over me, a warming. Still, it was the sort of thing that might easily have been snatched away by the next small annoyance, were it not for the strange event that transpired in the parking lot of Ricky's that day.

We were standing beside our cars, Chris by his door and I by mine, saying our goodbyes. Traffic was rushing by on Fraser Highway, making it somewhat difficult to hear. But as Chris raised his hand in a wave and beamed a last, broad smile, I distinctly heard him call out, "Yabba-ka-doodles!"

Yabba-what? What did he mean? What language was this? As we'd just been talking of Jewish matters, I wondered if Chris might be delivering some traditional Yiddish holiday greeting. I felt like Mary who, when hailed by the angel Gabriel, "wondered what kind of greeting this might be."

"What did you say?" I called back.

This time Chris threw back his head, beamed as brightly as if he were seeing an angel himself, and belted out, "YABBA-KA-DOODLES!"

Chris is not much given to spontaneous ecstatic utterances. Maybe he was just goofing off? More puzzled than ever, I left my car and walked around to where he stood.

"I don't get it," I said. "'Yabba-ka-doodles.' What does it mean?"

"Yabba-what?" said Chris.

"Yabba-ka-doodles. You said yabba-ka-doodles and I want to know what it means."

"Yabba-ka-doodles? I didn't say yabba-ka-doodles."

"Then what did you say?"

"I said, 'I'm glad we could do this.'"

"I'm glad we could do this?" I echoed blankly.

For a moment we stared at one another, listening to the sound of this inane sentence against the backdrop of the rapturous, ululant syllables of yabba-ka-doodles.

And then we burst into laughter—wild, hilarious, thigh-slapping gales of it there in the parking lot of Ricky's. It was so preposterous a mistake, so rich and gloriously unlikely. It filled us with that unlikeliest of qualities in this darkly unsettling world—JOY!—rich and glorious joy, as preposterously surprising as if Santa Claus himself—or his Yiddish uncle—had come thundering down out of the sky in his sleigh.

All the way home in the car I kept muttering, caressing, shouting that silly word—"Yabba-ka-doodles... Yabba-ka-doodles"—giggling and guffawing like a schoolboy. Talk about joy! More than happy, I felt drunk with joy for the rest of that day. And when Chris and I saw each other next, on Christmas Eve, we nearly jumped into each other's arms yelling, "Yabba-ka-doodles, brother!"

Who would have believed that so much joy could be contained in one crazy, purely imagined word? Later I wondered: Were my ears playing tricks, or was it possible that Chris, without realizing it, really did say *Yabba-ka-doodles*? Was he unknowingly used as a messenger of God to me, delivering the joyous news of Christmas in an angelic tongue?

Dr. Waltke, I think, would be amused. On Christmas Adam, 1999, I was transported to joy through a word I had mistranslated, a word that has now entered my vocabulary as a traditional Christmas greeting. Tiny Tim says, "God bless us, every one." But I declare to each and every one of you:

YABBA-KA-DOODLES!

(2000)

The Christmas Letter

One year I mailed the wrong Christmas letter to all our friends. When Hilda next door sprained her wrist, I offered to fold and address her letters along with mine. The two piles were side by side on the dining room table. Usually I clear off the table for this job, but this time I didn't, I just worked amidst the clutter. My whole life was cluttered, continually rearranged to accommodate Jack, and I was tired and distracted. Hardly had I sat down when Jack needed attention. When I returned to the task, somehow the piles got switched in my mind and the wrong letters went into the wrong envelopes, and then into the mail.

My first clue was the phone call from Joan.

"Mom, it's really nice to get all of Frank and Hilda's news, but I'd really rather hear about you."

We had a good chuckle about it. But when my brother Bert called a few minutes later and asked, quite seriously, if Jack's Alzheimer's might be contagious, suddenly it dawned on me what I'd done: Not just one, or two, but *all* my letters—and all of Hilda's—had gone to the wrong recipients. I was horrified, fit to cry. But just as I hung up, Jack came shuffling into the kitchen, as usual without his pants. All he had on was a clumsily-knotted tie (no shirt) and an old sports jacket he'd gotten inside out so that the big shoulder pads stuck out like wings. And that look on his face! Like a mischievous little boy who knew exactly what he was doing and was so pleased with himself.

Well—it was too funny and I burst out laughing. His face went stern and he turned away and padded down the hall. But I couldn't stop giggling. When you live with someone with Alzheimer's, sometimes you slip into their little world, and that mischievous expression crept right inside me. *So what* if I'd sent out the wrong letters? What did it matter? Maybe I'd *meant* to. Maybe at heart I was a practical joker. In any case, the neighbors' news was much cheerier than ours.

Naturally I had to re-send Hilda's letters to the right people. But I didn't worry about ours. Throughout the holidays our phone rang more than it had since the kids were teenagers. Some people wouldn't want this, but I loved it. Being cooped up with Jack all day had been driving me batty. Now, instead of writing some dumb letter, I *talked* to people. What a concept! I don't do the Facebook thing, or even email, so the telephone was the only way most people could find out what was going on in our lives. And I told them. Instead of consigning Jack to a couple of veiled sentences in a form letter, I told everyone exactly how bad he was and about all the funny things he did. I laughed and laughed, and did some crying, too. It was the best Christmas I'd had in quite a while.

By mid-January the calls died away and everything returned to normal. If you can call it normal when your husband goes to bed with a butcher knife under his pillow. I don't know how long he'd been doing it before I found out. He was definitely a sundowner—he got worse at night—and it seemed he was paranoid about someone breaking into the house. One evening I slipped into his room for a cuddle, and out comes this knife! He didn't know who I was—that was happening more and more—but thankfully he couldn't coordinate himself to launch a serious attack. Still, it gave me a good scare, and after that I gathered up all our knives and scissors and locked them in the garage.

We had a bad year, and when the next Christmas rolled around I had no heart for the annual letter. What was there to say? That Jack was now in diapers? That he regularly took all my jewelry and other valuables and hid them—a common Alzheimer's behavior called 'shopping'? Or that he liked to parade around the house with his boxer shorts on his head and stand naked in the bay window? Or maybe I could tell the story of him nearly stabbing me to death? No, the years of the Christmas letter were over.

But then that characteristic little-boy look of his flashed into my mind. I happened to be going through the stack of old Christmas letters we'd received, and I thought—why not? Why not send out *these*? Not back to the original senders, of course, but randomly to different people? After all, why shouldn't all these folks get to know one another? Why couldn't the whole world be one big happy family?

So that's what I did. After weeding out a few letters that were too personal, I sent out the rest with little notes such as, "John and Mary are so nice—I'd love for you all to meet." I had such a good time! And once again came the flurry of phone calls—some folks even dropped by for a visit—and once again for a little while our home filled up with life.

In the course of the following year Jack's silliness gradually passed and he settled into a deep trough, like a ship sunk in murky waters. No more puerile grins; no expression at all on that still-handsome face. More than ever that year, the Christmas letter was not a custom which at all lent itself to our situation.

But old habits die hard. One day when I got feeling goofy I sat down at the table and wrote a letter of outrageously good news. I'd won a Rolls Royce in the hospital lottery! Jack and I had gone on a cruise to Alaska! I'd discovered a secret manuscript of Jack's, a novel, which a publisher had accepted! And so on. I don't know, I just went crazy. And afterwards, reading that letter over and over, I couldn't stop smiling. I wasn't going to send it out, of course. But then ... why not? Before I could second-guess myself the red box at the corner had swallowed up a hundred letters.

Afterwards I felt terrible. What would people think? But when the phone calls started pouring in—the "reviews" as I called them—I knew I'd struck just the right tone. Nobody took my letter seriously, everyone had a good laugh. Except, of course, brother Bert.

By the following Christmas I knew I could write anything at all in the annual letter, and everyone but Bert would love me for it. Would love *us*. The letters were giving us a second life, a life we couldn't have anymore in reality. But on paper, the sky was the limit. A few people even said I should write a book.

So that year as I sat at the table with a mug of mulled cider and carols playing on the radio, and with Jack slumped beside the Christmas tree in the chair he'd always called his 'throne,' once again I let myself go and I wrote about the best Christmas I'd ever had, when I was ten years old. That was the time all my cousins came to visit and it was cold enough to skate on the lake; we skated and skated forever till it got dark and the sky filled with stars and we felt like stars ourselves gliding through the universe. With all the families there were so many presents we opened them all at once, not one by one. And Uncle Fred played Santa Claus so convincingly that for a little while I believed in Santa all over again. I told some stories about Jack, too, when he was ten, some things I knew about and others I made up. And it's funny, but whether I was telling the truth or not, the whole time my face was so wet with tears I could hardly see to write.

That letter brought more calls than ever. People loved it! And it had been good for me to write it. It unlocked something. So by the next Christmas when there really was nothing whatsoever to say, I found it easier than ever to write our letter. This time I did simply tell the truth. Yesterday I couldn't pry Jack's mouth open to give him his medicine and he bit me—hard! Last week I gave him a bath and he nearly drowned. This past year he spoke only two words, both beginning with F. And so on. I ended up writing quite a long letter, about fifty pages. By halfway through I knew I could never send it. But in the end I relented and made a digest version of ten pages, which I got Joan's husband to print as booklets. I mailed out two hundred copies. Interest was growing.

I needn't have put up a Christmas tree that year because my switchboard lit up like one. As Joan said, I was going viral!

Another year went by, this time with scarcely any change at all. Looking back, it was hard to believe that in a whole year so little could have happened. Jack was just more shrunken, more expressionless, more profoundly absent. That was all. Except I did sense he was more at peace. And, strangely, he had taken to wearing an outlandish red-and-gold-patterned housecoat. He must have gotten it from the grandchildren's dress-up box, though I couldn't recall seeing the thing before. And how he put it on I have no idea, since the rest of the time I had to dress him. But the moment I turned my back he would magically appear in this velvet robe and wouldn't be separated from it.

Other than that, there was nothing to tell in a Christmas letter. But for that very reason I felt excited to write it, precisely because our life was such a blank page—365 blank pages—on which I could write to my heart's content.

I began planning the letter in October. It was going to be about animals. News about all our family pets, past and present. All the cats and dogs that Jack and I and the children had had; Joan's hamsters; her daughter Jenny's goldfish; Benjy's boa and mice; even Bert's sourpuss pug; on and on. And suddenly I thought of our crèche, the olive wood set that Joan had brought from Israel, which I always displayed on the mantel. I pictured the mournful donkey, the proud camels, the dove with its burning eyes. Why not tell news of them too? Even better, why not bring all our family pets to the stable, gather them all in a great crowd around the baby Jesus?

Not that I wanted to make it religious. Jack had never believed in that, and whatever I once believed had been worn away by these last grueling years. But the story—the story kept drawing me. All of creation gathered around that cradle! After all, Christ's birth had been announced by a host of angels—but what about the animals? Weren't they like angels of the earth, barking and bleating and cooing their praises? Wasn't there some legend about the animals talking on Christmas Eve? Oh, the possibilities! I could hardly wait to get writing.

But alas, on November 14, the day before his birthday, Jack died. Pneumonia, the old man's friend, carried him away. The hardest part was having it happen in hospital. That broke my heart, that he couldn't spend his last days at home. The noise in that awful ward, and the night-long vigils—by the end I was ready to die too. Maybe I did. Certainly life since then has been vastly different. You have no idea how empty the days can be when a sick, crazy old man is gone. You'd think I'd have been glad, relieved. And I was. But oh, how I wanted him back! I wanted him the way he was before he got ill; or if not that way, then any way. Where was my meaning if not in caring for Jack? I kept seeing him sitting there on his throne, a bowed, expressionless lump, battered and beaten, a limp old ghost of himself—but still my Jack.

As for the Christmas letter, I decided to make it just two words: JACK DIED. Eight letters in bold black type as big as the page, maybe even bigger. Maybe just a completely black page.

That's how I felt.

One night, a couple of weeks before Christmas, I was sitting in the living room gazing at Jack's chair, trying to remember him. I don't know why but I couldn't. That chair was so vacant. I tried focusing on details, on any small thing I could recall about him, and little by little the picture filled in. Those ratty bedroom slippers; the baggy jogging pants (not always present!); that stupid red and gold robe. And then his face: the keen blue eyes (not the least faded), the thick brows, the white scar over his top lip, those big ears that always seemed, no matter how diminished he became, to be listening. And then his voice. What had his voice sounded like? It had been so long...

And all at once I heard him. Not out loud, but plainly in my mind, the phrasing, the cadence, that scornful little laugh, the manner he had of leaving sentences unfinished while arching his eyebrows meaningfully.

Before I knew it I was at the dining room table with a clean sheet of paper. Not that I meant to write the Christmas letter. No, I didn't need to. Instead, *Jack would write it!* His voice was inside me, clear and intense as the candle flame on the sideboard. I was possessed. His words came thick and fast like the snowflakes beating against the black bay window. I began to write:

Dear Friends,

Merry Christmas from beyond the grave! In case you haven't heard, I passed away in November. I'm sure you are all curious to know what life may be like here on the other side, but that is not what I wish to write about. I can tell you that I did not arrive here under my own steam. My steam was exhausted long ago, all of it. No, I was carried here.

Let me start by saying that throughout these past few years, despite all external appearances, I have remained much more lucid than anyone realized. In fact I've been fully aware—more so than ever before—only of different things. The way a swath of sunlight lay like spilt grain over the carpet. The soaring weightlessness of the garden roses. The complex texture of the underside of a table, so different from its surface. Such things I found deeply absorbing, as though I had never really seen this world before. Everything was so dazzling and intricate, so much more beautiful than I had realized, that I could not relate to it anymore. It wasn't so much that I could not read a newspaper or follow a conversation, as that something much deeper and more important was happening inside me. Something that demanded all of my attention.

For as my external world grew clearer, my internal world became clearer still. Such a floodlight was turned on within me that I felt I had never truly had an internal life before. I suppose it was like old Scrooge being visited by the three ghosts. Every day scenes from my life came before me—past, present, future. People think Alzheimer's is a loss of memory—but no, it is an intensification of memory, an overload. Waves of nostalgia so swamp one that even the present becomes a kind of past that can no longer be reached. It was as though I stood in the street at night, peering through a lighted window into my own home, but never able to enter. Such a stranger had I become to myself that I could not return to my old life, but neither could I see a way forward.

My theory is that I was learning to see with the eyes of the heart rather than the eyes of the mind. What else could I do but shut down my external faculties in order to give myself fully to this inner work? Wishing to divest myself of every encumbrance, I took to removing my clothes and standing naked in our front bay window. For Irene this was surely a great trial, but I was past all that. Naked had I come into the world, naked would I go. I was tired of hiding, of not being myself. I wanted to be seen, to make some gesture toward a radical change of apparel. To wait, to hope, in utter nakedness—I found this strangely soothing.

Until one day in January when I observed a stranger approaching the house—a young man with longish hair and a hungry gaze, oddly dressed. A hippie? A tramp? What with high snowbanks lining the road and the fading light, he was difficult to make out. But I was frightened, especially when the fellow looked me straight in the eye. I felt certain he would turn into our walkway and come right up to the front door, perhaps even force his way in. But he did not; he passed on by. I hadn't budged, except for my eyes looking away. I could not meet that disturbing gaze.

It was then that I began hiding all our valuables and sleeping with a knife under the pillow. I knew he'd be back, and now more than ever I had good reason to stand at the window, to make it plain that this house was guarded. And sure enough, every evening he appeared, walking slowly up the street, staring into our house, staring into me, almost pausing at our walk, then passing by. Biding his time, I presumed, until the watchful figure at the window should drop his guard.

My only defense, I felt, was my nakedness. Especially after Irene confiscated all of my weapons. How to protect *myself then? Only by letting this hoodlum know that I had nothing, nothing worth taking, nothing at all to hide. Even if it should come to a fight, I thought, a wrestling match, a naked man is hard to grasp. Brave words, you may think. But I don't mind telling you I was deathly afraid.*

Thus things stood for several weeks. I grew more and more agitated. It was very cold, blustery, with storm after storm, as though mirroring conditions in my own soul. Irene was beside herself trying to control me. I wanted to comfort her, to explain, but the situation was so perilous it was all I could do to contain myself. She couldn't have understood, she was oblivious, and of course each time she caught me at the window she threw shut the curtains and scolded me. She became so watchful (in her own way) that I had to miss a great deal of window time.

One evening in March, when she happened to be on the kitchen phone with Joan, I was at my post, undressed for duty, when I spotted the prowler at the end of the street. For some reason he always approached from the east, the direction of the cul-de-sac, though I was sure he didn't live here. It had snowed heavily that day, and now at dusk the whole world looked the same pewtery color, tall snowbanks merging seamlessly into low-hanging clouds as though we—the stranger and I—were inside a vast egg. His eyes, glaring into mine, seemed to fill the night. This time I held his gaze; I don't know why; something about this occasion felt different. It was not even a great surprise when, against custom, he stopped at the end of our walk, and then began slowly to approach. As he entered the blaze of light falling from the window, I saw clearly what he wore: a long, shapeless gown, velvety in texture and patterned in gold and crimson. I was astonished by the brightness of those colors. How strange! From a distance he had always looked such a shabby, shady character, but now he was radiant.

I no longer knew what to think, what to feel. I was still frightened, yes, but with a fear that was somehow calm, wonderstruck. I heard his tread on the front steps, then his hand turning the doorknob. We always kept the house locked but he came right in. A moment later he was in the room with me, not ten feet away. I braced for our encounter. But at this point he paused, searching my eyes as if seeking permission to come further. What sort of burglar asks leave of the householder? I was confused. Overcome by his presence, my eyes filled with tears. Hardly the brave front I had meant to put up! Yet my house with all its valuables faded to insignificance as I sensed that rather than resisting, I might simply surrender.

Seeing my dawning consent, he drew nearer step by step until he stood before me. I hung my head, the tears falling freely, but he touched my chin and lifted my face so that I had to look at him. And then he did something utterly astonishing. Untying the sash at his waist, he removed his sumptuous red and gold robe, reached behind me, and draped it over my shoulders, then gently placed my arms into the sleeves, folded the garment over my front, and secured the sash. I was so amazed, and it was all done so quickly and smoothly, that I could not react. Now he was naked and I was not. He had come not to take, but to give! Immediately I wanted to undo his gesture, to return the robe and cover his nakedness. But the look in his eyes told me that what had been done, was done. No more would I be naked, there was no more need, for he had seen me, and I him.

I knew him then. It all came thundering in upon me, the whole mystery of life revealed in a person. After that, I spent every minute with him. The time was short, I knew. The curtains were closing over this world, opening onto the next, and I was being ushered through. By what seemed to others a terrible disease, I was being healed. I became like the little child Christ set before his disciples and said, "Become like this...."

At this point in Jack's letter my pen ran out. I gave it a shake, but no, it was dry. I was about to get another when I felt such a strong sense of Jack's presence, I thought if I looked toward his chair in the living room, I might actually see him.

I did look—and there he was! Dressed in the old red-gold robe and looking like one of the wise men in our crèche. Imagine—Jack, a wise man!

But then I did a double-take and saw—it wasn't Jack.

Seated on Jack's throne, clothed in Jack's robe, and wearing a pair of Jack's boxer shorts on his head like a crown ...

It was Jesus.

And that look on his face—like a mischievous little boy!

I didn't know whether to laugh or cry. I did both. I nearly choked with amazement and joy.

When finally I settled down, Jesus leaned over and picked up something from the Christmas tree beside him. As he rose, I saw it was a small, oblong box, a gift wrapped in shiny paper with the same red and gold pattern as his robe. Approaching me, he set the gift on the table on top of Jack's letter.

And then he vanished.

That gift—it's back under the tree now, waiting for Christmas Day. I can guess what it is.

Maybe Jack will write that novel after all.

(2013)

Honorable Pigeon

Ever since the children had left, one of Nat's favorite remarks to his wife Midge was how empty the house felt without people in it. A big, jovial, red-faced bon vivant, he was forever bringing guests home from work. Usually there were a few foreign sales reps in town who were glad of the chance to escape their motel room and enjoy a home-cooked meal. In this way Nat had gotten to know a lot of people from all over the world. It was the part of his job that he liked best, and at home he was never more relaxed or expansive than in the presence of a third party.

This year, a few days before Christmas, he arrived home with a young Pakistani named Bashir and they sat down to one of Midge's beautiful roast goose dinners. Winking broadly at his wife, Nat remarked, "Usually at Christmas time around here we have partridge..." and he proceeded to tell the story of the big garish china partridge in a pear tree that they annually hauled out of the box of decorations and set in the place of honor on their mantel. Nat knew full well how hideous it was. Everyone agreed that the partridge looked like something extinct and flightless, and as for the pears, they had all fallen off, so the running joke was that the extremely corpulent bird had devoured them.

"You know, Midge, I don't think that pear tree ever will produce any more fruit," Nat would say every year. "Not with that big turkey smothering the life out of it." And then he would nearly smother himself, and her, with laughter.

Waving her diamond ring under his nose, Midge would reply, "Honey, it would be hard to improve on that first crop." Midge seldom laughed aloud, but she did wear a nearly permanent smile as if the corners of her mouth were hitched by wires to her ears.

On Christmas Day thirty years before, when presenting Midge with a heavy package, it had been all Nat could do to keep from bursting. He had stumbled across the thing in a thrift store window, and the monstrous appropriateness of this seasonal gift for his "true love" had tickled him nearly to death. And hadn't the look on her face been priceless!

"What on earth...?" she'd stammered.

"Take it apart!" Nat managed to choke out.

And sure enough, the bird, designed as a cookie jar, separated in the middle, and inside Midge found the diamond ring.

Ever since then, the unlikely partridge had made its annual appearance, pregnant with its symbolism of a long-ago Christmas engagement. In earlier years it had been filled with hard candies, but now that the kids were grown it held nothing but memories. Midge made no bones about her dislike of the bird, but to Nat this was just part of the fun. More than once she had told him that it seemed as though the partridge, more than the ring on her finger, were to him the real symbol of their marriage.

"Then wear the partridge on your finger!" he'd retort with a roar.

As Nat related this whole tale, Bashir smiled but did not laugh, and at the end, apparently nonplussed, he looked uncertainly at Midge. He was a pleasant, serious fellow with a round face, bright black eyes, and a refreshing guilelessness.

"Is the partridge, then, a religious symbol?" he asked.

Now it was Nat's turn to be nonplussed. Normally he liked to grill his guests about the politics of their country, finding out as much as he could about national affairs. But somehow Bashir kept turning the talk toward religion—a subject with which neither Nat nor Midge felt comfortable. But Bashir was very likeable and seemed quite at home with the topic. It seemed important to him to give his hosts some insight into what was involved in being a Muslim.

At one point he asked, "Tell me, please, what is your opinion of Jesus? I must tell you, very frankly, that I have never before been close enough to a true Christian to find out this question." Nat and Midge sat at either end of the rather long table, with Bashir in between. He looked expectantly from one to the other.

"Well-lll..." replied Nat, rubbing his chin. He considered himself a true Christian, alright, but that did not mean he knew what he thought about Jesus. It seemed to him an awfully private matter. "Jesus was a very great man..." he murmured. What more was there to say? He looked to Midge for help (something he seldom did), but she remained quiet. She was staring at Bashir with an almost frightened expression.

"It may surprise you greatly," said Bashir, "to know that the Holy Quran speaks most highly of Jesus, or Isa as he is called. We believe, as you do, that he performed many miracles, curing the blind and raising the dead. It is even said that he brought a clay bird to life. And he is the one who is to return at the end of time. Still, I must tell you, very frankly, that we do not hold Jesus in nearly as high regard as you do. I have heard it said, for example, that Christians actually worship Jesus as if he were Allah himself. Is it true?"

Again, an awkward pause. "I guess I would be of the opinion," said Nat slowly, "that that's maybe going a little too far...?" His voice trailed off and he looked toward the ceiling, as if hoping for support from above. When silence reigned, he added, "I suppose there are Christians and there are Christians."

"Well," said Bashir, speaking now with a tone of

greater boldness, "I must tell you, very frankly, that we find such worship of a human being most embarrassing and shocking. There is only one God, Allah, for all of us, and he is far from being a man.

"And one more thing," he pressed on with relentless matter-of-factness. "It is said that Christians worship not just one god, or even two, but three. How can this be so?"

Nat pushed back his chair from the table and wiped a hand across his brow. Bashir's question seemed unanswerable. Hoping to close off the conversation, Nat said simply, "I suppose each fellow has his own belief."

The two men smiled weakly at one another. Midge was as silent as a stone, and soon after this the evening drew to a close. Nat drove Bashir back to his motel, and in the car he found out a good deal about Pakistani politics.

*   *   *

Over the next few days Nat found himself thinking frequently about Bashir, recalling his shining eyes, his high lilting voice, and his questions concerning Christianity. What had he been driving at, exactly? In every other way he was such an agreeable man. He didn't seem the type to be a religious fanatic. How should Nat have responded? What would have been the Christian thing to say? He felt he had not been a very good representative of his religion.

He was reminded of another dinner conversation with a foreign guest, a Japanese man who had told an anecdote about one of his countrymen and a Catholic priest.

After hearing a talk by the priest, this fellow commented, "Honorable Father I understand; Honorable Son I understand; Honorable Pigeon I not understand."

Honorable Pigeon... In the days leading up to Christmas Nat couldn't get this phrase out of his mind. He kept muttering it, trying to tease out its meaning. He wished he could remember the joke.

He also found himself pondering Bashir's story from the Quran about Jesus bringing to life a clay bird. He imagined the Great Man tossing the clay model into the air before a hushed crowd, and everyone expecting it to smash to pieces on the ground—but it didn't! Instead it shuddered into glorious life, caught the air in its wings, and flew away! It seemed remarkable to Nat, amazing, to discover a story about Christ that he had not heard before. Could it be true?

*   *   *

When it came to church, Nat and Midge were two-timers: Christmas and Easter. Accordingly, arriving home late from the office on Christmas Eve, Nat expected to find Midge ready to go. But the house was silent and the door to the spare room was closed. One peek told Nat all he needed to know: migraine.

He sank down on the couch, loosened his tie, and stared at the Christmas tree. It would be no fun going to church by himself. But what was the alternative? The next day the kids would arrive and the place would be hopping. But to spend Christmas Eve alone ...?

He warmed up a frozen chicken pie in the microwave and listened to the all-Christmas radio station on headphones as he ate. He wracked his brain for someone he might call—but no, on this night everyone would be busy.

In the car as he neared the church, he considered driving right on by and maybe taking in a movie. But sitting in a theater alone seemed an even drearier prospect.

As he entered, a tall young man with pimples and a very wide mouth shook his hand and introduced himself as the guest minister. Uh-oh—this fellow wasn't even as old as Nat's son. And the minister should greet the congregation *after* the service, not before. But a children's choir was singing *Away in a Manger* and the church was radiant with candles, so that Nat, though he sat near the back, soon relaxed into the holiday spirit.

When it came time for the sermon, the young minister did not mount the pulpit but rather stood on the same level as the congregation—another bad sign. After calling the children to sit around him on the floor, he produced three objects: a large and powerful flashlight, an old-fashioned oil lantern, and a candle. After lighting the lantern and the candle and placing them on a small table, he switched on the flashlight, held it high over his head, and shone the beam out over the congregation.

"Think of this as our Heavenly Father ..." he began. And he proceeded to expound the doctrine of the Trinity. Though the explanation could not have been simpler—there were three different fires, but only one light—Nat had trouble following it because the flashlight beam kept hitting him in the eyes, almost as if that pimply fellow were deliberately targeting him.

"At the first Christmas," said the preacher, juggling his various fires, "God became a man in Jesus Christ, so that, believing in him, we ourselves might be filled with the Holy Spirit."

Nat had begun to feel physically hot, even to sweat. And while the sermon had opened in a casual, friendly tone, it was now winding up into an earnestness that Nat felt was out of place in church—at least in *his* church.

Midge needs me, he thought suddenly. *I should be at home.*

Abruptly he rose and slunk outside into an overcast evening as uncannily still as if everyone in the world had suddenly departed. Or gone to church.

Nat did not return home. Instead he let the car conduct him along King Street all the way into the center of town. Drawn by the magical forest of tiny white lights in the square, he parked and got out, thinking there would surely be some activity here, some life. But no—nothing. Not a soul. Behind a candlelit window something moved— a person? A ghost?

Buttoning his coat up to the neck, Nat sat heavily on a bench and folded his arms. He could not remember ever having felt so restless, so empty. He had no idea what to do. Worse, that minister's talk was buzzing around his head like a maddening insect. That fellow was exactly the sort of fundamentalist that Bashir had been upset about.

Peering into the empty square with its silent fountain, stilled for winter, Nat suddenly realized he was not alone. As if there were a slight breeze (though there was none), something like scraps of newspaper were blowing about. But it was not scraps of paper ... it was ...

Pigeons.

In the bedizened glimmer of the night about a dozen pigeons were strutting, flitting, pecking, and now one of them landed on the far arm of Nat's bench. He gave a start. The bird was so alive, so real, so *there*. The stole of iridescent green and purple at its neck seemed inordinately glamorous, opulent, for so otherwise plain a creature. Fastening its bright orange eye upon Nat, it cocked its head, as if about to speak. As if to ask a question...?

And then it flew off, taking with it, Nat felt unaccountably, a piece of his heart.

He continued sitting there on the bench for a long time, very still, letting something as soft and silent and silver as snowflakes fall all around him, and inside him, as if he were one with everything.

*   *   *

On Christmas morning he was up before dawn and could hardly wait for the day to begin. Midge was still barricaded in the spare room, however, and he knew better than to disturb her.

He thought of returning to the square to see if he

could find his pigeon, but instead he took a chair out to the back porch and did something he never did: simply sat. He sat and watched the morning come, its delicate colors displayed so beautifully among the feathery scarves of cloud.

When his son and daughter finally arrived with their broods, Nat had no need to don a red suit in order to inhabit with perfect merriment the soul of Father Christmas. He sang, he told jokes and stories, he bounced the little ones on his knee and gave horsey rides. He made blueberry pancakes for brunch, and when Midge appeared he caught her in an embrace and waltzed her around the kitchen (having carefully ascertained that her headache was gone).

After the opening of presents, Nat led them all in the traditional singsong, favoring more than ever before the more religious carols. But there was also *Frosty* and *Rudolph* and *Silver Bells* and, to wind things up, the noisiest, most rambunctious rendering of *The Twelve Days of Christmas* that any of them had ever heard.

As the last verse began, with its tumultuous descending recitation of all the twelve outlandish gifts, Nat took the china partridge from the mantel and held it aloft, precariously, as if daring it to fall, to hoots of mock concern from all around and even a "Nathaniel, be careful!" from Midge who was convulsed in laughter.

But Nathaniel was not careful. Instead, as the chorus reached its close with a sustained bellowing of *"And - a - par - tri - idge - in - a - pearrrrrrrr - treeeeeee!"* he threw open the sliding door to the back porch and heaved that big ugly monstrosity far out into the yard. Watching it sail through the air, for a moment he wondered if it might shake itself alive, spread real wings, and take flight. But no—it fell, and great was its fall upon a large rock in the garden. As it smashed—nay, exploded—there seemed to fly up out of the wreckage all manner of invisible winged entities: geese, swans, calling birds, French hens, turtle doves, angels, and at least one Lord a-leaping.

(2011)

The Giver

Christmas morning, 1995.

My daughter Heather is eight years old and we're sitting in the living room around the tree. We've barely begun to open presents, but already Heather is dragging out the one from Daddy, crying, "I want this one."

"No, Heather," I say for about the tenth time. "That's a special one that I'd like you to save until the end."

"But I want it NOWWWWWW!" she wails.

Already she's grabbing at the ribbon. What to do? Snatch the box away? In my mind I picture a vicious physical struggle over a Christmas present, a little girl hot with tears bolting furiously from the room, Karen glaring at me reproachfully, Christmas Day in ruins.

At the same time, I'm thinking about the contents of this box. This is a special gift and it's important to me that it be left until last. It's particularly important that Heather not open it in her present state: grasping, whining, impudent. Spoiled rotten.

"Heather, please don't open that now. I beg you."

"Daddy, don't be silly. It's my present. I can open it if I want."

Already she's tearing the paper.

"Heather—Stop! Please!"

But it's too late. The bare box is exposed and the lid is coming off. Now the tissue paper is parting....

Okay, okay, I tell myself. Lean back, take a deep breath. Get a grip. The special present is ruined, but it's not the end of the world.

And then, all at once—a miracle! Who would have dreamed that such a thing could happen?

Heather is crying! In fact, she is sobbing. As the contents of the box are laid bare, she sobs and sobs as if her heart would burst.

Karen and I lean closer, put our arms around her. All together we gaze at the object in the box, as still the crying goes on and on....

*   *   *

Now let me back up to the night before, Christmas Eve. It's getting on to midnight and after a busy week I'm longing for bed. But there's one more job I must do. It's a job that was supposed to be easy but, like most manual tasks I undertake, it's developed a bizarre complication.

I'm seated in a halo of light at my grandfather's old oak desk. In one hand I hold a wooden cross about eighteen inches long, and in the other a plastic figure of Jesus in a loincloth with His arms outstretched. I'm trying to get the two to fit together.

On the desk is a tube of contact cement and beside it a small bottle of epoxy. Both substances have utterly failed to accomplish their intended purpose. I'm about to go down to the basement to fetch the hot glue gun. But I can tell you right now, that isn't going to work either.

The problem is that Jesus is warped. His hands and His feet are not on a level plane, so that every time I try to stick Him down, He pops up again. This plastic is really tough stuff!

Finally I get so exasperated with the darned thing that I'm about ready to use nails. At that point, I turn the whole mess over to Karen, who of course with her womanly arts somehow accomplishes it easily.

And so to bed.

*   *   *

Only once before in her life have I heard Heather cry the way she cried that Christmas morning. The other time, we were in church singing worship songs. At least, Karen and I were singing. At that age Heather was more likely to be reading, drawing, coloring, fidgeting, talking, or rummaging around for food.

All at once, for no apparent reason, she burst into tears. Different kinds of crying have different sounds, and instantly I knew that this was no ordinary crying over a pinched finger or a thwarted desire. This was weeping.

Have you ever heard a child weep? The crying of angels, I suppose, could hardly have a sound more surprising, more holy, more heartrendingly pure.

It went on for a long, long time, and when it finally ceased our little girl's face looked like a freshly bloomed rose washed in dew in the first light of morning.

Later when we asked her what had happened, she said simply, "I saw an angel light." Back then I was working on a book about angels, and I'd mentioned to her that some people see angels not in the form of figures, but as colored lights.

Glancing up toward the church balcony that morning, Heather had seen a circular light composed of beautiful colors. This is what had touched her heart, and for long afterwards she referred to this experience as her "vision."

*   *   *

Now it's Christmas morning and once again I'm hearing the sound of my daughter weeping. Only this time it's not a vision she's seeing, it's something solid and tangible. An object.

The object Heather is crying over is a crucifix. Jesus on the cross.

Her crying is deep, savage, tender.

The crucifix is something she wanted. Asked for. I have one in my study that I received as gift at the age of fifteen on the occasion of my confirmation in the Anglican church. I did not become a Christian until fifteen years later, in the meantime sowing a lot of wild oats. But for some reason, wherever I went, I kept that crucifix hanging on my wall.

Heather, looking at it one day, asked if she could have one for her room. I was pleased. Overjoyed, in fact. I'd far rather give her Jesus than Barbie.

So off I went to the Catholic bookstore (really more of a jewelry or hardware store) to look at crucifixes. I couldn't find one that I liked. After all, it was two days before Christmas, hardly the right season. Easter stock was low.

In the end I had to buy the cross and the figure separately, which is why I spent Christmas Eve trying to affix Jesus to His cross and finding out that He didn't want to go.

*   *   *

Come morning, I can hardly wait for Heather to open her special present. But it has to be saved for last, I reason, after the orgy of materialism is spent. That way we can move easily into a time of family devotions. Every year this is a challenge, trying to slip the Bible in among the presents without Heather noticing.

This year, instead of the Christmas story from Luke, I plan to read the story of Good Friday and Easter. It will be a different sort of Christmas, a memorable one. But never in my fondest imaginings could I have predicted just how different and memorable this Christmas would be.

Heather's weeping goes on and on… and on and on…

The three of us sit there huddling on the couch until,

finally, the sobbing subsides. Heather still hasn't lifted the crucifix out of its box. Now she begins to touch it, delicately, exploratively, and eventually she takes it into her hands.

By this point the room is filling up with a kind of warm, rich, golden glow. All of us feel it. We're all teary, tenderized, bright-eyed. It's as if God Himself has opened us up like Christmas gifts, exposing our soft and real hearts and touching them with His fingers.

What happens next is no canned devotional time, but the most beautiful and spontaneous worship I have ever experienced. With God right there in the room, what else can we do but thank and praise Him and lift our voices in hymns and carols? We even get up and dance around the Christmas tree for pure joy.

Oh yes—Jesus will not stay on His cross today! He will not be glued down and hung on a wall! For close to an hour an eight-year-old girl completely forgets all the rest of her presents, still waiting to be opened, and celebrates one present only, the one gift that she suddenly knows to be better than all other gifts in the world put together.

What comes out of the box this Christmas morning is no mere crucifix, but Jesus Himself—Jesus alive, royally well, and bursting with happiness. More than a gift, this is the Giver Himself.

(1996)

Christmas in July

It was July 24, 1976, and I needed a Christmas tree. How could we have Christmas without a tree? At home the tree was always the center of everything.

But I wasn't at home. I was a hundred miles away on an island in Lake of the Woods, at a summer camp where I was in charge of a cabin of eight girls. Though I'd attended the camp myself for years, this was my first time as a counselor and things had not gone well. I couldn't control my nine-year-olds and I felt they disliked me, especially one with stringy red hair named Timmie who was taller than I was. With the camp's traditional celebration of Christmas in July one day away, I needed a win. I was responsible for decorations. I needed a tree.

In years past there had always been a tree. But this time, wouldn't you know it, we had a new director, Miss

Eva, who believed in "no-trace camping." Before, whenever we went on overnight canoe trips to other islands, we cut down little trees and lashed them to make tables, chairs, all kinds of things. I know it sounds scandalous now, but back then it was just what we did. This was Canadian wilderness and the trees went on and on forever.

All this changed when the word *conservation* entered the vocabulary. Overnight, it seemed, the supply of trees dropped drastically and now they had to be conserved. No-trace camping was the big buzzword. The teenager I was in 1976 did not care much for this idea. All I knew was that we needed a tree for Christmas and the powers-that-be were against it. Suddenly, cutting a tree was like cutting human flesh. But how could you have Christmas without the blood sacrifice of a young evergreen?

When I mentioned it to Ryan, he said, "Why don't you just cut one anyway? What's one tree?" Ryan was my first crush. He was our waterfront director and everyone called him Wonder Duck. To me he was no duck, but a golden haired god with eyes the color of seawater.

The only person I told about my crush was Shannon, our crafts director. She was helping my girls make paper ornaments—chains and balls and lanterns and snowflakes—and a star out of pine cones. When I whispered to Shannon how dreamy Wonder Duck was and how I thought I loved him, I wondered why she looked at me strangely.

*   *   *

On the night of July 24 I lay in my bunk and asked God to provide a Christmas tree. After all, He was supposed to be *Jehovah-jireh*, a name that means *The Lord Will Provide.* I'd learned this from Skipper, our chaplain who gave campfire talks. We called him Skipper because of his neat white beard that made him look like a sea captain. He was a great storyteller and with the flames dancing on his little round glasses he could hold us all spellbound. The night before, he'd told the story of Abraham preparing to sacrifice his son Isaac, and at the last moment finding a ram caught by its horns in a thicket. Abraham called that place The Lord Will Provide.

Alright, I thought—let Him provide a Christmas tree. I didn't think He would. I didn't see how He could. Even Jesus couldn't cut trees anymore. Conservation was bigger than God and He would just have to obey it like the rest of us. Still, I prayed. My need was desperate, and huddled in my sleeping bag on Christmas Eve in July, listening to a high wind outside, I prayed.

Little did I know that the answer to my dilemma would appear the next morning, lying on the path near my cabin. A beautiful little balsam fir, the ideal shape and size and covered with candles! Not real candles, but cones, dozens of them sticking straight up along every branch and glistening with sap like lit tapers.

I was stunned. Standing the tree up, I walked all around it. It was a little taller than me. It could not have been more perfect. It was almost like being in the presence of a person. But where had it come from? It seemed to have just fallen from heaven. Talk about a Christmas gift!

My girls were still sleeping, but I rushed into the cabin and woke them to come and see what The Lord Had Provided. We laughed and shouted and whirled about, and for the first time in two weeks I felt connected to them—even to Timmie, who danced as though her hair was on fire. Watching her, suddenly I was young again, just a little kid on Christmas morning, the vast abyss that separates the child from the teenager all at once bridged.

We carried that tree up to the hall like hunters in a hungry winter returning with a stag. Wonder Duck would be so proud of me! As we set it up and strung and hung our colored paper decorations, other campers and staff gathered around and I told the story again and again of the tree that had fallen from heaven. But where was Wonder Duck? He was usually in the middle of anything exciting.

At one point I had to get something from my cabin, and then I saw him, down by the water, sitting on the dock. With Shannon.

I was about to go and tell them my story, when I noticed they were holding hands....

Instantly I knew, of course, that I didn't have a chance against Shannon. She was too beautiful, talented, mature. And she and Wonder Duck, you could tell, were a perfect match. I tried to console myself with the thought that now I had something better than a golden Greek god. Didn't I have the Lord Who Provides, the God of heaven and earth who had personally answered my prayer? But no—what was a miserable little tree compared to the love of a lifetime?

Returning to the hall, I did my best to join in the celebration as the whole camp gathered around my tree and exchanged gifts—simple crafts of birch bark and stone and wood, wrapped in construction paper. And later on we sat down to a feast of turkey and stuffing and all the trimmings. To see such abundance appear on the tables, there on an island in the middle of the wilderness—well, in former years this had always seemed the purest magic. But now I could hardly bear to lift a fork.

After supper, when Santa Claus arrived, everyone but the littlest campers knew it was Wonder Duck. Santa had special gifts for the chief staff members: for Skipper, an admiral's cap; for Miss Eva the conservationist, an axe. And when Shannon came and sat on Santa's lap, the whole place erupted in whistles and catcalls. "She wants a kiss for Christmas!" shouted the boys. "Kiss her, Santa! Kiss her!" And he did. Santa placed a big wet kiss right on her mouth, and she kissed him back.

That's when I lost it completely. I was sixteen and never been kissed, never even held hands, and it seemed like such things could never happen for me. I was doomed to never have a boyfriend, never have a husband or family, and my insides would always be eaten by this raging, lonely ache.

Slinking from the hall, I went to my cabin and sobbed.

*   *   *

That night there was a campfire out at the point. The lake was completely calm and Skipper paddled a canoe a little ways from shore and spoke to us from there. Though it was a moonless night and we could barely see him, we heard him perfectly, as if his voice issued from the darkness itself or as if the black water were speaking. He said that the very first Christmas in Bethlehem would have been much like this one, because Jesus was probably born in March or April, not December, and that in any case the Holy Land didn't have snow. It would have been warm and green and the night would have been big and black and velvet just like this one, with the stars nearly popping out of the sky like a choir of angels themselves, and at least a dozen stars so bright that any one of them might have been the Christmas star.

As he talked I was watching the trees, those spires of spruce and pine and hemlock, each one seeming to point to its own individual star. My eyes fell on a majestic balsam fir at least a hundred feet tall. Standing all by itself, it seemed so lonely. It appeared to be gazing back at me, and looking up to its top I realized ... it wasn't there! The topmost tip, pre-decorated with its load of cones, stood now, I suddenly knew, in the dining hall—having been delivered first class nearly to my doorstep by last night's wind.

At that moment the full message of Christmas burst upon me, how God had sent His Son to earth—*for me*. I could feel it, just how it was the night Jesus was born. And it felt like He was being born *in me*.

Later, in my bunk, thinking of my tree—my ravishing, heaven-sent, cone-lit tree—my cup of romance was full. It was, there in the dark soft heart of summer, not only the best Christmas I'd ever had, but the first real one.

*   *   *

Thirty years later, two weeks before Christmas, I find myself recalling all this as I take the dog for his nightly stroll and discover, right outside our house, a surprise in the soft new snow. It's lying by our sidewalk, as though placed there for me. For a minute or so I simply stand and stare. I can't believe it. It's like seeing an angel. That great and holy night when I was sixteen comes rushing back to me and my eyes fill with tears. Before I even touch the tree, or caress its lovely branches, or stand it up and marvel, I know it's perfect. As I kneel in the snow, perfection pierces my soul like light.

It's not a balsam fir this time, but a white spruce, the very top of a big tree that cracked off in last night's storm and landed almost in our living room. No cones this time, but the branches sweep up and up in long beautiful arcs as though reaching for heaven. And later that night I watch in wonder as two handsome men, my husband and my son, carry the tree into our home.

(2006)

69

Miles

It all began the Christmas I was nine. I guess I put a little too much tape on my brother's present.

"What did you do to this thing?" Miles complained. "Encase it in concrete? I bet this crummy present isn't even worth opening. What's in it, rat poison? I don't even want it. Here—you take it."

With a flick of the wrist Miles winged the present straight at my head. Ducking, I heard it crash against the wall over my shoulder. So much for the ceramic spaceship piggy bank I'd spent two whole dollars on. So much for Miles. With a cry of outrage I picked up his present and took aim.

"Boys, boys!" yelled Mom. "It's Christmas."

It was no use. A moment later Miles and I were rolling around on the floor in a lethal embrace, and our big Christmas present that year was getting sent to our rooms.

Miles isn't my real brother. He was adopted after my parents gave up trying to have a kid of their own. A year later I came along. I couldn't understand why Miles got so angry. Any little thing could set him off, and that would get me going.

By the next Christmas I'd forgotten all about my over-wrapped present, but Miles hadn't. He decided to get me back by wrapping my gift in as much tape as he could get his hands on. Not just Scotch tape, either, but thick swaths of packing tape. He must have gone through three or four rolls of the stuff, making my present look like a solid mass of congealed glue.

"What's this all about?" I asked.

"Merry Christmas, Ben," said Miles. "I know how you love that stuff."

Scissors wouldn't cut it. I had to take the thing to the basement and saw it open. I have no recollection of what was inside, but at least that year we didn't fight. Miles was eleven and I was ten and we'd almost outgrown physical combat. We even got along some, at least on the surface.

After that, the Christmas present thing became a kind of game. He thought he'd paid me back and that was it. But the following year I put his present inside a wooden box and screwed it shut, then tied the whole thing with pretty ribbons of barbed wire, well knotted with pliers. I was disappointed when it took Miles only about ten minutes to get into it. Next time I'd do better.

By the following Christmas, however, I was the one

who forgot about the game. So it came as a complete surprise when Miles led me to the kitchen, pointed at the freezer, and told me to open it.

"You're giving me food?"

"Just open it."

Inside was a huge block of ice. In the middle of the block, far away and blurry like something appearing through thick fog, was what looked like a small scrap of red Christmas paper. I heaved the block out of the freezer. It must have weighed fifty pounds.

"What am I supposed to do with this?"

"It's up to you," said Miles. "Put it in a glass of pop, maybe? Or toss it in the back yard and wait till spring."

Again, I've forgotten what that present was. All I remember is the ice. In fact for the next few Christmases I have no idea what we gave each other; I recall only the wrappings. Each year they became more ingenious, more outlandish, more impenetrable.

One year I really did encase Miles's gift in concrete.

The next year he welded mine inside a metal box and buried it in the back yard, where I had to locate it with a metal detector.

And then there was the year when Global Positioning was all the rage.

Another year the town did me the favor of re-paving the road in front of our house, and Miles had to bribe a friend in the public works department to cut through the new pavement.

He got me back good for that one—by sinking my next present in the lake. In the middle of winter I had to cut a hole in the ice, and get my cousin Jake to suit up in his diving gear to retrieve the thing.

And so it went, year after year of this jocular, faintly sinister ritual. As a kid I didn't give much thought to what was really going on between Miles and me. He hung out with a different crowd, his behavior got wilder and wilder, and we communicated less and less.

Around eighteen he got into some real trouble. First drugs and shoplifting, then a break and enter. Finally, in a bizarrely botched hold-up, he wounded a police officer and was sent to maximum for ten years.

That was the end of fiendishly wrapped Christmas presents. Ever try smuggling a concrete box into a prison cell? No, Miles had finally outdone me and won the game, or war, or whatever it was. From now on he himself was the hidden gift, inaccessibly wrapped in steel bars. The few times I visited him, what was there to say? There was no getting to him.

At twenty-one I "got religion," as they say, and I began to pray for Miles. Prayer, I figured, was better than a hack saw, better than any Global Positioning System. I prayed with great faith, expecting dramatic results. Nothing happened.

Several years later, while going through the motions of the usual strained visit with Miles, I happened to mention that our parents were moving.

"What? Selling the house?" He looked startled.

"Yeah, it's too big for them now."

After a thoughtful pause, he said, "Well, I might as well tell you. You know the big oak tree in the backyard? Take a metal detector and sniff around the trunk, about six feet up. You'll find a surprise."

"What—*inside* the tree?"

"Yeah. It'll be all overgrown now. I don't know how you'll get it out without cutting the tree down. But there, now I've told you."

One January Miles had bored a hole into the core of the tree and inserted a small object. By Christmas, he reasoned, the wound would be nicely healed. But that was the year he went to prison, so he never told me.

As it turned out, I didn't have to fell the tree, but I did make a mess of it. When I finally retrieved the present, I was awed. It was an engraved Rolex watch. Probably stolen, but still—Miles had never given me anything so personal. The engraving was of my initials entwined with a cross. Touched, I thanked him sincerely. And the more I thought about it, the more I wanted to give him something as meaningful in return. But what?

Around that time our dad, an aeronautical engineer, happened to land some work on the Canadarm for the International Space Station. One thing led to another, he was able to pull some strings, and that Christmas I proudly told Miles that his present was in orbit around the earth.

I knew he was impressed. As a kid he had been intensely interested in space and always said he wanted to be an astronaut. I could hardly keep from revealing what his gift was: a splendid star sapphire. But of course I couldn't tell, even though I knew his chances were slim of ever retrieving it, and this made me slightly uneasy.

However, the following year Miles was released on probation, and one of the first things he did was to contact Robert Thirsk, the Canadian astronaut who had aided my mission. One night around two a.m. the phone rang.

"I gotta to hand it to you, Ben. You almost got the better of me this time. But that thing you gave me—it's real pretty." After a pause, Miles added, "Thanks."

That was all he said. But I heard a change in his voice, and after this all our talks were more relaxed.

A few months later he re-offended. It was just selling pot, but that was enough to land him back inside.

And so another year passed, and another Christmas rolled around. I went to a party at the prison and Miles looked in fine form. We swapped stories about childhood and chuckled away as if we'd always been best buddies. I wondered what he was so happy about.

Just as I was leaving, he tapped me on the shoulder. "By the way, maybe you've heard about the new mission to Mars next year? Well, your Christmas present will be going along."

"Mars?" I said in astonishment.

"Yeah. After orbiting Mars it's going on to some of the other planets, and eventually it will leave the solar system."

Miles's grin was so wide I thought the top of his head would fall off. And then he started laughing, laughing so deep and long that there was no more talking to him. That's how I left him, standing beside the twelve-foot Christmas tree in the prison with his shoulders thrown back and his face aimed at the sky, looking like a perfectly free man.

I have no idea what's on that spacecraft to Mars. I guess I'll never know, any more than I can know what's wrapped up inside my brother. That cross on the back of my watch: Was it just for me, or did it mean something to him too? Who knows?

The best gifts have to wait for eternity.

(2000)

The Ghost of Christmas

W.R. Wheeler was what his daughter Rita called a "buttonholer." He fastened onto people and wouldn't let go until he had told them more than they ever wanted to know about Jesus Christ. He was not above pointing his long, bony index finger like the barrel of a loaded gun directly at the center of a man's chest, while resting the other hand companionably on the fellow's shoulder, ready to clamp down like a vise should he try to wriggle away. That, at least, was Rita's persistent image of him.

She was certainly right that, whether you were a dinner guest in her father's home or a stranger waiting at a bus stop, W.R. had but one thing on his mind: to tell you how to get saved. Or, if by chance you were saved already, he could be just as insistent about helping you find the Lord's will. As even his closest friends joked, "W.R. loves you and has a wonderful plan for your life." After all, what else was there to talk about besides God? Who had time to chatter away about politics and baseball, or to be suave and urbane as if pleasantness alone could ensure one a place in heaven? Was not life like a puff of smoke, like a flower of the field that bloomed one day and withered the next? The cashier who rang up your groceries on Friday morning, smiling and perky, might be dead Friday night, without ever having known the love of Jesus. The human predicament was desperate, catastrophic. Every moment eternity hung in the balance; staggering issues clamored for attention. If most people insisted on spending their lives frantically avoiding those issues, what better service could W.R. perform than to bring the eternal verities patiently but pressingly back to their attention? If W.R. had a childlike faith, he also had a child's capacity to aggravate.

Always at the back of his mind was God's warning to Ezekiel: "If you do not speak out to dissuade the wicked man from his ways, that wicked man will die in his sin, and I will hold you accountable for his blood." W.R. did not want to be responsible for any man not knowing the way of salvation. For him this was more than a matter of religious duty. After decades of missionary work in Korea, the gospel simply welled up out of him irrepressibly. He talked automatically of the Lord the way others talked of the weather, and as others recited jokes, W.R. recited God's Word. He breathed the Scriptures. "A beautiful day, W.R.," someone might greet him, to which he would reply heartily, "Amen! The Sun of Righteousness has risen with healing in His wings!" And he would be off and running.

He'd had some astounding successes. One of his favorites was the vacuum cleaner salesman who had knocked on his door one day and ended up staying for a month while W.R. discipled him. Now the man was pastor of a large church in California. Another time a young customs official had made the mistake of asking W.R. if he was carrying any liquor in the car. That fellow ended up working with Wycliffe Bible Translators in New Guinea.

There were dozens of such tales. In fact, if one could possibly have totaled up the number of people W.R. had led to the Lord, taking into account that new converts would in turn carry the message to others in an ever-widening network—well, it was simply staggering the impact that one man could have for the Kingdom of God. While W.R. took great comfort in this thought, he knew also that he was only a farmer scattering seed. Much of the seed was bound to fall by the wayside among rocks or thorns, but some, he knew, would fall on good soil and produce a crop of fifty or a hundredfold. It was his job to broadcast the seed; it was the Lord's job to make it grow.

W.R. Wheeler even looked like a farmer. His face and neck and hands (and those parts alone) were brown as dirt from a life spent largely outdoors, trekking to far-flung villages and preaching in the open air. He was tall and skinny as a post, and about as wooden in the way he walked, and when he stood still he seemed to lean somewhat, as though facing into a strong wind. His Adam's apple jutted out like a bone swallowed the wrong way. And his eyes had the look of someone who searches the skies, checks the horizon, forever peers into the far distance. It was a look of eager anticipation combined with great long-suffering.

Of late, however, W.R.'s tremendous confidence was wearing thin. Instead of giving thanks for all that the Lord had done through him in his long life, he was increasingly preoccupied with what the Lord was not doing. He found himself bothered by the barren soil. Was there really nothing to be done about it? Had he himself, perhaps, contributed to its barrenness?

His thoughts focused particularly on his daughter Rita. His five other children were born-again Christians, serving the Lord in various parts of the world. His two oldest sons had even followed him to Korea and were this moment working on additions to the school and hospital complex he had built, as well as preaching and leading Bible studies just as he had done for forty years. One other son was a missionary doctor in Africa, ministering not far from where the heart of David Livingstone was buried. As for W.R.'s two youngest daughters, they were not, admittedly, leading lives that were dramatically evangelistic. They had settled down with good but unambitious husbands and were raising families. With their color television sets and their microwave ovens, W.R. found them, frankly, rather dull. They had never caught the missionary vision. But at least they knew the Lord, and that was the main thing.

With Rita, however, it was a different story. Rita was

the sole holdout. While the other girls were quiet and obedient creatures, pretty and feminine, Rita was a large, big-boned woman, stubborn, outspoken, and raucously jovial. Where had this one come from? She seemed of a different cut entirely from the rest of the family, although perhaps the truth was that she was so much like her father that neither of them could appreciate the resemblance. If W.R. was an evangelist for the Lord, then Rita practiced her own brand of evangelism, and it was decidedly not a religious one.

Rita had made one big mistake in her life. At twenty-five she had let a man sleep with her—a man she had known only a few hours who did not even care for her body, let alone for her, but only for a night of sex. Of course Rita had known this; she was not stupid. But she had quite simply been overcome by desire. Even as a teenager, before putting on weight, she had not had many dates. So it had been a moment of weakness, that was all, like reaching for a chocolate éclair. It could have happened to anyone. But the result was a child.

W.R., who had recently returned from Korea after a five-year absence, had seen Charlotte only as a baby. When the Mission Board forced him to retire (that was a story in itself), he determined to settle down in the same city as Rita, largely with the motive of having some impact upon this granddaughter of his (and even upon Rita herself) before it was too late. In fact he had a dream in which he felt the Lord promising him success if he went to live near his wayward daughter. Accordingly, he purchased a small house in a neighboring suburb, a broken-down thing held together mostly by years of grime. W.R. was a frugal man who appreciated a bargain.

Rita met him at the airport, and for the first few days things went extremely well. She bent over backwards to help her father get established. Together they cleaned the whole house in three days, scrubbing until it gleamed, working shoulder to shoulder and joshing around like old army buddies. They both were garrulous and shared a robust and eccentric sense of humor. Charlotte, tiny as she was, joined eagerly in the work. She could scarcely carry a pail of water without spilling most of it, but she was a bright, well-behaved girl and W.R. took an instant shine to her.

Having finished the inside of the house, they moved outside to scrape, paint, nail, and share secrets of carpentry as towering white clouds scudded like tall ships across the vast midwestern sky. It was the height of summer. Evenings were cool and luminous, and after work the three of them would sit in the backyard around a hibachi until the mosquitoes drove them indoors. Then, with Charlotte asleep, Rita and W.R. would stay up talking and talking in the manner of family members who, having little in common anymore, nevertheless shared in their mutual past a certain lost innocence. In particular, they reminisced fondly of Rita's mother, gone these twenty years.

Strange as it might sound, there were even ways in which W.R. felt closer to Rita than to any of his other children, though he would never have admitted this himself. For in the final analysis, what real fellowship could believers have with unbelievers?

The trouble began, naturally, when W.R. started his buttonholing. How would Charlotte like a storybook about an exciting hero named Jesus? Did she know there was such a thing as salvation? And wouldn't she enjoy coming to church with her old grandpa?

Rita hit the roof. One of these conversations, right under her nose, she let pass. But the second time it happened she stood up from her lawn chair, a loaded hamburger dripping ketchup down her arm, and gave W.R. one of her notorious "teacher stares," grim enough to stop a locomotive. She taught junior high and brooked no nonsense from anyone, including the principal.

For a few tense moments nothing was said. The mother boiled, the little girl crept to the edge of her chair, and Grandpa looked a portrait of innocence. Once Rita gained a semblance of control, she said—speaking in measured tones as if counting out W.R.'s allowance—"Dad, we're happy to have you here. But there will be no discussion of religion in this family. You know the problems it's always caused between us. Charlotte wants a grandpa, not a propagandist."

Rita had learned well from her father. The only way to handle W.R. was to be more assertive, more intimidating, than he was.

And so a line was drawn. At least Rita had drawn her

line; it was not yet clear where W.R. would draw his. He decided to limit his evangelizing to private conversations with the girl, explaining carefully that it might be better if mother didn't know when they had talked of "certain matters." But of course mother did know; she grilled her daughter on every detail of her times alone with Grandpa. In her strong-willed, big-hearted way she loved the old man, but when it came to this business of religion she trusted him no more than one of her junior-high boys. He had a one-track mind and she was determined that Charlotte not be swallowed up in his fanaticism. What if the girl rebelled one day and actually became a Christian? Charlotte was all she had. How could she stand to have her own daughter side against her, just as the rest of the family always had?

Soon there came a second confrontation with W.R., in which she told him pointblank that if he ever again so much as breathed the name of Jesus around Charlotte, she would cut off their visits entirely. "I'm not fooling, Dad. I'm not having you pump my daughter full of your pious blarney." Rita had a way of planting her feet, arms akimbo, that made her look like the entire defensive line of a football team.

W.R., however, was not inexperienced as a quarterback. His whole life had been devoted to smuggling the gospel past all opposition, and there was something in this second warning of Rita's that served only to whet his zeal. He considered it a healthier thing when people openly resisted the faith rather than pretending to be Christians when really they were not. Indeed the very extremity of Rita's reaction might even be a sign that she was closer than she knew to surrendering. Besides, had not the gospel always thrived under persecution? At least now the battle lines were clearly drawn, and W.R. warmed to the task ahead. He prayed up a storm; his Adam's apple worked overtime. Fully confident of the inherent power of the gospel, he set about evangelizing his granddaughter more brazenly than ever.

The third confrontation was a calm one: a long, cool, rational talk. A meeting between generals. From the start W.R. took the high ground, pointing out to Rita how totally unreasonable were her demands. The gospel was the plain truth and could not be suppressed. Did she expect Charlotte to go through life without ever having to deal with the great questions of faith, without ever thinking it through for herself? Did she expect to keep her in the dark about Jesus Christ, the most famous man in history? Did she really think she could protect her daughter from everything she herself did not agree with? Besides, he argued, his Christianity was so much a part of him that he could not possibly be silent about it. Take that away and he was nobody. Did Rita want Charlotte to have a nobody for a grandfather? A fake, an impostor? Or would she be allowed to get to know her grandpa in 3-D and technicolor, as the full-blooded old rapscallion of a missionary that he was?

W.R.'s case was so convincing, so watertight, that he began to believe he was winning over his daughter. She listened to him so patiently, grew so very quiet, and in the end offered no further arguments—except, as it turned out, the argument of total intransigence. For finally she looked him straight in the eye and said, "Dad, it's plain that when it comes to religion you are not a sane man. You are determined to infect Charlotte with your bigoted views, even against the wishes of her own mother. Therefore, since you cannot control yourself, you leave me no choice but to forbid you to have anything to do with her. From now on you are not to try to see Charlotte under any circumstances, and until you agree to change your mind and refrain from proselytizing, I'm afraid you are no longer welcome in our home. I'm sorry, but I cannot see any other solution. Perhaps you will come to your senses."

And that was the end of that.

Initially W.R. did not really believe she could be in earnest. He had not seriously considered that it might come to this. Of course the gospel was bound to attract opposition; deep and determined hostility was to be expected. Had not Jesus warned, "A man's enemies will be the members of his own household"? But the willful severing of blood ties—that was not a thing to be done lightly. Surely, given time, the storm would blow over.

But it did not blow over. Three times in the next two weeks W.R. phoned his daughter and remonstrated with her. But always her answer was the same: W.R. was the one who was making things difficult, not she. If he were a sex maniac, or insisted on giving Charlotte drugs, then her reaction would have been the same. She was simply setting clear limits, as any parent had to do these days. It was up to W.R. to respect those limits. Parents, not grandparents, must have the final word in a child's upbringing.

One day W.R. showed up on Rita's doorstep and was actually turned away. By his own daughter! How many times had he changed her diapers? And now he found himself standing on her step in a September drizzle, the door shut in his face. He couldn't get over it. The thing just wouldn't sink in. Clearly, as unsavory as it might sound, his daughter must be in the grip of the Devil. Or could it be the Lord Himself who, for reasons known only to Him, had hardened her heart as He had done with Pharaoh?

"Blessed are those who are persecuted for righteousness' sake," Jesus promised, and on one level W.R. did rejoice at being rejected on account of the gospel. But deeper down, he agonized. A month passed, then two. He threw himself into the work of the local church but could find no peace. The image of his little granddaughter haunted him. He pleaded with the Lord to show him what to do, but no clear answer came. Should he just give in? But that was unthinkable. To accede to Rita's demands was to deny his Lord, his very soul. Had not Jesus said, "He who denies me before men, I will deny before my Father?" So his hands were tied. It was utterly inconceivable for him to carry on a relationship without ever talking of Christ, without any bold witness to His love and glory. It was like trying to avoid the word *and* or *the* in conversation or to get along without any vowels. What was left to say?

For Rita's part, teaching junior high had inured her to battles of the will. Could any human beings on earth be more ornery than pubescent teenagers? But Rita prided herself on being able to hold her own against any of them. She planted her feet and refused to budge; it was as simple as that. And the same methods that worked in the classroom she applied to the larger arena of life, treating the world as a school and other adults as students. When it came to her father, therefore, it wasn't that Rita had disowned him, she had simply sent him to the hall to cool his heels. When he was good and ready to behave himself, he could come back. W.R. was a powerful, persuasive, stubborn customer; if Rita gave him so much as an inch, he would swallow her whole. Perhaps the very secret to her strength of character was this lifelong opposition to her father, this capacity for outmaneuvering him.

Both father and daughter tended to view things in black-and-white terms. But while for Rita this made for simplicity, in the present crisis W.R. found himself squirming amidst a growing complexity. Charlotte had started first grade, and as the long, light-filled summer days shrank away into fall the old man tormented himself with the thought of all the precious moments he was missing in the development of his granddaughter. She would be learning how to read. Soon she would be able to study God's Word for herself. But would the estrangement from her Christian grandfather turn her away from Christ forever? And what kind of lies would Rita tell the child about him? That he was nothing but a religious nut, a dangerous old fool to be avoided like the plague? How impressionable was a young mind! And then there was the question of Rita herself. Where had W.R. gone wrong with her? All these years he had prayed unceasingly for her conversion, but of course being on the opposite side of the globe had made it much easier to leave her in the hands of the Lord. Now, in his retirement, he was brought face to face with his failure as a Christian father.

Uncharacteristically, W.R. began to give way to depression. He brooded, lost his appetite, grew listless. Never had he faced such a trial. He had endured difficult situations, been under enormous stress. But he was an optimistic sort, not easily discouraged even for an hour. Why was he affected so grievously now? Part of the problem, undoubtedly, was his forced retirement. No more carrying the gospel to the ends of the earth, no more living on the very cutting edge of the kingdom. Now he was stuck in this backwater of an American suburb, out in the boondocks of faith. His sons had even joked that he would be getting a color TV and a microwave himself, and taking up lawn bowling and cribbage. Increasingly such thoughts oppressed him.

Still, there was no reason to stop trusting in the Lord. No reason was good enough for that. What business did a Christian have moping around? "Rejoice in the Lord always," said the Apostle. "And again I say, rejoice!" But more and more W.R. could find no joy, no peace. Though he searched the scriptures for consolation and direction, somehow it was the passages of warning and censure that lodged in his heart. "If a man know not how to rule his own house," wrote Paul to Timothy, "how shall he take care of the church of God?" At such words W.R.'s whole ministry came before him in question. Had he preached the gospel to others, only to be disqualified himself? Had all his years of witnessing been without love and therefore worthless? Was he nothing but sounding brass, a tinkling cymbal?

For the first time he could ever remember, W.R. experienced a prolonged inability to pray. Rather than pouring out all his concerns in a flood of words like a little child to his Father, he tended now to sit mute before the Lord, both his tongue and his heart frozen tight. Sometimes he felt nothing at all, other times he was a tangled mess of hurt and confusion, even moaning and groaning out loud like an animal. Occasionally he even yelled at God, bawling Him out for not answering. What on earth was going on? Was he losing his mind? Or worse, his faith? A man who insisted on fretting, who would not let go of his problems and surrender them to the Lord, was a man who did not believe.

Another month went by, and another. Snow came, melted once, then came to stay. The daylight dwindled and the night sky grew black as an open grave above the white earth. The stars were brighter than in summer, but also farther away, and they shone with a cold light.

On one of these nights, just a week before Christmas, W.R. was poring over his Bible, following each line with his index finger as he always did. He was in the first chapter of Luke, beginning a study of that evangelist's incandescent account of the first Christmas. But first came the story of Zechariah, the father of John the Baptist, and all at once a peculiar feeling crept over W.R., almost a kind of spell. It was like that uncanny experience when some ordinary sound (running water, for instance, or the flickering of a fire) seems transformed into clear, audible music, as though a marching band may be winding its way through distant streets. Yet what W.R. heard on that December evening was not music, but rather the voice of the Lord God speaking to him, saying, "Behold, thou shalt be dumb, and not able to speak, because thou believest not my words, which shall be fulfilled in their season." It was the twentieth verse, in which Zechariah, seeing a vision of the angel Gabriel and yet doubting the divine message, was struck dumb, unable to speak another word until the angel's promise had come true.

W.R. stared at the page, his mouth dry and hollow. Though he knew the story well, this time as he read it something moved inside him, shifted, like plates of the earth's crust or like a fetus moving in the womb. There was a kick, a pang of queasy pain but also of wonder, and then a slow subterranean explosion as though some hard wad of congestion deep inside him were being dislodged, blown apart. "The word of God is quick and powerful," wrote the author of Hebrews, "and sharper than any two-edged sword, piercing even to the dividing asunder of soul and spirit, and of the joints and marrow."

And then something new came flooding into W.R.'s heart, something new and great and inexpressibly wonderful.

The very next morning, the annual children's Christmas pageant was presented at W.R.'s church. This year it was a mime; instead of the excruciating woodenness of children reciting lines, not a word was spoken. There was only the dreamlike solemnity of small bodies draped in bath towels shuffling back and forth across the stage. The congregation craned their necks to see, chuckled, exchanged wry and puzzled glances. But W.R. covered his face and wept.

The message for him was all too clear. For whatever reasons, the privilege of speech had been taken away. The thing he had most depended on all his life could not be used. He was like a boxer with both hands tied behind his back. Like Zechariah, he had the most wonderful news to share with the world, and especially with Rita and Charlotte. But he could not open his mouth. Yet might the Lord still make use of him, just as he had used Zechariah, working through a man's silence even more powerfully than through his speech?

For the next few days W.R. was like a patient emerging from a long illness. The daylight hurt his eyes; his legs felt like rubber. The world seemed such a vast and bewildering place. He had planned to visit two dozen hospital patients in the week before Christmas, but he could not summon the energy. His stomach was unsettled and he ate little. He felt strangely tender, inside and out, and often on the verge of tears. All he wanted to do was to sit still in a chair and be with God, immobilized by wonder. For the root of despair, when finally exposed, begins to shrivel, and its wizened detritus is the kernel of joy.

Two days before Christmas W.R. phoned Rita and told her he was ready to give in. He had been wrong, he admitted, stubborn as an old mule. Would she forgive him? And couldn't they spend Christmas together? He promised to respect her wishes and say nothing to Charlotte about religion. They would just have a nice day, play some games, eat some turkey, make up for the months of hurt.

If Rita had been a believer, she might have fallen on her knees and thanked God for this miracle. As it was, she was inclined to be skeptical. The granting of forgiveness could be harder than the asking, and having established a safe distance from her father, she would have been happy to carry on as if he were still in Korea.

Nevertheless, he was her father and it was Christmas. And there was no mistaking the tone of sincerity in his voice, the ring of genuine repentance. Had a miracle indeed occurred? Might the old goat really learn to bite his tongue?

Oh, the power of Christmas to draw together families,

those wiliest of enemies! There it sits in the dead of winter, a pagan feast taken over by the Christians and then secularized, a season both peaceful and tumultuous, garish and holy, in which warring nations lay down their arms while families take up knives and forks and sit down together to eat. People who have hardly anything in common gather in the soft glow of candles and colored lights to gnaw on the same carcass, to wear one another's gifts, to wrack their brains for something to talk about. Christmas: a sacrament in which believer and unbeliever share alike.

By the time the day arrived W.R.'s period of religious ecstasy had mysteriously passed. He knew it was over from the moment he laid eyes on the enormous plastic Santa Claus, complete with sleigh and reindeer, set up on the lawn of Rita's house. He eyed it with the same disgust he had felt towards all those tawdry statues of the Buddha that littered the Far East. To W.R., Santa even bore some resemblance to the Buddha; both were roly-poly pig-men whose pasty faces gleamed with slovenly, self-satisfied smirks that people mistook for joy. Mentally composing a sermonette, W.R. warmed to his topic. No mere effigy, this plastic Santa Claus was an idol, a powerful alien god riding in a chariot. And like all idols he was an empty invention of man, a clay-footed technique for supplanting the one true Lord. A pagan leech, he sucked glory from Christ. For it was not Santa Claus who bestowed gifts at Christmas—it was the Lord Jesus! As W.R. rang his daughter's doorbell, suddenly he realized why Santa wore a red suit: It was because he was the Devil in disguise!

Rita, teacher that she was, had decorated the whole house lavishly. There were lights inside and out, festoons of crepe paper, strings of popcorn, wreaths, mistletoe, Christmas cards everywhere. A foil angel crowned the tree, but otherwise W.R. noted an obvious and studied avoidance of all religious symbols. Well, he had promised to say nothing. At least Rita was not averse to playing Christmas carols on the stereo, the kind of thing with "O Holy Night" and "Here Comes Santa Claus" back to back, sung by a choir of orphan children.

Father and daughter embraced, but not without holding back. Forgiveness, as it turned out, was not a business to be transacted over the telephone. And when little Charlotte ran into his arms, W.R.'s heart sank. Here was a child who might never know the Lord! How could her grandfather, on Christmas Day of all days, keep such a secret? Right then and there he nearly broke his resolve. As a young man, before heading out to Korea, he had felt called to take the gospel to Islamic nations, but two governments had thrown him out. He just did not possess the subtlety for such a task. And now, he thought gloomily, being in his own daughter's house was worse than trying to work with Muslims.

Somehow the day unfolded, with the opening of presents, the playing of games, a walk in the new snow. Between Rita and her father there remained, not an open coldness, but a stiffness that grew the more strained the harder they sought to conceal it. Rattling on in their garrulous fashion, even guffawing over queer jokes that no one else would have caught, nevertheless behind it all they watched one another with gazes slow and wary, distant as cats.

Were it not for Charlotte, the day would have been a disaster. But she, thank God, behaved exactly as a six-year-old child on Christmas Day should, bubbling around the adults like a silver stream rushing through a burnt-out woods. Her favorite present was a box of pick-up sticks that W.R. had brought from Korea. It was the Asian version with sticks made of ivory and ornately carved in different patterns. For over an hour while Rita prepared supper, the girl and her grandpa stretched out on the living room floor and took turns dropping the delicate white sticks in haphazard piles and then picking them up, using the longer hooked piece to extricate each stick without disturbing any others. It was a game requiring considerable coordination, and while the old man's crooked bony hands trembled like aspen leaves, Charlotte proudly held her pink and perfect fingers rock steady, screwed up her face in histrionic concentration, and deftly won round after round. Just being with the girl and basking in her girlishness, W.R. relaxed more than he had all day. Parched places deep inside him were watered. Perhaps even for Charlotte the real game consisted less in winning than in seeing how long she could keep her grandfather captivated.

Finally it was time for Christmas dinner, a feast of feasts with both ham and turkey, potatoes and stuffing, three kinds of vegetable, and all the other trimmings. The food shone as if with its own inner light. There were Christmas crackers and special napkins, tall candles, and a red-and-green tablecloth. Rita had spared no effort. Yet as the they sat down to the glittering repast, once again W.R. felt a sinking of the heart. Why so much food for just three people? And what good was such lavish external preparation if the heart also were not prepared? Could turkey, even a moist slab of breast with sweet crinkly skin, satisfy the soul? To top things off, Rita did not even pause for grace— a concession she had never denied her father in the past.

So, he thought: *This is how things will be.* Even the little he had would be taken away. Again he nearly broke his resolve. He thought of rising to his feet and praying to Jesus, crying out to the Lord in his loudest voice. For a moment he let himself be mesmerized by a vision of the melodrama of this action. The whole meal would be ruined. Rita's sumptuous preparations would wither away to ashes, exposed in all their hollowness. Perhaps the very roof of the house would collapse upon them in judgment, and the plastic Santa go up in flames.

But W.R. caught himself. Was it zeal for the Lord's Name that moved him, or vindictiveness against his daughter? Swallowing his pride, and then a mouthful of turkey, he exclaimed, "Delicious! Best bird ever! Rita, you're as fine a cook as your mother." He forced himself to be pleasant, talkative, even exuberant. But how hard it was! Whatever special grace had buoyed him up during the past week, it was gone now. The Lord, it seemed, had withdrawn His hand, leaving W.R. to love this rebellious daughter of his as best he could, in his own strength, and to express that love in an emasculated language, in words without vowels.

Partway through the meal, predictably enough, even the thin protocol of politeness gave out and a ponderous silence descended on the table. To W.R. it felt as though every possible avenue of conversation (except of course the gospel) had been explored up and down twenty times, utterly exhausted, thrashed to living daylights. Every word now was like a massive weight that had to be pulled up from the bottom of the sea. Even the chatterbox Charlotte was strangely becalmed, as for what seemed an eternity the three of them sat in the festive room as if each was all alone, hopelessly cut off from the others.

At the same time, there did almost seem to be a fourth presence with them at the table, invisible, yet mutely dominating. It was like a prisoner in chains, allowed home for this one day in the year but destined to be returned to his cell by nightfall. Or perhaps it was like a senile elderly person whom the family had finally decided to ship off to a nursing home the next day. It was a presence that cried out with reproach, shrieking like any ghost.

For an excruciating interlude there was no sound at all save breathing and chewing, the grim scrape of cutlery on bone china, and the orphan choir grinding out "The Twelve Days of Christmas." Finally, when the silent shrieking had attained an unbearable pitch, it was little Charlotte who spoke, who broke the deadlock. She gulped her milk, heaved a white-mustached sigh, and pointing her fork at W.R. like a microphone, asked him point-blank, "Grandpa, why is today called Christmas?"

If the plum pudding had suddenly exploded in the oven, it could not have had a more dramatic effect. The child's question came like a peal of thunder, crashing out of the blue into the dining room just as if, indeed, the roof might be collapsing. Did the little girl have any idea of what she had said? Did she herself grasp, however dimly, the overwhelming significance of that word *Christmas*? Did she deliberately seek to scandalize her elders? Did she sense the power she had over these two sullen adults, and would she now exploit it for all it was worth? Or did she, like her grandfather, merely wish to acknowledge the presence of the mysterious uninvited guest?

Who can say what animates the mind of a child?

For long moments the mysterious question floated above the table, as W.R. stopped his chewing, sighted along the silver shaft of the fork into his granddaughter's inscrutable blue eyes, and sincerely did not know what to say. To such a blunt query there was only one reply, a simple, clear, and precise answer. But he could not give it. He glanced down at Rita, as though seeking permission to speak, but her face told him absolutely nothing. She looked as if she had just swallowed a sharp bone but was not letting on. Desperately W.R. wrestled with himself, until finally he lowered his eyes to the table and said quietly, "Perhaps your mother could give you a better answer than I could."

Surprisingly, his voice carried no subtle shade of sarcasm, no rancor, not the slightest hint of blame. What came out, instead, like a bright flow of water gushing miraculously from a rock, was a tone of pure humility. The old man was simply defeated, exhausted from the struggle, utterly powerless.

Still Charlotte's question hung in the air. Or rather, the answer hung there, like one of the pinned ivory sticks in the game, a delicate white rod, balanced precariously, that no one dared to touch. But now it was up to Rita; it was her move. And all at once, inside her too something gave way, something was defeated. It had been a trying day (though not nearly as trying for her as for W.R.), yet despite all the strain and the uncomfortable silence during supper, she had found herself warming to her father. Never had she seen him so self-controlled, so patient, so meek as he had been that day. It rather awed her that this man who, she thought, would never change, had clearly changed.

And perhaps that is why, when finally she spoke, it was to say to her little daughter, "Today is called Christmas, Charlotte, because it is the birthday, or mass, of Christ. Like your grandfather, Jesus Christ was a good man, a great man, who suffered a great deal. His goodness and his suffering brought something new into the world—a gift so marvelous that the world is still trying to understand it. The best word we have for it is *love*—and that is what we celebrate today."

W.R. gawked. His own Rita was talking about the Lord! And with a note of softness, even reverence. After all, she could have made a cynical reply. She might have answered haughtily, mordantly, with a toss of her chin as if to say, "Your grandfather worships this man, but you and I know better." Or she could have spoken matter-of-factly as one does reciting statistics. But no, instead her reply came seasoned, just as W.R.'s had, with a radiant humility, something so unexpected that it clearly caught even Rita off guard.

Tension, like a shamed animal, slunk from the room. The plum pudding, a sacred family tradition, Rita carried in on a platter as ceremoniously and triumphantly as a haggis, and W.R. poured brandy (of which he never touched a drop) onto a spoon, warmed it over a candle until it ignited, and poured the liquid fire over the nearly black pudding as the three of them leaned forward, eyes shining, to watch it blaze. Genuine laughter broke out, Charlotte's face glowed like a little angel's, and the orphan choir started into "Silent Night."

There was no more talk of Jesus that evening. And yet, and yet ... it was as though the Lord Himself, like a master goldsmith, had devised the perfect setting in which the mere mention of His Name might shine like a spectacular jewel, a diamond on a black velvet cloth.

(1983)

The Anteroom of
the Royal Palace

Many centuries ago there lived a man who devoted his life to roaming the earth in search of all its most magnificent works of architecture. He had been to Rome, to Athens, and to other great ancient cities, and he had even journeyed to the Orient (something unheard of in his day) to view its splendid temples and palaces. Wherever there was rumored to be a grand or unusual edifice, there the traveler bent his footsteps.

Born into a family of builders, and independently wealthy, at first the man had intended to travel only for a few years, with the idea of steeping himself in the design and construction techniques of a wide variety of cultures. But everywhere he went he heard stories about new wonders that lay just beyond: a fabled citadel on a mountaintop, a golden pagoda at the end of a certain road, or an entire city of green marble on the other side of a sea. He found such tales irresistible, and wanderlust drew him ever onward.

Like most travelers, it was not only that the new and the unknown tugged at him—it was that the old and familiar pushed him away. And disillusionment, once surrendered to, has a way of furring the eyes like cataracts, until one day a man may wake up to discover that whatever he looks at, new or old, gives more pain than pleasure.

It was in just such a world-weary state that the traveler found himself one winter, late in life, while sojourning in a Mediterranean land. Jaded with grand spectacles, he had come to settle in a single humble room in the one inn of a small village, where he determined to stay put for a while and try to unravel the riddle of his life. For the thought came to him hauntingly—now that his own porticoes were sagging, his own columns and foundations giving way—that a human might by nature be not only a traveler, but himself a building, his every beam and stone stamped with an unquenchable yearning for permanence.

One afternoon, while sitting in the village square by the well, he chanced to fall into conversation with a peasant who was drawing water there for his sheep. As always with strangers, the traveler began to give a glowing report of his adventures, talking easily and enthusiastically about all the exotic places he had seen. (After all, if one could no longer experience real joy and wonder in life, the next best thing was to talk as though one did.)

"Well, well," nodded the peasant, having listened attentively to the whole account. "It sounds as if you've seen just about everything there is to see in the whole world. And I suppose you've taken in our local attractions too, have you?"

"Oh, yes—to be sure!" chuckled the traveler, catching the joke. "I'm afraid you haven't much to boast of around here."

"Ah, but on the contrary," responded the peasant in apparent earnest. "Have you not seen our Royal Palace? It's right here in the village, and I can assure you there isn't anything to match it in all the earth. If it's grand buildings you're after, then this is the thing to see."

Scratching his head, the traveler looked around at the collection of homely boxes that made up the tiny village, and at the empty rolling hills beyond. Was the old fellow daft? There was certainly no palace here. Even the largest building in sight, the inn where the traveler himself lodged, was a mean and unimaginative structure.

Seeing his bewilderment, the peasant beckoned with his staff and said, "Come, let me show you. It would be a shame to journey as far as you have and to miss seeing the greatest attraction of all."

So with that, driving the sheep ahead of them, the two old men set off together through the winding laneways until they reached the outskirts of the village. There they halted, as the guide gestured toward a clump of ramshackle outbuildings behind a row of abandoned tenements.

"There," he announced with curious finality. "There is our Royal Palace."

The traveler rubbed his eyes. Was he looking in the wrong place? But no—his new friend was pointing, unmistakably, to what appeared to be the very last and least of all the buildings in the village. Apart from a few rock doves flying in and out of crannies in the walls, the structure looked uninhabitable, unfit even for livestock. And beyond lay nothing but fields of stubble rising up to the desolate hills. Only the wind seemed at home here, moaning and sighing with that eerie sound it reserves for deserted places.

The traveler, uncertain now what manner of man he might be dealing with, remarked cautiously, "It doesn't look like much from here."

"You're right," responded his guide. "From here you wouldn't know it from a hole in the ground. But what you're actually seeing is just the facade of the Royal Palace. To view the Palace itself, you must go inside."

Accordingly, the two men went forward until they were standing beneath the sloped roof of a most precarious-looking lean-to. Sunlight filtered in dusty curtains through loose boards, and the straw scattered about the earthen floor was dirty and mildewed. In one gloomy back corner a door was visible, hanging askew from a single hinge. Apparently it led into a stable.

"I'll have to be about my business," advised the peasant. "But you just go on ahead and have a look around. Right through that doorway you'll find an anteroom. Wait there, and after a while you'll be attended to."

"Attended to?" inquired the surprised traveler.

But already the old man was gathering his sheep and herding them off along a narrow path that wound through the grain fields up toward the barren hills.

"I'll return for you shortly!" he called back merrily with a wave of his crook, and soon the other was left all alone with the doves, the moldy straw, the cool quiet shadows and curtains of dusty light, and the piping wind that crept ghostily through the rafters with an almost-human sound.

Well—what did he have to lose? Stepping gingerly toward the back corner and swinging open the door, the visitor entered into the darker interior of what looked to be a cowshed. Here, a single pencil-shaft of sunlight lanced through a crack in the very apex of the roof onto the earthen floor. The traveler stood still, blinking, peering into the shadows.

What in the world was he doing here? Allowing himself to be hoodwinked by an old prankster? Perhaps it was a fitting conclusion to a lifetime of futile wanderings.

As his eyes adjusted to the dimness, the first thing he noticed was an unusual knothole on the farthest wall. Perfectly circular and curiously bright, it was haloed by a distinct sunburst pattern in the surrounding wood. Drawing nearer, he saw that the old planks held other intriguing designs, and the longer he studied these the more fascinating they grew. Indeed, hidden amidst the swirls and ridges of the wood grain were shapes of ferns, trees, birds, and animals, so that all in all the effect was like that of a large mural. Suddenly the odd thought came to him that the scene might portray the original forest from which these very boards had been cut! Not only that, but before he quite realized what was happening, the flat surface of the wall seemed to recede and to take on three-dimensional depth, until all at once he felt himself to be standing, incredibly, in the sun-shot reality of a Mediterranean forest of cedar, fir, oak, with a cloud of brilliant songbirds threading the lacework of boughs. And there, not twenty yards off, stood a small antelope gazing at him with eyes as solemn as an angel's.

Recalling with a start that, as perfectly real as this looked, it could not be so, the amazed visitor took a step back. But immediately his attention was drawn to a second wall, where once again the flat surface melted away beneath the swirling image-rich patterns of the wood grain—until now the vista that unfolded was that of a great mountain with a majestic waterfall leaping from its heights into a valley decked in the luminous gold and crimson robes of autumn. The whole scene was more vibrant and gorgeous than the grandest of Byzantine mosaics.

"My word!" exclaimed the traveler. "What remarkable work this is!" For it struck him that such breathtaking dioramas could not possibly be attributed to chance designs in old boards, but only to the consummate artistry of some master craftsman. And all the more admirable it was for having been so cunningly concealed.

The observer was not given long to reflect, however, as he was distracted by a sound—a familiar, tremendous roar that encompassed him as completely as if he were hearing his mother's heartbeat in the womb. Turning toward the third wall, he discovered himself on a long sandy beach with thunderous combers higher than himself breaking, dissolving, bowing to the shore and then washing glassily right up to his sandaled feet. And all at once he felt it— the cool, curling water laving his soles! For some time he stood there, lost in wonder, letting the waves carry all his thoughts away.

Finally, however, it was the fourth wall that displayed the most marvelous tableau of all. For here, as the visitor glanced back at the rude doorway through which he had entered, in a twinkling he was transported bodily back to the wooded hills and valleys of his own birthplace. Once more he stood high upon a favorite lookout, his native city spread out below garbed in the sapphire sash of its shining river, which seemed to lead toward the ends of the earth. And once more he felt, as he had so often as a boy, the thrill of the wide world spilled at his feet like treasure and just waiting to be explored. So full of poignancy and nostalgia was this scene, so charged with the shimmering magic of childhood, that it moved him to tears, and he hung his head as the memories flooded in.

Even as he cast down his eyes, the very straw on which he stood was transformed into field upon field of golden wheat tossing in the wind, while in another direction appeared chains of lakes with turquoise waters through which rainbow-colored fish glided like jeweled shadows. And elsewhere the humble dirt floor gave way to spectacular canyons and gorges or to flower-filled meadows or broad plains alive with game.

As if all this were not enough, when at last the observer lifted his eyes overhead to where the one ray of light traversed a chink in the peak of the roof, he was surprised to see that this was not a beam of sunlight, but a star, dazzling in its splendor! And off among the darker slopes and rafters shone the full moon, the planets, and all the heavenly host, unfurled to infinity upon the imponderable velvet of deep space.

Overwhelmed with awe, he fell to his knees and bowed his face into the musty straw. Never in all his travels had he beheld such stupendous artwork, so perfectly realistic, so rich with grandeur. How was it possible?

At that moment, the stocky frame of his peasant friend appeared behind him, his raised shepherd's crook forming the silhouette of a question mark in the doorway. Turning toward him, the visitor implored, "Tell me, I beg you—what place is this? And who, pray tell, is the Master Builder of this grand Royal Palace?"

"Why, friend," replied the shepherd, "don't you know? You are in Bethlehem, and this is the Royal Palace of Christ the King. But listen: What you have seen so far is only the Anteroom of the Palace, and I assure you, it is nothing compared to the Throne Room! Come, won't you follow me and meet the King Himself?"

(1985)

A Subtle Change

The evening was winding down. The group had just finished planning its Christmas party for the following week, and Josh and Carol, always the first to leave, were already on their feet.

Penny, curled up in a corner of the sofa, suddenly remarked, "I don't believe you people."

Everyone stopped and looked at her.

"What do you mean?" asked Stewart.

"What I mean," replied Penny after a significant pause, "is that there's something different about me. Radically different. I've been sitting here all evening, biting my tongue, waiting for someone to comment, and no one has. No one's even noticed."

Everyone peered at Penny more intently. Carol even sat down again to gaze at her longtime friend.

"Something different?" said Stewart, removing his

glasses. "What do you mean?"

It was Stewart's favorite question. For three years the group had met together every Wednesday evening to study the Bible, and at some point in the discussion Stewart could be counted on to remove his glasses, point them at someone, and ask, "What do you mean?" More often his exact words would be, "What exactly do you mean?"

Stewart happened to be sitting right next to Penny on the couch, with the pointing arm of his glasses just inches from her nose. Penny smiled as if at a private joke.

"I mean, Stewart, just exactly what I said. There is something fundamentally different about me tonight, and none of you has noticed. If a person you've known this long suddenly makes an obvious change, don't you think you'd notice?"

"Your sweater," said Josh. "You got a new sweater."

"Don't be silly," Penny replied. "I've worn this thing a dozen times. You must be blind, Josh."

"This change you're talking about," inquired Stewart, "is it external or internal? Is it something on the inside?"

Penny threw back her head and laughed.

"What on earth are you thinking, Stewart? That I've gone and had my gall bladder out or something?"

"Well, it's possible."

"And I'd expect you to notice that? To comment on it?"

"I just needed to clarify," said Stewart. "So it's something external? A change in your appearance?"

"Yes, yes!" Penny nearly shrieked, unable to believe Stewart's obtuseness.

"Is it to do with make up?" said Josh. "Rouge or eye shadow or something?"

"No, no, no," said Penny. "Well, maybe. Come to think of it, I did use a new shade of eye liner today. But that's not it. I wouldn't expect you to notice that."

"Did you get a new Bible?" suggested Carol.

"No, no," said Penny. "My appearance, my *personal* appearance. *Look* at me."

Penny thrust her neck out like a goose and swiveled her head, peering exaggeratedly at every person in the room.

"I know what it is," said George. "I've known all along."

All eyes turned to George. The newest member of the group, he was a painfully quiet guy. Especially during the Bible study discussions he normally said nothing at all. Now he was leaning forward and gazing at Penny.

"You've known all along and you haven't you said anything?" said Josh.

"I was curious to see if anyone else got it."

"Alright, what is it?" asked Penny. "Tell me what's different."

"Glasses," said George. "You've got new glasses. And very becoming they are, too."

"That's it!" shouted Penny.

"Of course, of course," said the others.

"Oh, now I see," said Stewart, putting his own glasses back on.

"I wonder why we didn't notice?" said Josh.

"I'll tell you why," said Penny. "It's because I paid a thousand dollars for these beauties, and they're only the hottest thing on the market. Everybody in Europe is wearing them, but here they're brand new."

They all drew closer to Penny to inspect her new glasses. Entirely rimless, the frames consisted of two nearly invisible, pencil-thin shafts of flexible titanium. Removing them, Penny twisted the frames every which way to demonstrate how indestructible they were.

"They're so light," she said. "It's like wearing nothing."

"If you'd worn nothing we would have noticed," said Josh.

"Oh, Josh," said Carol.

Everyone was glad that George had been the one to pick up on Penny's new glasses. He was so quiet, it was hard to know how to include him in the group. He and Penny had dated for a while, but Penny had broken it off because their views of religion—and especially of Jesus—were so divergent. Why such a person would join a decidedly evangelical Bible study group was not such a great mystery. Presumably he was still interested in Penny.

"Well done, George," said Josh. "Good work."

"It still seems odd," observed Carol, "that no one else clued in."

"I'm actually delighted," said Penny. "Not to notice someone's glasses is a high compliment."

"Why don't you get contacts?" asked Stewart.

"Too much hassle. Why get contacts if I can have glasses nobody sees?"

"Hey, this gives me an idea," said Josh. "How about if next week everybody shows up with some subtle change to their appearance? Then we make a game of guessing what's different."

"And I'll bring a prize," added Carol. "For the person who stumps everybody."

"Oh, that's fantastic!" said Penny. "I know exactly what I'm going to do."

So it was decided. Next week everyone would come to the Christmas party having made some subtle change.

"But wait a minute," said Stewart. "Just wait a minute. We need some rules. I mean, for one thing, the changes have to be exterior, right? Obvious and physical."

"But not too obvious," said Penny. "We have to have something to guess about."

"Sure, but you can't change your attitude or something like that."

"In your case, Stewart," commented Josh, "I think everyone would be delighted if you changed your attitude."

Stewart gave Josh one of his blank looks.

"But don't you see what I mean?" he said.

The following Wednesday the group met at Penny's place. The aroma of mulled apple-cranberry cider filled the small apartment, and Penny had also made a big bowl of her special crème de menthe chocolate trifle. Over the mantel of the gas fireplace a string of white lights blinked on and off, while the stereo played Vince Guaraldi's "A Charlie Brown Christmas."

Penny, a grade four teacher, had brought home a lumpy-looking manger scene molded from different colors of plasticine. Carol, examining the figures, commented that it was difficult to tell the shepherds from the wise men.

"Or, for that matter, from the camels," noted Josh.

"The wise men have crowns, silly," explained Penny.

"In that case," said Carol, "there are eleven wise men here."

"The Bible never says there were three. Most of the boys wanted to make wise men, so I let them."

"The magi weren't even there at Christmas," said Stewart. "They came a year or two later."

Everyone groaned because Stewart made this same comment every year.

"The Bible doesn't mention any animals, either," Stewart added, as if deliberately soliciting further groans.

"For once, Stewart," said Penny, "couldn't you just entertain a bit of childlike imagination?"

"This is a Bible study group," he replied. "I just want to encourage good exegesis."

"Exegesis: a scholarly term for the execution of Jesus," quipped Josh.

Throughout this time no one made any mention of

the game that was to be played that evening, though secretly they all studied their neighbor to see what subtle changes had been made. Ron and Margaret, a couple who had just returned from a holiday and didn't know about the game, left the room for a few minutes to make their changes.

After the demolishing of the trifle and the singing of Christmas carols, George, who had hardly spoken all evening, suddenly asked if it wasn't time for the game to begin. He was sitting on the edge of his chair with his hands tightly clasped between jiggling knees.

"I know," said Josh. "Penny has new glasses."

"Ha ha," said Penny. "Wouldn't you be surprised if these were actually different from the ones I wore last week?"

Everyone peered very closely at Penny's glasses.

"Just kidding," she said.

"Wait a minute, wait a minute," said Stewart. "We need some rules here. I have it all worked out."

Stewart explained that the guessing should not be a random free-for-all but must proceed in orderly fashion.

"One guess per person per person," he said. "Process of elimination. Each guesser gets one chance to go first. We go once around clockwise, then run off the finalists. Straight guesses, no clues."

Everyone looked at Stewart as if he was speaking Swahili, but in the end they did it his way.

First on the hot seat was Josh, whose change was so obvious it was guessed immediately. He had shaved off his beard. Everyone congratulated him on his boldness and his fresh new face.

"I knew you'd all guess," he said. "Except for Carol. Can you believe it, I shaved this morning but my own wife didn't notice until just before we left for the party?"

"Honey, I was so busy today," Carol apologized.

"I'm just thinking," mused Penny. "I wonder how many of the changes tonight will be permanent?"

"Not mine," said Stewart, and everyone turned to him.

"What—your underwear's backwards?" suggested Josh.

"It has to be external," reminded Stewart.

They went all around the circle without anyone guessing. Stewart's secret had to be left for another round.

Next came Penny, who also nearly stumped everyone. Clothes, hair, jewelry were all guessed, but it was none of that.

"This is so weird," she said, "having everyone stare at me like this."

Finally George, who had the last turn, correctly guessed that Penny had drawn a tiny, reddish mole—more like a pimple—on her neck. No one, of course, was surprised that George had detected such a minuscule change in Penny's appearance.

After this the game went more quickly. Ron, who always wore shirts with a buttoned collar, had undone the buttons. Margaret was wearing her socks inside out. Carol had turned her wedding ring around.

"Is that symbolic of something?" asked Josh.

By the time it was George's turn, his knees were not just jiggling but bouncing up and down with excitement.

"It's something about your knees," said Josh. "You've had springs surgically inserted in them?"

Immediately the knees stopped, but still George looked ready to explode.

"It's not that," he said.

"You swallowed a stick of dynamite?"

"No, no. Well, not exactly."

"What do you mean 'not exactly'?" said Stewart.

"Forget it," said George. "That's not it."

In the end George too managed to stump the whole group. And so it came down to a final round between him and Stewart.

Clearly very proud of himself, Stewart kept saying, "You'll never guess it."

"Are you sure it's something visible?"

"Yes, yes, of course."

"Let's see your hands," said Ron. "Why are you hiding them?"

"I'm not hiding them," said Stewart.

"You are too. You've got them half tucked inside your sleeves. Pull up those sleeves."

With obvious reluctance, Stewart pulled up his sleeves. Several people got out of their seats to inspect his hands, which Stewart extended palms up.

"Turn them over," said Ron. "Let's see the backs."

As Stewart turned his hands, there were audible gasps. Each wrist was marked by a clear line of thick, black hair, below which the skin was perfectly smooth and white. Stewart had shaved all the hair off the backs of his hands.

"I don't believe it," said Josh.

"That is so weird, Stewart," said Penny. "It's just plain weird."

"I almost had you," said Stewart. "It wasn't fair to get me to pull up my sleeves."

"George wins the prize," said Carol.

"By the way, what is the prize?" Margaret asked.

"It's a book by Mike Mason," said Carol.

"Who?"

"Mike Mason. I don't know who he is. Someone gave it to me and I couldn't get into it."

"A recycled prize," said Stewart. "I should have known. What's it called?"

"*The Mystery of Marriage*," said Carol.

"No wonder you couldn't get into it," said Josh.

Finally the group turned back to George. A plain-looking man to begin with, George normally blended right in with the furniture. Detecting a subtle change in such a person was doubly difficult. Tonight, however, there did seem to be something different about him. Everybody felt it, but nobody could see it.

"I know," said Josh. "You're not wearing your nose ring."

Everyone laughed, and for a while things got completely silly.

"It's the tattoo—he had it removed!"

"No, no—he's wearing a toupee!"

George, surprisingly enjoying all the attention, giggled like a schoolboy. For once he did not appear shy or reserved but even became the life of the party.

"Are you sure it's something visible?" asked Stewart.

"I can see it," said George. "If you can't, I don't know how to help you."

"Is it something really small?" asked Carol.

"No, it's actually quite big."

"What part of your body should we look at?"

"What a rude question," said Josh.

"Everything," replied George. "This change affects everything."

Gradually the room grew quiet. The search, far from narrowing, seemed to be expanding, taking on an aura of mystery. People sensed that the game was drawing to a close. George had well and truly stumped them all.

"We give up," said Stewart. "You'll have to tell us."

George, clearing his throat, rose to his feet. Though trembling, he was not behaving at all like the George they all knew. If there had been a microphone he might have seized it. Instead he walked over to the manger scene, picked up the tiny figure of the Christ child, and cradled him in his hands. The figure was an unlikely pastiche of red, green, purple and yellow clumps of plasticine.

"Three days ago," he began, "I was passing by the manger scene downtown. I was thinking about our game, wondering what kind of a change I could make, and I happened to look at the baby Jesus. He didn't appear to have anything different about him, but suddenly I saw the one thing that sets him apart. I can't explain how, but suddenly I knew that Jesus is God. Who would have expected God to come to earth as a baby?"

George's voice was breaking, but he went on.

"The Bible says that a believer is a new creation in Christ. The old has gone, the new has come. Therefore the person you see standing before you, including my body, is not the same as what you saw last week. I live no longer, but Christ lives in me."

For some time no one broke the stunned silence in the room. The only sound was the soft on-off ticking of the white Christmas lights on the mantel. Finally Carol, in a hushed whisper, breathed, "What a Christmas present!"

Stewart shifted uneasily.

"But wait a minute, George," he said. "Just wait a minute. Do you really think this is fair? I mean, the rules..."

"Stewart, stuff it," said Josh. "George, this is fantastic news!"

"Wow!" said Carol. "Wow!"

Suddenly everyone was on their feet, crowding around George, pumping his hand, clapping him on the back, embracing him. George beamed. His pent-up excitement released, he looked taller, glowing, more handsome.

Penny, overcome, was the one person who had remained seated. Finally she too rose and approached George. Placing her hands on his shoulders, she gazed into his eyes. Her own eyes were wide and glistening.

"George, I'm so glad ..." she said. "I know how hard this whole thing has been for you."

And then she wrapped her arms around him and held on for a long time.

Eventually Carol said, "I'd say it's time to give George his prize."

"Looks like he's already got it," said Stewart.

(2002)

Sometimes I Tremble

On Christmas Eve Ed Harper strolled down the street thinking how pleasant it was to be a five-point Calvinist. Not that the four-pointers were excluded from salvation, but that fifth point—limited atonement—was the one that really separated the men from the boys.

A light snowfall feathered the dusk as the last of the shoppers scurried about on their materialistic errands. Ed himself, though he deeply disapproved of the season's commercialism, was on his way to Dempster's Department Store to pick out a gift for his wife. As far as he was concerned, every day was a day to gather around the true Christmas tree, the cross of Jesus Christ, and to open eternal gifts. And this day, as any other, his primary mission was to do soul business with anyone the Lord might put in his path.

Having paused to empty his change into the Sally Ann bucket and to chat with the bell-ringer (a sister from church), Ed rounded the corner onto Main Street to be greeted by a strange sight. A big black man dressed in burlap was coming toward him, dragging a large cross along the sidewalk. It left a long, dark gash in the new snow.

Hadn't Ed seen something about this on the news the other day? Could it be the same fellow? Attached to the cross was a placard announcing in crudely-drawn red letters shadowed in black, "REPENT, FOR THE KINGDOM OF HEAVEN IS AT HAND. MT. 4:17."

The man was half a block away, just passing the nativity scene by the Episcopal Church. Ed was struck by the contrast: cross and cradle. Not that he approved of nativity scenes, nor of decorations in general. Nor did he condone mawkish public displays of religious fervor. Still, the cross-carrier was obviously a brother in the Lord, and Ed felt drawn to have a word with him.

"How do you do, brother? Christmas is a fine time to proclaim the gospel."

The man did not stop, and Ed, reversing direction, fell in step beside him.

"Every time's fine for that," the man returned. "The end draweth nigh." His deep bass voice sang with the drawl of the South; he was a long way from home. Despite the cold, his face was glossy with sweat.

"Can I ask where you're headed?" Ed ventured.

"Just passin' through, son," came the sonorous reply, "and sowin' the word as I go." He indicated a large leather satchel slung over his shoulder. Inside were a dozen or so placards inscribed, presumably, with various scriptures. By his own account the pilgrim put in eight-hour days bearing his burden clear across the continent, changing placards now and then as the Spirit directed.

"I just feel the Lawd has called me to carry my cross," he reported. "Now and then folks stop to chat, just like you. But mostly I let the Lawd do the work."

Despite reservations, Ed was impressed with such wholehearted discipleship. Noticing that the bottom end of the cross was badly worn and splintered, he asked, "How long does one of these things last?"

"All depends, son. I had one cross lasted me three years without showin' any wear. Another cross'll peter out in a few weeks. It's just a mystery."

The thought of wearing out one cross after another, nailing together a new one, and trudging on in all weathers, through mud and gravel, up hills and through cities— Ed's mind boggled. He'd once seen a picture of a similar pilgrim with a wheel attached to his cross. But obviously dragging showed deeper devotion.

"How long you been doing this good work, brother?" Ed asked.

"Nigh on thirty years, son. Thirty years tomorrow. The Lawd's been good."

"You began on Christmas Day?"

"It was the Lawd's timin', not my own. I just answered the call."

Thirty years, thought Ed. Three decades of lugging a

cross from one side of the continent to the other. Come to
an ocean, turn around and head back. Talk about perse-
verance! The black man had an aureole of pure white hair
encircling a face puckered like a baseball mitt. He looked
to be in his sixties, which meant he would have taken up
his cross at about the same age Ed was now. Ed wondered
where he himself might be thirty years down the line.
Still selling window coverings in his father's store? It was
a good job, but no way to advance the gospel. The old man
wouldn't permit his son so much as to breathe the name of
Jesus in the store. Ed dreamed of the day when the Lord
would tap him on the shoulder and send him to the ends
of the earth.

As the two men trudged along, the younger sounded
out the older on various points of doctrine. These wandering souls, Ed knew, often wandered in their theology as
well, but this one's beliefs rang true, at least as far as they
went. His knowledge of five-point Calvinism was scant,
and Ed had to explain why the four-pointers felt the fifth
point took the edge off evangelism. Why share the gospel
with those who were predestined to reject it? To Ed this
was no problem, for looking into the eyes of a stranger,
who was he to judge whether this was a person Jesus had
died for or not? Though Ed tried to explain this point to
his comrade, the elderly man couldn't seem to grasp its
importance.

"Say, son," interrupted the latter, "you sound like a
right eager young feller. How'd you like to take a turn at

carryin' the cross? I don't mind sharin' it with you."

As the man stopped and began to unshoulder his burden, without thinking Ed took a step backward. Seeing him flinch, the other said softly, "Don't worry, son. It doesn't bite."

Ed froze. He truly did not know what to say. What was the problem? What was he afraid of? Surely not a stick of wood? Surely not the cross of Christ? Everyone in town knew Ed Harper was a radical Christian. He had always been ready to share his testimony with anyone who cared to listen, and often enough with those who did not. He thought of his faith as subtle, muscular, resilient, capable of winning any argument. He had backed many a sinner to the wall. Why shouldn't he carry an old rugged cross down the main street of his home town? Why did just the thought of this make him feel weak in the knee, exposed, pinned?

"What's the trouble, son? You ashamed of Jesus Christ?"

"What? Me ashamed? You don't know me, brother. Here, hand that thing over."

With a lurch Ed laid hold of the cross. He was surprised to find the shaft not smooth, like a tool handle, but rough and square and too large to lie comfortably in the palms. It was also heavy. The blond wood bore dark stains where the owner's sweaty hands had held it. Like a baseball player with an enormous bat, Ed hefted the cross, ran his fingers along the wood, eyed the stains. He found himself studying, for a little too long, the object's simple construction. Three long nails joined the two beams, and more nails fastened the rude placard-holder at the top.

"Maybe you want to change the scripture?" asked the man. "Here, let's have a look-see. The Lawd'll tell us which one to use."

With a sigh of relief Ed set the cross aside, resting it against a trash barrel, while together they flipped through the placards.

"How about this," suggested the man, straightening up and reading: 'This is a faithful saying, and worthy of all acceptation, that Christ Jesus came into the world to save sinners; of whom I am chief. One Timothy One-Fifteen.'"

"Too long," muttered Ed.

Eventually they settled on the one Christmas verse: "'Unto you is born this day in the city of David a Savior, which is Christ the Lord.' Luke 2:11."

"That was my own first verse," reflected the man.

As he was changing the placards, Ed voiced an afterthought. "Listen, brother. Would you mind if we turned the corner here and went down this side street? I feel a nudge that way."

"Nudges are awful important," said the man. "The Lawd can do more with a nudge than you or I with a mountain of shovin'."

Then he handed Ed the cross, saying, "She's all yours."

Again Ed was surprised at its weight. He found it

difficult to straighten up beneath it. At the first step he
nearly lost his balance. Surely the thing didn't need to
be quite so large and cumbersome? No matter how he
shifted it, he couldn't seem to keep the edges from biting
into his shoulder. He wished he had a pad or something.
Meanwhile his companion had begun singing in his low,
rumbling bass the verses of *Were You There When They
Crucified My Lord?* Didn't he know any Christmas carols?

As Ed moved slowly forward, he rounded the corner
to avoid his father's store in the next block. Thankfully no
pedestrians were in sight. A few cars passed, vehicles he
recognized, but he carefully avoided looking at the drivers.

Suddenly two men emerged from a shop, farmers Ed
knew casually. If they'd come into the store they would
have greeted him pleasantly, but now, after a mildly
puzzled glance, they passed by without speaking. Ed did
not meet their eyes but stared straight ahead. Sweat was
starting to trickle down his forehead into his eyes.

Midway down the block Ed caught sight of some
unbelieving friends from high school. Against his will
he found himself turning his face from them, bowing his
head, even angling the cross slightly so that the placard
shadowed him. Even so, one of the group paused, then
stepped closer to get a better look.

"Hey, guys!" he sang out. "Getta loada this! Crazy
Ed's at it again. Don't you ever give up, Ed?"

Mercifully, the rest of the group had already turned
the corner, immersed in some talk of their own, and the

straggler ran to catch up.

Ed's comrade interrupted his singing long enough to quote—savoring each word as if it were a morsel of sugar pie—"Blessed are they which are persecuted for righteousness' sake, for theirs is the kingdom of heaven."

More than ever now Ed was struggling with the weight of his burden. He shifted to the other shoulder, but no position seemed satisfactory. He wished he had observed the old fellow more closely at the start, to see how he had done it. But then, he'd been at this for a long time and must be in pretty good shape.

"Say, brother," Ed asked. "Do you ever get tired doing this?"

"Well, son, look at it this way. You're a fit young feller. Ever do any runnin'?"

"Sure, I was on the track team in school. Once ran a marathon."

"Ever get tired?"

Ed answered with silence.

"We're in a race, son. And the Devil takes the hindmost."

Ed pondered this. In his spiritual life he was used to being a frontrunner. Why at the moment did he feel like the hindmost?

More of Ed's friends and acquaintances passed by, and more judgments, he felt, were registered. He knew people regarded him as a loud-mouthed fundamentalist, but now it seemed he had crossed some entirely different line. In the tip of a hat, in a slightly twisted smile, in the light sarcasm of a "Well, if it isn't Ed Harper!" lifelong relationships were being altered. It wasn't that Ed cared so much, really, what people thought or said about him. The hard part was not being able to talk back and defend himself. He would have liked to carry another placard with a written explanation of what he was doing.

The snow was coming down harder now, its cold fingers investigating inside his collar. He kept wanting to scratch, to wipe his face, to check his watch. But the weight and unwieldiness of the cross took the work of both hands. It was like being in a pillory. He didn't dare put the thing down until he'd carried it a decent distance. He had his pride.

But all at once he recalled the reason he'd come to town in the first place: a Christmas present for his wife. Dempster's would be closing soon. Being Christmas Eve, they might even close early.

"Say, brother," he asked, "what time is it getting to be?"

"Now don't you worry about that," replied the man. "The Lawd Jesus didn't have a clock on Calvary."

Doggedly Ed carried the cross a block further. Then, abruptly, he put it down, hard, sliding it off his shoulder and shoving it toward the black man. The latter had to catch it before it dropped.

"Listen, brother," Ed croaked, "I've got things to do. But it's sure been a pleasure working with you. A real pleasure."

"Son, it's always a pleasure to serve the Lawd."

Saying a hasty goodbye and scurrying away, Ed glanced at his watch. To his amazement, only fifteen minutes had passed! It had been the longest fifteen minutes of Ed Harper's life. As it turned out, he had plenty of time to get to Dempster's. He was just about to disappear around the corner when the black man called after him.

"A happy Christmas to you, son! I sure have to hand it to you. Why, it was ten years before I got up the nerve to do this in my own home town."

(1998)

The Family Upstairs

When my husband's business went south, we lost our lovely home and had to downsize to a two-bedroom apartment in an older building called the Ebenezer. I had a lot to get used to, having never lived in an apartment before. It was small and dark and the layers of grime were generations deep. We'd had to sell off most of our things and it seemed impossible to arrange our remaining furniture in a pleasing way. Stan was forever shifting things around until it drove me crazy. Jennifer complained that even the food smelled strange in that cramped, grubby kitchen. And of course we ate different things. Though we'd moved only a few miles, it was like a foreign country. I didn't know anyone, and to be honest, didn't want to. We just didn't belong there.

Mr. Dickens, the superintendent, gave me the creeps, puttering around unshaven in his dirty undershirt. And that's how it was with everyone: dowdy, unseemly. Even when they did dress up, heading off to work or to some event, they seemed so sad. They all looked like they'd had the stuffing knocked out of them.

One of the hardest parts was laundry day. I hated walking down the hall with all our dirty things and never knowing who you were going to meet or even whether you could get a machine. There were three small laundry rooms, one on each floor, so you traipsed from one to the other and took your chances. You washed on one floor and dried on another. Once I had a whole load stolen from a dryer. You don't know what something like that feels like until it happens to you.

The heaviest blow came in December when I opened the Christmas box. The movers must have dropped it and every last thing was smashed, including my special favorite, a nativity scene of Italian porcelain. It had been a wedding present from Stan's parents, and when he saw all those beautiful figurines shattered beyond repair, I could tell he was shaken. As for me, I cried and cried until there was nothing left in me. Nothing.

Jennifer cried too. But then, she'd been crying all fall. The smallest thing could set her off. There were no other pre-teen girls in the building and she kept to her room and gained weight. I suggested we make snowflakes or popcorn strings or *something* to put on the tree, along with the few other things that had survived the move, but neither of us really had the heart for it. I guess the thought of trying to celebrate Christmas in this dingy hovel was too much. So our tree remained bare.

All December it rained and rained and I seldom went out. We didn't see many friends; that old life of ours was gone. We hardly even talked to one another. The only neighbors who interested me were the people above us in #248. In the evenings they played music, old dance tunes like the ones Stan and I remembered from our lessons. The upstairs lights cast their shadows onto the lawn, accompanied by the shuffle or thump of their steps above. The old songs broke my heart, but the dancing shadows—there was something so beautiful about that. Whenever I could, I sat and watched them, though Stan scolded me. He said all I did was sit around the house. But all he did was hang out with Mr. Dickens, with whom he'd struck up quite a little friendship. What he saw in that man I can only imagine. A nice change from the insurance racket, was all he said. In any case, it was through Mr. Dickens we learned that the people upstairs were newlyweds with a baby boy. Most of the Ebenezer's tenants were either old men or single moms, but this was an actual couple. A family.

The building was practically cardboard, so we heard their dishwasher, microwave, shower, and TV almost as clearly as our own. Stan, naturally, had a lot of trouble sleeping, and he kept complaining about the noise from their bedroom directly above ours. He claimed they stayed awake till all hours, "up to their tricks." I knew what he meant but I never heard anything myself. I had my pills and I was dead to the world.

From the shadows on the lawn and the tread of steps, I had formed the impression of extremely large people, and I took to calling them Mr. and Mrs. Santa. When finally I saw them, on one of my laundry rambles, it gave me quite a start. I wouldn't have known them except that they were at the door of #248, balancing bags of groceries and fumbling for the key. They turned out to be slight of build, fine-featured, dark-complexioned. He had a full beard, but she looked so young—a teenager. I put my head down and hurried past.

The one other time I saw them, they were outside in the rain under a chestnut tree. She carried the baby in a sling and held a sky blue umbrella. Her head was tilted back, cradled in the crook of her husband's arm, and he was tipping water drops from a large leaf directly into her wide open mouth. They laughed, and then they hugged and kissed and spun around and around. They looked so *happy*, so gloriously in love. I couldn't help staring.

That night I had an idea. It was crazy, I knew. But it gave me something to do, and to look forward to. I guess I wished they could live up to their names—Mr. and Mrs. Santa—and somehow give us what they had. So I sat down and wrote them a letter:

"Dear Tenants of #248: In our annual Christmas gift exchange, your names have been drawn to give an anonymous gift to the family in #148. In turn, an unknown resident will give a gift to you. Please don't break this beautiful custom, and please don't discuss it with other residents, as we wish to preserve the anonymity of the givers. Thank you and Merry Christmas!"

I signed it, "The Christmas Committee of Ebenezer Apartments."

After slipping the note under their door, I took my umbrella and caught the bus for downtown. I already knew what to buy them. I'd seen it the week before at Bolton's China Shop. It wasn't exactly the same as my own set; some of the figures were postured differently. But it was hand-painted Italian porcelain and the similarity was remarkable, even down to the facial expressions. The biggest difference was that the baby Jesus, instead of being tightly swaddled, had his arms thrown wide in blessing. I liked that, and I thought the family upstairs would like it. All the way into town, and all the way home again with the precious package on my lap, I could scarcely keep from smiling.

Of course it was a terribly extravagant present. I couldn't have bought it for myself. But I had some money set aside that Stan didn't know about, and the urge to do this just bubbled up irresistibly. Besides, I couldn't help thinking: *I wonder what they will give us?*

The morning before Christmas Eve, I sat at the kitchen table wrapping the present when Stan came home unexpectedly. Quickly I finished taping the paper and began cutting ribbon for the bow. Casually I mentioned the gift exchange.

"I suppose you got them some tacky gewgaw," he scoffed.

I chuckled to myself. If only he knew what I was wrapping up for total strangers!

About eleven that morning, as every day, I heard footsteps overhead and the door of #248 opened and closed, signaling that Mr. Santa was heading downstairs to collect his mail. Quickly I scooted up the opposite staircase and deposited my gift in front of their door. A few minutes later, as I listened from below, their muffled tones of surprise thrilled me. I imagined their comments as they unwrapped the tissue from one piece after another—the radiant Mary, the humble Joseph, the magi in their sumptuous robes, the rough shepherds, the ox and donkey with their holy eyes, and of course the baby Jesus.

Not long after that, Stan came back from a chat with the superintendent and informed me that Mr. Dickens knew nothing of any gift exchange. Oh dear—I hadn't thought of that! I had to confess how I'd arranged it myself—just so we'd have something special to put under the tree.

"Sick," was all Stan said at first. But in no time we were into one of our awful rows, which ended with him storming off again to his beloved superintendent. "Alright, then—go to the Dickens!" I shouted after him. All my joy drained away. I felt like one of those delicate figurines who had fallen off the truck. What a crazy idea was this gift exchange! Even the thought I had cherished all week—*What will they give us?*—seemed now so empty. They would give us some tacky gewgaw and Stan would laugh in my face.

That evening it turned cold and the moon came up

full and achingly gorgeous with that alien beauty it has. Stan stayed away and Jennifer cried and cried. I felt like kicking down that stupid bare tree and pitching it out the window.

Not until the next day, Christmas Eve, as the three of us sat around the table after supper, did a light knock sound at the door. When I rose to open, no one was there. But I looked down and saw the gift. As big as a bread box, it was handsomely wrapped in gold foil with silver stars and a red bow. I knelt to read the card: "Merry Christmas to #148." Lifting it, I could not believe how hefty it was.

Carefully, walking slowly and formally as in a processional, I carried it to the table and set it down.

"Gift exchange," I announced. "For us."

Stan regarded it dubiously, but Jennifer's eyes were large and incredulous, as if to say, "Things like this don't happen to us."

"Well, aren't you going to open it?" said Stan.

I wanted to save it for Christmas Day. But I couldn't; I was too excited. That box was the best, brightest thing in our apartment. In our lives. As I plucked at the ribbon, my fingers shook, and the foil paper rustled like tiny wings.

"Maybe it's a bomb," said Stan.

With the paper half off, I stopped. They had used the same box I had used for their present.

"Bolton's China," read Stan. "Not bad."

Before proceeding, I smoothed and folded the paper.

"Come on, Mom," urged Jennifer.

I parted the box flaps and we all peered inside. Tissue paper. Lots of it. I took off a first layer, and a second. Then I felt something hard. And small. Covered in tissue. I removed it and unwrapped it.

We all stared.

"My word!" said Stan.

It was a porcelain figurine of the baby Jesus, just like the one from our old nativity set, except his arms were thrown wide.

"Mom, he's so beautiful!" whispered Jennifer.

Stan was already unwrapping another item from the box—this one a dark-skinned king in a purple robe. Then Jennifer found a lamb.

The figures were exactly like the ones I had given to the family upstairs. I was dumbfounded.

"Who gave you this?" demanded Stan.

I just shook my head. I didn't know whether to laugh or cry.

We kept going, taking turns unwrapping one gorgeous figure after another. When I got to Mary, right at the bottom, her face so radiant, I broke down completely. All the tension and darkness of months and months—I sobbed it all out.

"How did they know, Mom?" said Jennifer. "How did they know we'd lost this, and how much we loved it?"

Finally I managed to whisper, "A miracle."

In the hush that followed, I gathered up the whole set and arranged it on a velvet cloth by the window. No one spoke. We all just sat and basked in the glow of those holy figures. Even the bare tree shone; not one more decoration was needed.

Strangely, it was an hour or two before it occurred to me to wonder why the people upstairs hadn't wanted my present. Did they truly not like it? Come to think of it, what if they were Jewish or something? Was that the problem? Well, I might never know, but it didn't matter. All I knew was that the holy family had returned to our home.

That night it snowed, a light fresh dusting that covered everything cleanly like a sheet. Christmas music floated down from upstairs and the couple's shadows glided around like skaters on the frozen lawn.

Suddenly Stan grabbed Jenny's hand, then mine, and led us outside and began twirling us around and around until Jenny laughed—a sound pure and crystalline as the snow itself. Oh, it was intoxicating—whirling with my family through the white night, dancing in the shadows from above.

(1999)

Christmas Rocks

I was with Ronnie when he made the decision. We were at Polo Park, a big shopping mall in Winnipeg. A real palace of lucre. Everything gleamed and sparkled; cellophane reigned supreme. Ronnie observed that the purpose of this marvelous substance wasn't just to keep things airtight or protected but to draw the eye and do a number on the brain.

"I can't take this anymore," he said. "This place is one big junkyard, except all the junk has been cleaned up and polished and has a price tag attached." We'd been wandering around for a couple of hours and still hadn't bought a thing. Another day, perhaps, we might have found all the right presents for the people on our list, had a good time, and gone home happy. But somehow today the whole mall scene was giving us the heebie-jeebies. Disheartened, we'd sat down on a backless bench next to a little tree. One of those typical mall trees that tug at the heartstrings of all sensitive beings, like the sight of a shoeless begging child when you're on your winter vacation in Mexico.

"Poor thing," said Ronnie. "She'll never grow an inch. The same thing happens to trees in here as to people. They turn artificial."

It was true. Looking around, I couldn't see a single genuine smile on a face anywhere. The hordes of shoppers were like wandering ghosts, wearing looks of grim determination, mechanical frenzy. Only a few children seemed really alive, although not even they outshone the leering trinkets in store windows.

"Mike," said Ronnie, "I have a good notion not to buy any presents at all this year. What do you think? Maybe I'll just wrap up a few old rocks."

Now Ronnie, you ought to know, is a writer, as I am. Writing is a seat-of-your-pants profession (literally), and it's a rare writer who doesn't have some superstition, ritual, or talisman to keep himself in tune with the muse. Maybe it's a lucky pen, an old typewriter, a faithful dog who lies at his feet, or three-and-a-half cups of coffee (no more, no less) in a certain chipped mug.

Ronnie's thing is rocks. He works on a ping-pong table in his basement, a surface occupied by just four things: his Underwood, a can of Coke, reams of paper arranged in neat piles (his *piling system*, he calls it), and about a hundred rocks. The rocks are various shapes and colors but all are small enough to sit in your hand. Though many hold down stacks of paper, as far as Ronnie is concerned they're not paperweights. They're just rocks, and he works around them as comfortably as a gardener in a rock garden. Whenever his writing gets stuck, he picks up a rock, handles it thoughtfully, and after a while the words flow. For years he's been collecting rocks from beaches and streams and odd places all over the world where his travels have taken him. His criteria are a mystery to me. These aren't gemstones or fossils or rarities and most of them aren't even pretty. They're just Ronnie's rocks, geological plain janes, and each and every one of them is his favorite. So when I heard his idea of giving rocks for presents, I understood.

"Ronnie, I wish you were serious. I wish everyone would stop all this crazy buying and just give rocks for Christmas. The economy would collapse but we'd all be a lot happier."

"It's true, Mike. Christmas has become a festival of *getting*, not *giving*. It all goes back to those three wise men. What was the baby Jesus going to do with gold, frankincense, and myrrh? Mary and Joseph likely turned around and sold the loot. Nobody thinks about that. Instead we all want to be wise men and give rare and precious gifts, however useless they are. Now you take the shepherds—those guys didn't give anything. Nothing but their attention, their being there. The best things in life you can't wrap up in fancy paper."

Ronnie could really talk when he got warmed up. Just listening to him, my spirits were perking up. Even the leaves on our little tree seemed a bit brighter and greener.

Across from us, a fat man in plaid pants was leaning on a glass counter, absorbed in picking out a pocket calculator. There were about thirty different models to choose from. We guessed he was trying to decide if his wife would need logarithms to tote up the grocery bill.

"Let's get out of here," said Ronnie. "People can say what they like—that I'm cheap, selfish, whatever—but I'm giving *rocks*. It's all I can think of that might mean something."

"Maybe it will only mean something to you," I suggested.

Grimacing, Ronnie pointed a finger at me. "Look, this time of year everyone rushes around trying to alleviate their guilt. We give out of inadequacy, not generosity." Already we were on the other side of the big glass doors and hustling across the parking lot. "The beauty of rocks—even more than making stuff with my own hands—is that rocks take the focus away from the gift itself and put it squarely on the act of giving. Suddenly there's no place to hide."

Soon we were in the stream of Portage Avenue traffic. For a long while Ronnie said nothing as the dreary, glittering city drifted past. It was a frosty sunny Saturday a few days before Christmas and everybody and his dog were out shopping. On this one day, we knew, some merchants would do a third of their entire year's business.

Where were we headed? Did Ronnie have a plan? All I knew, watching him hunched over the wheel, eyes burning, threading his way along the river of metal, was that I loved him.

"Ronnie," I declared, "you're the most original person I know. The idea of giving away your very own rocks—I think that's the most stupendous Christmas gift ever!"

Ronnie shot me a glare. "My *own* rocks!? Mike, I wouldn't dream of parting with my own rocks." Then, softening: "Not that I couldn't. But after all, they're *my* rocks; they wouldn't mean the same to anyone else. No, I'm not wiggling out of Christmas shopping that easily. What I mean to do is to find brand new rocks, ones appropriate for each person. A big job, but a lot can be accomplished in a short time with pure motives."

Ronnie fell silent again, saving his energy for the task ahead. Turning north onto Main Street, he kept driving until the clutter of civilization gave way almost suddenly to the dramatic breadth and clarity of open prairie. Yes, I thought, here was God's own great mall, where things didn't have to be wrapped in cellophane or foil to make them enticing. Finally I asked Ronnie where we were going.

"The place to get good rocks," he replied, "is where they're made: by the shores of a great body of water. Lake Winnipeg is one of the truly great lakes of the world. If Jesus had been Canadian he would have walked on it. So I thought we'd take a little spin out to the fishing village of Gimli. It's the Capernaum of Manitoba. Such a place gives birth to wonderful stones. I have a couple from there myself that would knock your eyes out."

Overlooking Ronnie's unfortunate phrasing, I remarked,

"I'm afraid your rocks all look alike to me."

"You could say the same of gold-plated Cadillacs, Mike. Or babies. There are days when everything looks the same as everything else. Like the Preacher said, there's nothing new under the sun. But that's the voice of despair. The truth is that everything, all the time, is as fresh and different as it could possibly be. It's all in the eye."

Eventually we arrived in Gimli and found a spot on the beach about a mile beyond town. As if responding to Ronnie's words, the air looked so crisp and sunshiny that each and every molecule seemed to have a wink in its eye, and it was the same with the frozen lake that stretched white and shimmering into pure infinite distance, pure horizon. For a long time we stood silently, gazing out, asking ourselves some version of that question, *Who am I? And what is my place in this vast scheme?* until finally we turned and smiled at each other, realizing, *Hey, I'm me, and my place is right here.*

The only sound came from an open stream that trickled down the snowy beach. It looked so cold it seemed about to freeze before our eyes. The water was clear as a night sky, and peering into the stream bed I thought of Thoreau's image of "the sky, whose bottom is pebbly with stars," for it was covered with the most amazing array of rocks and stones. The long-lost tomb of a pharaoh could not have been more dazzling, and the transparency of water suggested the most elegant of glass display cases at Tiffany's. There were stones of all shapes and sizes, and the combination of wetness and winter light and sparkling cold brought out their colors with stunning vividness. They were red and pink as only rocks can be red and pink; never were there blacks so elemental as these blacks; even the grays were like some color no one had ever imagined. The only thing I could think of more real or beautiful was human eyes.

"Oh, Ronnie!" I gushed. "How did you ever find this spot? Have you been here before?"

"Never. I couldn't find gold or silver if my life depended on it, but for granite and quartz I have a prospector's nose."

It was mid-afternoon, the sun low and casting long sepia shadows, so without delay we set about our shopping spree. Having decided on rock gifts myself, I was gripped by the wild notion that Ronnie's inspiration might well be the founding of a great tradition. Every custom, after all, has to start somewhere. Who had hung the first Christmas stocking? When was the first tree brought into a house and decorated? Who first linked mistletoe with kissing? Many Yuletide customs had only the most tenuous of connections to the true meaning of Christmas. But not so with Christmas rocks. Wasn't Jesus born in a cave? The very manger He was laid in was probably a stone trough. And wasn't the church founded on a rock?

"And didn't Mary rock her baby boy?" added Ronnie.

We discussed all this as we hunted in the stream. Centuries from now, we dared to speculate, people all over the world would go out at Christmas to collect rocks. No more trinkets, no more fancy frivolities, no more of the scandal of RV keys under the tree. Instead people would reverently tell and re-tell the story of the two young writers whose simple pilgrimage to a lonely beach at Gimli had broken the back of the great decadent beast of Western materialism. Perhaps this very stream, virginally pure, would be immortalized.

The task of collecting proceeded thus: Holding the image of an intended recipient in our minds, we would concentrate on loving that person, appreciating their goodness and wishing them well. We looked for stones that would, mysteriously, be just the right size and shape and weight and color to fill up whatever might be lacking in these lives that were dear to us. In this way our Christmas shopping became an act of prayer—which, come to think of it, is just what gift-giving ought to be.

Each time we spotted a suitable rock we'd take off one mitten and reach a bare hand down into the frigid stream. The water was so cold it burned the skin. There was pain in acquiring these gifts. There was cost. After an hour our hands were so numb they seemed to be turning to stone themselves.

More and more we worked in silence. But every so often Ronnie would straighten up and break into a paean: to creation, to Christmas, to his mother, to his girlfriend Mabel, or else to the very rocks. He had his own philosophy of rocks, a cosmo-esthetic petrology.

"People who don't like modern art," he observed, "haven't looked closely at the real world. Each of these stones is a tiny sculpture, perfectly crafted, more abstract than a Brancusi. Much has been made of Stonehenge—but what about the stones in this stream? Haven't they also been placed here, set up on this particular beach through a fantastic feat of engineering? 'Sermons in stones,' said Shakespeare. Maybe the reason Jesus refused to turn stones into bread was that the stones, just as they are, are so eloquent."

What a preacher Ronnie would have made! There on that spectacular beach, with the snow glistening and the stream flashing its crinkly smile at us, with our pockets full of shining bits of the earth's crust and the light deepening over the lake as the sun descended until everything looked engraved in winter-equinox pewter—in such a setting it wasn't hard to believe that Christmas really was coming— that this old world, flawed and broken as it was, had become the womb of God and was soon to be delivered.

Ronnie and I finished our Christmas shopping in the nick of time, just before the light died. We had even found a few extra rocks for people we hadn't intended to get presents for. So we counted it a successful day, and not until later that night would I begin to feel like Jack in the fairy tale, who was sent out to the fair with a valuable cow and returned home with a bag of worthless beans. Would my rocks produce a stalk leaping up to heaven?

We were about to return to the car when I noticed

Ronnie pause and grow thoughtful. Reaching deep into his pockets, he drew out all the stones he had gathered and held them in cupped hands. For a few moments he gazed out at the darkening frozen lake dusted with a patina of snow glowing silver in the twilight. Then with two swift motions he swung his right arm up and back and hurled all those painstakingly-collected gift-rocks far out into the wide-open mouth of the horizon. They fanned out like flocks of little sparrows in the air and landed with a hollow clatter on the ice like so many worthless shards of pottery.

I was stunned. When the last stone lay still, everything was very, very quiet—much quieter than it had been before.

"There," said Ronnie. "You hear the lake declaring the hollowness of my gifts?" Then he stooped and gathered another two handfuls of stones from the stream bed, stuffed them in his pockets, and we walked back to the car in silence. I was too perplexed to speak.

Only when we were on the highway heading back to the city did I blurt out, "I don't get it! We spend a whole afternoon choosing special rocks and then you go and throw them all away. Why?"

Ronnie was the same color as the night. His words seemed to emerge from the bottom of a well.

"Mike, I was taking myself too seriously. There was nothing special about those rocks. All that matters is that I put the effort into looking for them. These other rocks will do just as well and no one will be any the wiser. In fact,

I may even get some small store-bought presents, too, but now I'll do it with the right attitude. After all, nobody can ever really *give* anything to anyone else. God does the giving. The best we can do is stand in awe."

Well, I could sort of follow Ronnie's thinking, and I sort of couldn't. All I knew was that I wasn't about to throw away my own precious rocks. And so we drove on through the night, and as we came into the city with its myriad lights, we might have been a stream flowing through clouds of stars.

I felt privileged to be on Ronnie's Christmas list that year. I still have the mug he gave me (now chipped) and I have his rock—the one selected not by him but by God. They both sit on my desk, and sometimes when my writing gets stuck, I pick up that stone and feel its weight, and its lightness, and remember that day on the beach at Gimli forty years ago. And then the words flow.

(1981)

The Festival of Lights

Some years ago I was transferred to a little town in northern British Columbia to be the Postmaster. The post office was like an old railroad car—a narrow, draughty, wooden structure that, like the rest of the town, lay for three months of the year in the shadow of the mountains, with no sun at all.

My first day on the job, a young man entered and said in a high trembling voice, "Sir, I have reason to believe that I haven't been getting all of my mail." His name was Josh and he had bright red hair and buck teeth. A few long hairs straggled from his chin.

I took Josh's complaint seriously and investigated the matter. But nothing appeared to be out of order. Therefore when he came in again and asked, "Do you think I'm getting all of my mail?" I was able to assure Josh that yes, as far as I could tell there was nothing amiss. This time I noticed a slight cast to one of his eyes.

159

When Josh next came in, and the next time too, immediately upon seeing me he asked, "Do you really think I'm getting all of my mail?" Nothing I could say seemed able to persuade him that every indication suggested he was indeed receiving all the mail coming to him.

His concerns, however, did not stop with me. Soon he was writing official letters of complaint to my superiors. I received envelopes stamped 'URGENT! *Reply Within 48 Hours.*' Countless forms had to be filled out in quadruplicate. While the volume of Josh's mail (mainly flyers) remained unchanged, my own mail increased. Finally a postal investigator flew up to the remote little town to see what there was to see, and I had to entertain him.

Meanwhile, whenever I saw Josh coming I would slip into the back room. If I noticed him on the street I would cross to the other side. When it did happen that I was forced into conversation with Josh, I could barely stand to look at him for disgust. His long front teeth were yellow as a beaver's. There were holes in his clothes, and sometimes bits of food clung to the corners of his mouth. The hairs on his chin were particularly unsightly. And always he greeted me with, "Do you really think I'm getting all of my mail?" My answers became uncharacteristically abrupt, even rude.

Other people, I noticed, treated Josh tolerantly, kindly. Why couldn't I do the same?

One day I was getting my haircut at the little barber shop next door to the post office. It was the tiniest building in town, but the barber was a big square-shouldered man with a bushy black beard who reminded me of a bear. He looked as if he ought to have been out in the woods hewing down Douglas firs rather than in here snipping hair. Most of the time he just sat in his chair and dozed, or looked out the window at the passing show. Without mentioning Josh's name or particulars, I described to him the case of the young man who seemed convinced he wasn't getting all of his mail.

The barber stopped cutting and gazed out at what I suppose is one of the most spectacular views of mountains anywhere in the world. "Josh is no different from anybody else in this town," he reflected. "I watch them go by on their way to the post office. Some folks pass a dozen times a day. The way people flock to that building of yours, you'd think the mail came in every hour. Boredom is what it is. There's nothing to do here. If you ask me, everybody's just waiting around to die."

Eventually I learned that Josh was a resident of Mountview Home, a permanent care facility for mentally challenged adults. I also discovered that he wrote poetry, and had sent away to some publishing enterprise which promised to review and find markets for his work. This, no doubt, was the reason he scanned the mails so closely. I was a poetry lover myself and I could just imagine the sort of rubbish he wrote.

As time wore on I began to dream about Josh. While I had grown adept at avoiding him during the day, at night I met him more and more regularly. In one dream he was the Postmaster, in a blue uniform, behind a grille which turned out to be the bars of a jail cell. I was in the cell.

One morning upon awakening the thought came to me forcibly that I hated him. And immediately on the heels of that thought came another: Yes, I did hate him— because he was making me hate myself.

December brought incredible falls of snow. Several times the town was all but buried. At night the sky lay close overhead, deep and glossy as the sable pelt of some enormous animal. Stars jumped from it like matches just lit and flaring. Often I found myself lying awake long after midnight, and I would get up and sit in the kitchen with a drink and peer out the window. Where the mountains were, there were no stars.

That year the town purchased new Christmas lights for Main Street. The installation was to be celebrated by a "Festival of Lights" with band, choirs, speeches, and a "blessing of the lights" by a local minister. In preparation for the dramatic switch-on, all the merchants were to leave their lights off. The whole thing struck me as a bit mawkish, but as the barber had observed, there was nothing to do in this town, and so after work I ambled down to a very dark town square for the ceremony.

As always happens at such affairs, something went wrong with the PA system. The delay was long and it was a cold night, and the crowd huddled around the band shell began stamping their feet to keep warm. In the gloom in their bulky winter coats they looked ghostly, subhuman, like a herd of cattle in a boxcar, or like shades waiting to be ferried to the underworld.

But when the big moment finally arrived and all the lights flashed on at once and the band struck up *Hark! the Herald Angels Sing*, I must admit there was something rather thrilling about it. As I basked in the magical glow and listened with real enjoyment to the music—just then I happened to catch a glimpse of Josh. We were both on the outskirts of the crowd, and when I saw him making his way toward me my first thought was to get away. But then I felt something, almost like a hand on my shoulder, and I thought no, it was Christmas, and for once I would stay put and be pleasant to this fellow. Perhaps, I hoped, in the spirit of the season, he too might temporarily suspend his long-standing feud with the post office.

He came straight up to me and peered into my face, uncomfortably close. So close that I could smell his breath, see his whiskers gleaming silver in the lights. "Do you think I'm getting all of my mail?" he piped.

And suddenly, strangely, rather than being irritated, something in me gave way. Josh's entire face seemed to glow, not only with reflected light but with some inner radiance, fresh and innocent, like that of a youth—or a saint.

"Yes," I replied. "I feel certain you are receiving all of your mail. And aren't the lights lovely? And isn't it an absolutely beautiful evening?"

For a few moments we chatted, having a nearly-normal conversation amidst the myriad glistening lights as the band played like a company of the heavenly host. Later, walking home through the snowy streets, I felt happier than I could remember. As I looked up at the velvety darkness of the mountains, they seemed suddenly close and intimate.

And then I slept like a baby.

(1988)

Born With Wings

Staring at the white ceiling, Mary felt the scanner sliding around in the warm goo smeared over the mound of her tummy. The screen of the ultrasound swarmed with shadowy shapes, like pieces of a puzzle that wouldn't quite fit together. Then she saw it: the tiny head, the feet, the hands. All moving.

"Look!" she cried. "He's waving at us!"

Dave, shaking his head in wonder, said, "It's like a picture transmitted from Mars. Like the little guy is calling out, 'Soon be home, Mom and Dad! My rocket's on its way!'"

The technician, talkative until then, was staring intently at the screen.

"This must be such a lovely job," said Mary. "Meeting new moms, watching them see their babies for the first time. You must just love it."

The technician did not respond.

"I mean," said Mary, "isn't it just grand?"

The scanner slid back and forth, the image swam. Finally the technician replied, in a voice strangely remote, "Every job has its hard parts."

With these words, a different feeling crept into the room, like a breath of the Martian atmosphere.

"Is something wrong?" asked Mary.

Having intended to stay in the city and do some shopping, Dave and Mary Tressel changed their plans and headed straight home. All they were told was to see their own family doctor, Sharon Walker, that same day.

It was a long drive back through the blaze of fall colors that now looked shocked, unnatural.

*   *   *

Dr. Sharon made room for them as soon as they arrived. While Andy, their two-year-old, occupied her swivel chair and worked on a gigantic sucker, Sharon sat beside the Tressels so that she could hold Mary's hand.

She had to tell them that their baby, according to the ultrasound, appeared to have no kidneys. *Renal agenesis*, she called it, or *Potter Syndrome*. The condition was very rare; Sharon had never seen it before. It meant, among other things, a lack of amniotic fluid so that the lungs would not develop properly. The baby could not survive outside of the womb. Naturally, a second scan would be needed to confirm the diagnosis.

It was quite a while before anyone noticed that Andy was smearing grape sucker all over the leather chair. To Dave it seemed bizarre to be vexedly cleaning up the sticky mess of one child while choking back tears over another, not yet born.

*   *   *

Dr. Phelps, the obstetrician, peered at the grainy, motile form on the ultrasound screen and said, "I'm looking for two little shapes, Dave and Mary, about this size, but I'm not seeing them. They should be right here."

The Tressels nodded. With a magic marker you could draw those shapes onto the screen, thought Mary. Then they would be there.

Dr. Phelps outlined their options: Induce premature labor now; wait and hope for an early delivery; or carry to term. In the last case the baby might be born alive, but would die soon after.

"What's the point in that?" asked Dave. "Why wait at all?"

"Only to be absolutely certain," answered Dr. Phelps. "Some people believe in miracles. Another thing to consider is that right now the baby isn't suffering. Up to the point of birth, this is a healthy, comfortable child. I just want you to be fully aware of your choices. Immediate induction is an obvious route, but it's up to you."

"Does induction mean abortion?" asked Mary.

"In this case, I don't think so," said Dr. Phelps. "No, I wouldn't call this abortion."

In the end the Tressels decided to wait another month, just to see. Who could tell what might happen in a month?

"Just say the word," assured Dr. Phelps, "and we'll proceed."

*　　*　　*

"I don't want it, Dave!" cried Mary. "I want it out, out, out!" The deformed thing felt like a foreign body inside her.

"Well, then, we'll just pull the plug," said Dave. "Simple as that." He stroked his wife's hair but he would no longer touch her tummy. Even Mary shrank from touching herself. And certainly there was no more talking to it. What was to say?

But still the nausea continued, even worse than with Andy, and the wakeful nights, and on top of this Mary developed a series of bladder infections. And all for what? It was much worse than just being sick.

At the same time Mary kept thinking: The doctors are wrong. The machine is wrong. Everything is all right.

*　　*　　*

So they hung on for the month, somehow, not knowing why. And then something changed.

On Dr. Sharon's advice Mary attended a support group meeting of mothers who had lost their babies. The women sat in a circle drinking coffee in a church basement. As Mary walked in, every eye was on the bulge of her pregnancy.

"Looks like you're in the wrong place, honey," said an icy voice.

Mary was prepared to be ashamed, but not ostracized.

"No, no," she choked, "you don't understand ..."

As she spilled her story, the women surrounded her with tears and hugs. Every one of them wanted to touch her tummy. And suddenly there was another person in the room—almost as though her baby had just been born.

Explaining it later to Dave, Mary said the other women had made her feel lucky. Their babies had all died unexpectedly, without warning. But Mary *knew*. And now, in the time remaining, she and Dave had something that none of the other parents had had: the profound privilege of getting to know their child. Of saying goodbye.

*   *   *

From then on, the pain was different: before, like a black hole; now, a star excruciatingly bright.

They gave their baby a name so they could start using it right away. The gender being indeterminate, they decided on Chris, to suit either a boy or a girl. Chris was twenty-three weeks old and the Tressels began to behave like a family of four.

They were living in a trailer parked in a friend's drive-way, waiting for their new house to be finished. Curiously, the close quarters were no strain; in fact, since facing the news about Chris, they got along better than ever. Love was something they really needed now. It was not that they felt closer, exactly, but they talked more. About everything. They talked to Chris too. Often they addressed their baby as though Chris were as old as themselves, or older. As though Chris could understand things that they could not.

The kitchen window of the trailer looked out over acres of flat stubbled fields ending in a distant line of purple hills. In the late autumn sun the fields shone an exquisite pale gold, turning silver at dusk. It was the longest and loveliest view Mary had ever enjoyed from any house she had lived in. Sometimes she thought that she did not want to move anywhere else at all.

*   *   *

They told their family and closest friends. And one Sunday they stood before their church to ask for prayer. But still there remained the problem of how to handle the many others—the women on the street who came up to Mary to coo over her pregnant tummy like doves. She learned to smile sweetly and say, "Yes, Chris is gaining nicely."

One day Rhonda Sutherland came for coffee. She was thirty-five, a few years older than Mary, and a widow. Everyone knew that Rhonda had nursed her husband through cancer, but what Mary did not know was that she had also suffered a stillbirth. Her mother, too, had died of cancer, and a sister had been killed in a car accident. Everyone, sooner or later, had to pass through the valley of the shadow, but Rhonda seemed to live there. She had a look in her eyes. It was the look of a wounded bird as you pick it up in your hands, and at the same time it was the look of an eagle. Rhonda had no use for funeral parlors and the modern way of death. She herself had washed and dressed her husband's body. "He was my own flesh," she said simply.

In a short time Rhonda and the Tressels became good friends. Listening to their darkest thoughts, she could pronounce them normal. Neither Dave nor Mary had had anything to do with death. Now it was as if they were being initiated into some secret society. Or was it, rather, that all their lives they had been sworn to a conspiracy from which now, at long last, they were released?

Many of the same feelings still swamped them: despair, disgust, anger with God. And there was the same treadmill of questions: *Why? What had they done? What kind of people were they, that the fruit of their loins should be cursed?* Increasingly, however, it seemed that all this was contained within something larger, as if they too were held in a womb. Desolation took on an aura. Mary really did feel like a woman expecting.

*   *   *

December came. It seemed crazy to get a real Christmas tree, with barely room for it in the tiny living room. But Chris, Mary felt, deserved one. It would be her child's only Christmas.

They decorated the tree entirely with angels: straw ones, quilted ones, crystal ones that made rainbows in the sun. For the topmost ornament, a friend of Dave's had welded a small but rather fierce, apocalyptic-looking angel in dark metal that gave Mary a strange comfort.

It was while gazing at the tree one evening that she felt the first labor pains. Chris was premature, just thirty-three weeks, and to Mary this came as an extraordinary mercy. After all the early anguish over whether or not to terminate this pregnancy, finally the decision was made for her. Finally the darkness would end and she would see her child, would hold Chris in her arms and look into those eyes and speak her love. And then who could tell what miracle might occur? This was the thought that kept her going through a long night and an even longer day of preparing to give birth to death.

Often she had fantasized about a Caesarian: slipping into unconsciousness and waking up when it was all over, as from a dream. But afterwards Mary would be glad for the pain of this labor, glad for every stab of it. For it was the pain that made it real. She really did have a baby.

*   *   *

Chris was born at nightfall on Christmas Eve. Right up until the end things were easier than they had been with Andy, but since Chris was breech, the final pushes were horrendous. Who could blame this baby for not wanting to come out? Dr. Sharon was struggling, and for a few panicky moments it seemed as if this were a perfectly normal baby who suddenly was in danger of being lost.

But he was not lost; he was right here, right now, with them in the room, a boy, alive. Tiny and silent yet big as life. And so beautiful! There was no doubt about that. Dave and Mary were prepared for a thing from Mars. The books had described the external marks of *Potter Syndrome* as "wide-set eyes, large ears, parrot-beak nose, spade-like hands, wrinkled skin." But really he wasn't like that at all—not to them. He was just their child, a gorgeous baby boy. And so warm! How could something this tiny and doomed have so much life in him?

His only problem was that he could not breathe. He kept trying, but his undeveloped lungs would not take the air. "Breathe, you sucker!" chanted his parents in urgent whispers—"Breathe!" But he did not. He was not made for this world. There was no miracle.

Except this: Dave and Mary's great fear had been of a ghastly death—but it wasn't. A beautiful baby, Chris died beautifully. A kicker in the womb, and even during delivery, now he made no struggle. Just once he shivered all over, as if shaking something loose. Otherwise he lay peacefully on his mother's breast with his tiny mouth opening now and then in a perfect O like a choirboy's, as though about to pronounce one of the names of God. No gasps or ugly noises. No noise at all. Just once he made a faint coo in his throat that sounded, amazingly, like "Mom."

Mary kept thinking about something Sharon had told her. Just before leaving for the hospital, the doctor had tried to explain to her own daughter, four years old, why this would be such a difficult birth. God wanted Chris for an angel, she had said, and so He planned to take him right now.

"Mommy?" the little girl asked. "Does that mean Chris will be born with wings?"

*   *   *

He lived for about half an hour. They were feeling the heartbeat in the clamped umbilical cord when the beat stopped.

After that, Chris and his parents were left alone. They cried, cuddled, kissed him, sang Christmas carols, told him how proud of him they were, how much they loved him. They told him all about themselves, about his big brother Andy, and about the great wide world. They told him everything they could think of, including all the things he would miss: riding a bike, first day at school, holding hands with a girl, marriage, children of his own.

But you didn't have to be here for ninety years to have a life. In half an hour you could have light, truth, everything important. This was what they told him and they knew it was so. They knew him to be wiser than they were because he was so obviously full of love. He was like some unimaginably ancient sage, someone who had always been and now always would be.

They stayed with him for several hours. A nurse brought a basin and Mary gave him a bath. He smelled so fresh and good, just like the newborn he was. They mar-

veled at his tiny fingers and toes, his perfect body. Gradually his skin, at first wrinkled as an old man's, grew smoother
and cool to the touch. He was almost more lovely in death.
They dressed him in a newborn sleeper and Sharon took
pictures.

Later Dave and Mary would pore over every detail of
these images, so steeped in pity, mystery, love. There they
were, smiling like any normal family in the garish light of
the flash, their own faces so wan and haggard that Chris
looked better than they did.

The head nurse, Pat O'Hara, was an imposing woman
who normally ran a tight ship. But in the case of the Tressels she told her staff, "Bend or break any rule for them. It's
going to be tough enough."

The parents asked for a private room where they could
spend more time with Chris. Not until the wee hours,
when it was clear that Mary needed some sleep, was he
taken downstairs to the morgue.

As she left that night Sharon said to them, "It's been
like having Christmas and Good Friday all in one. Now
may we have your Easter too."

*   *   *

The moment Mary awoke on Christmas morning she
wanted to hold him again. Some of the nurses clucked and
would have stopped her, but Pat barked at them to bring
the lady her baby.

"Are you sure this is what you want, Mrs. Tressel?" inquired the nurse who held the cold, stiff little bundle. "He's not like he was last night ..."

But yes, this was definitely what Mary wanted. It was all she wanted for Christmas. She wanted him hungrily, more than anything else in the world, more than her own life. She really felt that if she could not hold her baby again she would die. Or maybe she was dead already, and only his touch could bring her back.

She kept him all morning, first in bed with her, and later in a bassinet. He seemed to be merely sleeping; at times she could almost see him breathing. When Dave returned, again they talked and talked with Chris, telling him the whole history of the world, and what a hero he was, telling him things they didn't even know they knew. Now was their time with their son, and with savage love they redeemed every moment of it like people holding back a flood.

Andy spent that morning opening gifts with his grandparents. When he came to the hospital, upon seeing his little brother he began to jabber excitedly, ecstatically, like a seer speaking in tongues. He cuddled Chris, kissed him over and over, tickled him, even beeped his nose. Like his parents he could not get enough of him, could not get enough touch, hug, chatter, gaze. For all of them it was less like a first meeting than a reunion. They had been separated through a long, long war and now were met again.

*   *   *

Visitors began arriving in the afternoon. First family and a few close friends; then, as word got around, others came. All day long they practically stood in line to get in. If anyone expected something weird, a sideshow, that changed the moment they entered the room and saw the mother and baby.

Said one person after another, "He's so beautiful!"

And they all brought gifts: frames for baby pictures, a book of remembrance, stuffed toys. One friend even set up a small Christmas tree. It was as if the whole town decided to have Christmas in the Tressels' hospital room.

In their wildest dreams Dave and Mary had not imagined such an event. Before, they'd had no idea they would even want to touch this baby, let alone show him off to the world. Now, inexplicably, they were as proud as any new parents. They felt caught up in the unfolding of something too large to comprehend, something with a mind and will of its own, as if Chris himself had taken charge. Could even such a waif as he dictate a last will and testament? Sway history, change the world?

When Dr. Sharon arrived to make rounds, she found Pat O'Hara in a Santa hat, planted in the middle of the hall directing traffic. For a normally stone-faced woman, the head nurse was fairly beaming.

"Sharon," she crowed, "we're having ourselves a regular old-fashioned Irish wake!" She made it sound like the greatest party she had ever attended.

*   *   *

On Boxing day, after a second night in the morgue, Chris was brought to Mary once more, still dressed as a newborn. He looked darker now, grayer, and Mary tucked the blanket more tightly around him so he wouldn't catch cold. Then Dave came and took him away to drive him to the city for the formality of an autopsy.

Most of that day Mary lay in bed and stared out the window. A few starveling snowflakes drifted down out of a leaden sky, turning later to drizzle. The debacle was nearer now, but still Mary held it back. Things were still okay. During the night, awake at three, she had thought, *He's just down in the morgue; I could go and see him right now.* Soon he would be in a lab in the city, and she could go and see him there, too, if she wanted. Then the next day Dave would bring him back and she would hold him again.

Rhonda, hearing this, responded, "I'm not sure you know what you're saying, Mary. It will be three days by then, and they'll have cut Chris open ..."

But Mary knew what she knew, what she wanted. Death's glory rested upon her and there was nothing she did not know.

*   *   *

She did not, however, get to hold him again. A carpenter friend of Dave's made a coffin and painted it white. Rhonda lined it, not with white satin, but with a cotton baby print.

This was how Mary saw him next, asleep in his little coffin-cradle in the church sanctuary just before the funeral. She had been right about one thing: it was amazing how good Chris looked, even without the attentions of a mortician.

Was this the miracle?

Andy, the moment he set eyes on his brother, once again launched into ecstatic jabbering. But this time it was unnerving, and when finally he had to be pulled away, he fell to wailing. From that point on the funeral was a nightmare. Guests were arriving and death's decorum seized the family like a social rigor mortis. All that week there had been the sense of a pattern, of steps to be followed, a ritual unfolding in an almost orderly manner. But with this most formal ritual, the pattern strangely broke down, fell to bits like a rotten piece of lace. Christmas was gone and now came the slaughter of innocents.

Somehow they held on, no longer in their own bodies but watching from afar, from Mars. It was the only way they could stand the lid being closed on their baby, and then the drive to the cemetery and stepping from the car as onto another planet where not one thing was familiar. Dave carried the casket all by himself, so appallingly light it was, so much lighter even than the bassinet or car-seat it should have been, and as he set it down by the grave side he looked so desolate, as if there were not one other human being, not even Mary, in all the universe save for himself and the contents of this box.

The few words of the service having been swallowed up in the tall bare trees and dispersed to the wind, there came the hardest part of all. Not until they watched the tiny white coffin being lowered into the dark hole did Dave and Mary experience fully how utterly finished was this dread transaction. Their breasts, their whole bodies, imploded like eggshells, and then like two little old people, shriveled husks that might have been whirled about like dry leaves, they hobbled back to the waiting car that would take them away down the long tree-lined drive as the frozen gravel crunched beneath the black tires like tiny bones breaking.

*   *   *

For a while the Tressels had a steady stream of visitors. People from the church brought meals, did favors, asked how they were and really meant it. After a couple of weeks, however, the river of kindness mysteriously dried up. Life began to go on as usual—on the outside, while on the inside little had changed. As the holiday season faded and January descended like a gavel, Dave and Mary often found themselves still at the lip of the grave, gazing down at the white box as it sank away.

Mary kept having dreams about Chris, dreams of holding him, how wonderful he felt. But then she would awake to find herself scrunched up like a fetus and clutching a wad of blankets.

Mary's mother stayed on after the funeral. It was good to have her around, though she wasn't the sort of person one could talk to. Unable to restrain herself, Mary would say things like, "All I want is to go out there and dig Chris up and hold him. Just once more."

"Oh, dear, no," her mother would say. "You don't really mean that."

But yes, Mary did really mean exactly that. Not that she would have done it; but she did mean it.

This was when Rhonda's friendship became most vital. She would drop over and regale Dave and Mary with stories that, in any other setting, might have seemed grisly. At times the three of them would laugh until their sides fairly split. Over what? Oh, the curious fate of Aunt Bessie's ashes, or the time Uncle Herbert's coffin slipped off the bier. That sort of thing. It felt so marvelous to laugh right in the face of death.

And yet, Mary wondered, what really was so funny about it all?

*   *   *

Besides the cemetery, Mary had three shrines that she visited again and again. One was a lock of Chris's hair, the only physical piece of her child that she could touch whenever she wanted. Unspeakably soft it was, like something not of this world.

Secondly, before leaving the delivery room they had made plaster prints of Chris's hands and feet. Infinitely expressive, piteously small, they stood as large and irrefutable evidence that someone had really been here, had made his mark on the world.

Finally, among all the plants and flowers delivered to the church, one gift stood out: a quilted angel with the face of a baby. Like the lock of hair and the plaster prints, here was something solid to see and to touch—although whenever Mary looked at that face, she dissolved.

*   *   *

Then another gift arrived.

About a month after the funeral, Mary glanced at the photograph of Chris on the mantel, and all at once she seemed to be looking right through the picture, past it. What she saw was not Chris a few hours old, but Chris a month old, as though he had actually grown. Before this, she had imagined him at different stages, but now she *saw* him.

Recalling Dr. Sharon's words about Easter, Mary felt then that Chris was not really dead but alive. He had his own life and he would live it out.

From then on, she would be working around the house, or sitting with a book, and she would glance up and see him. Older now, exactly as he should be: crawling, sitting up, taking his first steps, opening his first Christmas present. This never happened without a stab of pain, but the pain was not all there was. Even years later she might glance out the window at boys playing ball across the street, and Chris would be among them—a normal, healthy kid full of vim and mischief and elemental joy. She would not have to imagine him that way; she would *see* him. He would come to her.

*   *   *

That year the Tressels sent their Christmas cards late. They signed them, "Dave, Mary, and family."

Not until well into the new year did they feel ready to play the recording of Chris's funeral. As they listened, what at the time had seemed sheer chaos began to assume a design, a meaning. The simple words of their friends loomed large as though written in fire across the sky.

What especially touched Mary was a verse from Psalm 139, read by Dr. Sharon: "You formed my inward parts; You shaped me in my mother's womb; I will give thanks to You, for I am fearfully and wonderfully made."

Hadn't she read in Isaiah that very morning—"Does the clay say to the potter, 'What are You making?'"

"*Potter Syndrome,*" whispered Mary, feeling the great hands around her and her child. "*Potter...*"

As she said the word over and over, praying it, slowly it opened to her like the door of a vault, like the lid of a casket full of radiant jewels.

(1991)

Twenty-one Candles

Yes, Mr. Church,
There is a Jesus

In September of 1897, a now-famous editorial was published in the "Question and Answer" column of *The New
York Sun*. It was written by Francis Pharcellus Church,
a Civil War correspondent for *The New York Times* who
later joined *The Sun* as a writer specializing in "theological
and controversial subjects."

A question had come from a little girl, Virginia
O'Hanlon, who had scrawled on a slip of pink paper the
following note:

> *Dear Editor,*
>   *I am eight years old. Some of my friends say there
> is no Santa Claus. Papa says, "If you see it in The Sun,
> it's so." Please tell me the truth: Is there a Santa Claus?*

Let's picture the scene, back there in old fin-de-siècle New York City, as Francis Pharcellus Church, in eyeshade and arm bands, tilts back in his swivel chair with his feet cocked on the desk, eyeing sleepily the stack of correspondence beside his sleek new Underwood. Outside, perhaps, it's a gorgeous, sun-spangled, preposterously un-Christmassy autumn afternoon—the sort of day when Mr. Church would much rather be stretched out on the green grass of Central Park, let's say, and soaking up some real sun, than be cooped up in a dreary office of *The Sun* building with the Venetian blinds casting their jailbird pattern of dusty golden bars across the faded green expanse of his desk blotter. It's the sort of day when Santa Claus himself might have peeled off his red suit and headed for Coney Island.

But the world does not stop for a little sunshine. No, there are newspapers to put out, questions to be asked and answered, controversial theological subjects to be specialized in. And so, having fiddled as much as possible with his pipe, Mr. Church sighs, pushes up his arm bands, and finally chooses one letter, at random, from the middle of the pile. It's a pink, squarish envelope containing a single folded sheet of lined notepaper covered with the awkward, penciled printing of a child. Even at first glance, there in the dreamy golden haze of mid-afternoon, the page seems almost to be moving, dancing, filled not so much with words as with tiny bony arms and legs and round, round faces in bowler hats, as though each chiseled letter were a little animated stick figure.

And that's when it happens. The magic descends, the moment of inspiration, as suddenly one ragtag reporter is reminded of how much he loves sitting in this cramped office and banging out answers to all of New York City's myriad queries. Oh, the thrill of flattening a question mark into a period—or better still, of straightening it out into an exclamation point! And on top of that, to have one's every word backed up by such a venerable authority as *The Sun*! Yes, it beats slogging through ditches in the Civil War. And so, snapping a clean sheet of paper into the Underwood, old Pharcellus rattles off his reply:

> *Virginia, your little friends are wrong. They have been affected by the skepticism of a skeptical age. They do not believe except they see. They think that nothing can be which is not comprehensible by their little minds...*
>
> Yes, Virginia, there is a Santa Claus. *He exists as certainly as love and generosity and devotion exist, and you know that they abound and give to your life its highest beauty and joy. Alas! How dreary would be the world if there were no Santa Claus! It would be as dreary as if there were no Virginias...*

So it ran, this legendary assertion of the reality of Father Christmas and of the surpassing worth of all that he represents. Bravo, Mr. Church! Your name has been forgotten, but your deft and eloquent handling of a controversial metaphysical subject was destined to be immortalized in American yuletide folklore. And how many newspaper columnists may boast as much?

But wait a moment. Even granting that a certain jaded hack may have been particularly inspired that day, fired by the earnestness of a child's plea—even so: Did he have any idea of what he was about to do? Could he possibly have guessed that this one short article of his would have the effect of distilling, for an entire culture, the fundamental significance not only of Santa Claus but of Christmas itself? What if Francis P. Church had known that he would be the one to draft what may well be the definitive statement on the meaning of religion in contemporary Western civilization?

Or what if he had foreseen that his next twenty minutes of hunting and pecking would one day be viewed by the world as vastly more important than all the rest of his life's work put together? In the sudden, clear knowledge of the sort of immortality that would be his, might he have called upon his Santa Claus, and could the man in red have saved him?

So much, then, for the scene in the newspaper office that historic day. But what about the other half of this quaint story? What about that other precious Rockwellian scene that would have transpired a few days earlier—the scene around the dinner table in the household of Virginia O'Hanlon and her *Sun*-worshipping Papa? As it turns out, the grown-up Virginia has herself left us an eyewitness account of it, as told to an audience of college students some forty years later:

> *My parents did everything for me that any parents could do. Naturally I believed in Santa Claus, for he had never disappointed me. But when less fortunate little boys and girls said there wasn't any Santa Claus, I was filled with doubts. I asked my father, and he was a little evasive on the subject.*
>
> *It was a habit in our family that whenever any doubts came up as to how to pronounce a word, or some question of historical fact was in doubt, we wrote to the "Question and Answer" column in* The New York Sun. *Father would always say, "If you see it in* The Sun, *it's so," and that settled the matter.*
>
> *"Well, I'm just going to write to* The Sun *and find out the real truth," I said to father.*

And that is exactly what eight-year-old Virginia O'Hanlon proceeded to do—never guessing, of course, that her innocent question was destined to make her a figure almost as famous as Santa Claus himself (or at least as famous, let's say, as Frosty the Snowman). Neither did she suspect that henceforth her entire life was to be shadowed (or is *haunted* too strong a term?) by those celebrated words clacked out on the typewriter of Francis Pharcellus Church:

Not believe in Santa Claus! *You might as well not believe in fairies!... * No Santa Claus! *Thank God, he lives, and he lives forever. A thousand years from now, Virginia, nay, ten times ten thousand years from now, he will continue to make glad the heart of childhood.*

And so it happened that a chance exchange in newsprint became the stuff of near immortality.

Unfortunately, in the case of poor old Mr. Church himself, it is a question of some theological controversy whether or not he also ended up as the stuff of immortality. For of his ultimate spiritual condition, all we can say for certain is that he died in 1906.

And Virginia O'Hanlon—who was destined to earn a Master's degree from Columbia University and a doctorate from Fordham, and to go on to a long and distinguished career as a teacher and administrator in the New York City school system—she also, lamentably, became a victim of death in 1971, at the age of 81.

As for *The New York Sun*, it died in 1950.

Death, death, death. Alas! If the grave, that inscrutable place where no sun shines, could open its thin lips and speak, what might Mr. Church say now in his "Question and Answer" column?

> *Dear Mr. Church:*
> *I don't know whether this letter will ever reach*

you. But I need to know: If you see it in The Sun, *is it really so?*

My papa says, "Nothing's for sure except death and taxes." He also says, "If you see something written on a gravestone, it's so."

What about it, Mr. Church? Are you happy up there in the North Pole, wrapped in the snowy, everlasting embrace of Santa Claus?

Oh, to be sure, all those wondrous qualities extolled by our columnist—the love and generosity and devotion that give our lives their "highest beauty and joy"—they all, amazingly, keep on keeping on. But is that all there is to say? Is that the only news that's fit to print?

So much death, death, death. One can't help wondering what Santa himself might have to say about it.

Dear Santa:

I'm in my 50's. Most of my big friends say there is no God, or even if there is, he's as nebulous as you are. But my minister assures me, "If you see it in the Bible, it's so."

What do you think, Santa? Have you ever read the Bible? I'm writing to you because, as nebulous as you are, most people seem to like you more than they do Jesus.

Pray tell: Is there really a God? And is He Jesus

Christ? And did He rise from the dead? And is He really alive forevermore?

> *Santa, I'm counting on you. Please tell me the truth.*

(1986)

Seven Candles

My name is Emily, and this is a story my Daddy told me many times when I was around five. He always told me a bedtime story. He knew stories about everything. If an ant crawled across the floor, Daddy could tell a story about that ant. There wasn't anything under the sun that didn't have its own story, and Daddy knew them all.

The first time I heard this one was on a snowy night just before Christmas, when the power went out in our house and Daddy brought a candle into my bedroom. I'd never had a candle in my room and I thought it wonderfully exciting.

As I snuggled into my bed I said, "Daddy, can you tell me a story about that candle?"

"Of course, Emily," he answered. "That just so happens to be a very special candle."

Daddy said it was quite an old candle, dating from the time when he was a boy and his family lived in a cabin on an island just off the coast of British Columbia. There was a summer camp on the island, and Daddy's family used to stay there year round to take care of the camp. In the summer months the camp was alive with children swimming and playing games and having campfires. But for the rest of the year it was deserted, and the only people who lived on that part of the island were Daddy and his family. Except for a gas generator, used sparingly, they had no electrical power, so it was all candles and lanterns.

Winters were long, wet, cold, and could be stormy. There was a small boat for going back and forth to the mainland, but when the wind had its way they could be stranded for days. One year, feeling a touch of cabin fever, Daddy's family decided to go to Hawaii for Christmas. But who would look after the camp while they were gone?

Fortunately, Daddy's father had three brothers who said they'd be delighted to spend their Christmas holiday on an island. These men, my great-uncles, were all unmarried and liked to pal around together. Like many uncles they were big, hugely interesting, and had had many adventures. So big were they that the three of them could not sit together on a couch. As for being interesting and having adventures, that is what this story is about.

Daddy's uncles were named John Quagmire, Harry Gooseface, and Pasquale Three-Legs. John Quagmire was the sensible one. He did not speak with a British accent or wear a pith helmet, but he acted that way. He was the tallest, and thickly-built rather than fat. Harry Gooseface was definitely fat and he did not like his name (who would?), so people called him HGF. In my family there was a standard joke about HGF, which was: Do you know how Uncle Harry goes to Montreal? He just rolls over three times.

Pasquale Three-Legs had fought in the war and lost one of his legs. It had been replaced by a wooden leg made from a freshly-cut branch of an apple tree. The wood was so fresh that it continued to grow after being attached to Pasquale's thigh. It even sprouted a second branch downwards from the knee, which Pasquale cut off to make it level with the first. He said three legs were better than two, for the extra one improved his balance.

So these were the three uncles who came to stay in the island cabin for their winter holiday. When Daddy met them on the mainland he said his heart was in his mouth as he watched these huge men climb into the little boat to make the crossing, for it was a rough day and the waves licked hungrily at the gunwales. But HGF just laughed his famous laugh into the wind and shouted, "Our flesh may be heavy, but our spirits are buoyant!"

Their first night in the cabin, when the uncles went to turn on the gas-powered generator, it didn't work. They tried everything but to no avail. Even John Quagmire, the practical one, who knew all about motors, had no luck with this one. Not until after Christmas (when none of them cared anymore) would they discover that the secret lay in one tiny switch that had to be activated with a screwdriver because the toggle had broken off. Daddy's father swears he had explained this, but perhaps his brothers' spirits were so buoyant that they were above such trivialities.

In any case, throughout the holiday they were stuck without power or lights. Not only that, but though they searched high and low they could find only one small candle. Undaunted, always ready for adventure, the uncles built a blazing fire in the big stone fireplace and sat around it after supper to discuss their situation. Many were the ingenious schemes the three seasoned gentlemen advanced for cooking, keeping warm, and making lights. But by midnight it was all sounding like just a lot of hot air (which according to Daddy's father was what many of his brothers' adventures amounted to.) Finally they rolled into bed and slept soundly under the feather quilts.

When the sun came up there was no more need to worry about lights. Or warmth, for that matter, since the uncles were so large that even sitting still, without any fire, they could keep warm quite nicely. But as the afternoon shadows lengthened and it came time to make tea, once again the talk came around to the question of power. Thoughtfully they considered their one small stub of candle, all but used up from the night before. Should they relight it now? Or perhaps save it for Christmas Day?

Just then there came a knock at the door. This in itself was highly unusual, as their only neighbors lived on the far side of the island and were not expected to visit. As one the three uncles rose to see what adventure might await on their doorstep. And who should be standing there but a delightful old lady in a white apron and bonnet. She looked just like a grandma. Her face was brown and merry like that of a dried-apple doll, creased with the loveliest crinkles and all the sunny warmth of eighty summers.

"Hi, boys!" she greeted the three large men (no spring chickens themselves) who crowded around the doorway. In one hand she held a basket which she lifted up for them to inspect. "I'm selling candles. Do you boys happen to need any?"

Sure enough, the basket held an assortment of beauti-fully-colored candles.

"What luck!" exclaimed John Quagmire. "You bet we need candles! How much are they?"

"You may have this basketful for the price of a smile," said the old granny.

At this, the three uncles' faces lit up with the broad-est, beamingest smiles. It was just as if they were little boys again and their own dear grandma had waved a tray of fresh-baked cookies under their noses. They could not get over how beautiful the candles were, especially their un-usual colors—colors none of them had ever seen before, with no obvious names.

"Look at this one!" cried John.

"And this one!" cried Pasquale.

"But this one is even brighter!" cried HGF.

So entranced were they that they completely forgot the presence of the merry old woman. By the time they re-membered her, she had vanished.

"Oh dear!" said John Quagmire. "Grandmother's gone and we didn't even invite her for tea!"

"And it's rather a stormy day," observed Pasquale. "Where could she have got to?"

Peering down the trail to the beach, they saw just a flash of white bonnet disappearing around a bend.

"After her!" called HGF, and they all set off. But Pasquale Three-Legs, of course, was impeded by his wooden appendage, while John Quagmire had an abhorrence of quick movement. So it was HGF who, by rolling down the steep hill, reached the beach first. But even he was barely in time to glimpse the old lady in a small rowboat already far out to sea. When the others arrived, panting, her bonnet might easily have been a whitecap on the windy main.

They all thought the incident most odd. Yet what could they do but return to the cabin and enjoy the gift cast into their laps by the old woman of the sea?

Naturally the first thing they did was to make tea. With dusk already turning the windows to dark mirrors, they gathered around the basket of candles and considered which of the wonderful colors to light first. There were seven candles to choose from, and settling on a yellow one, they set it in the holder and struck a match.

(At this point Daddy always explained that though he would refer to the colors by common names such as *yellow* or *red*, these names were merely approximate. In fact the 'yellow' candle was like yellow only in the way that blue can be greenish, or red like purple.)

As the match touched the wick of the yellow candle, a strange thing happened. Immediately it burned with such an unusual brightness that its light not only drove night from the room but even seemed to bring on day. At the same time the room grew warmer and warmer, then positively hot, until what could the uncles do but take off their shirts and stretch languidly in the delicious sunshine? They felt so fine that they opened all the windows to let in the warm breezes and the sound of lazy surf far below on the beach.

At least, they *thought* the beach was far below—until suddenly a huge wave came crashing right through the windows! It was very blue, very salty, and very warm—much warmer than these north Pacific waters ever got even in summer—and the uncles moaned and squealed with delight as their ample bodies were exquisitely drenched. Pasquale Three-Legs, whose taste for adventure was keenest, yelled, "Bathing suits, lads!" and they bounded upstairs to change. By the time they returned the entire living room was awash with surf, spray, sun, sand, and shells. It was a tropical paradise! And oh, what fun they all had! HGF found that he could float without effort in the soupy brine, and the others took to climbing all over him as if he were an inflated rubber whale. All day they laughed and cavorted more riotously than a dozen little boys.

As the candle burned down, however, the waves diminished in size and the sunlight waned. Eventually the water receded completely, leaving the room as dry as before.

The last trace of delicious warmth fled with the candle's final flickerings, so that the men had to shut the windows and put their clothes back on. And there they sat in the dim, cool room with just enough glow from the fireplace coals to light one another's faces.

"Well, well, well," they all said. "Now *that* was an adventure."

And so they went off to bed and crept under their feather quilts and slept. And a very good sleep they had.

In the morning, they all thought it wiser to make no reference to the experiences of the evening before. For who could say whether they might simply have nodded off before the fire and had a lovely dream? However, as they gathered in the living room, they found a few broken shells and a sprinkling of sand.

"Aha!" said Pasquale. "We shall have to talk about this!"

So there was much to discuss over breakfast. Most importantly: What to do about the other candles? John Quagmire, true to his name, remained cautious and skeptical. He was the sort of fellow who, once loosened up, could be a barrel of laughs. But he wasn't easily loosened.

"Dreams—or whatever that was last night—can be both good and bad," he kept saying. "What if the next candle isn't such a pleasant one?"

"Ah, but what about adventure?" argued Pasquale.

As for HGF, he had so enjoyed their watery romp that he was all for lighting the next candle right away in broad daylight! But instead they waited for dusk and for tea-time before selecting a second candle, a beautiful blue one which reminded them of the tropical sea they had played in. Might they return there?

But this time as they fixed the blue candle in the holder and touched a match to it, nothing seemed to happen. The flame shed a glorious radiance throughout the room, but otherwise appeared to burn normally. Naturally the uncles were disappointed, but also somewhat relieved. After all, nothing is quite so threatening as the prospect of having spontaneous fun. So the men relaxed, tipped back in their rocking chairs, and prepared for an uneventful evening.

Presently John Quagmire, hands folded on his tummy and gazing up, commented on how very, very blue was the ceiling of this cabin.

"Not only blue," responded Harry thoughtfully. "Don't you notice those large patches of white, too?"

At this Pasquale Three-Legs nearly jumped out of his chair, shouting, "Those are clouds!"

Indeed the white patches drifted lazily across the expanse of azure which, quite clearly, was sky. Though the walls of the cabin remained in place, its windows still dark, the ceiling was transformed into a gorgeous sunlit empyrean. Again the room grew warm and the men removed their heavy sweaters. Pasquale, with his sharp eyes, was the first to notice a tiny white dot that seemed to be circling in the distance. Slowly, slowly it approached, growing larger and larger until it became plainly recognizable as a bird. And then not just a bird but a great, majestic, pure white eagle.

These men had seen eagles, but never an eagle like this one. So close it swooped that it seemed about to crash the cabin to bits. But no, it landed gently, folding its wide wings and perching on the back of Pasquale's rocking chair, from where it peered down squarely at Pasquale out of one of its eyes. And Pasquale knew beyond any doubt that the bird intended him to climb on its back.

Always the adventurer, without a thought he mounted the huge white eagle which immediately lifted off and soared up, up, and away into the airy distance, leaving John and HGF craning their necks. Not to be outdone, HGF recalled a large kite he had seen in a closet. Seizing this, and handing the cord to a dazed-looking John Quagmire, HGF took a big breath (so as to make himself even more buoyant) and climbed onto the kite as it lifted off the floor in the summer breeze and sailed into the blue.

"Hold on tight!" he yelled down to John.

"Hold on tight yourself!" John yelled back.

So John paid out more and more cord until eventually HGF caught up with Pasquale and the two of them put on a fantastic display of swoops and rolls and loop-de-loops high above in the spacious air.

(At this point Daddy always cautioned me that kite-riding was something that should never be attempted, unless one happened to have the proper sort of kite and was under the direct supervision of an experienced, sufficiently foolhardy adult.)

It wasn't a bad way to while away a summer's afternoon. But all too soon the blue began to fade, and John noticed that HGF was sinking down and down on his kite. John reeled in for all he was worth, until finally the kite came wafting into the cabin just as the roof beams closed back in overhead, and HGF landed with only a bit of a bump in front of the big stone fireplace. It was just in time, too, as the blue candle had that very moment burned out.

But where was Pasquale Three-Legs? Why hadn't he returned? Had the ceiling shut him out forever? For some time there were two very anxious uncles occupying two busy rocking chairs and staring glumly at a third chair that was very still and empty.

At long last the front door banged open and in strode Pasquale Three-Legs crying, "Greetings, lads! I've just had the ride of my life!"

Red in the face and quite out of breath, Pasquale flopped into his chair and, after a few gulps of tea, proceeded to tell the others the whole story of his amazing flight. And what a tale it was! In fact it took him all the rest of that evening and long into the night to relate it, and so there is hardly space to repeat it all here.

(Daddy told me this part only once, and then it covered several bedtimes, for it turned out that Pasquale felt he had been away not just for an hour or so, but for months. When it comes to adventure, Daddy said, it seems to be the rule that the more you want, the more you get. And Pasquale had a big appetite.)

It was late the next morning before the three uncles appeared for breakfast, once again wondering whether the events of the previous evening had really and truly taken place. So they were surprised (though not quite as surprised as the night before) to find on the ground just outside the front door a large, white eagle feather.

"Aha!" said Pasquale, inspecting it closely. "If I were to count the barbs on this feather, I bet there'd be one for every day I was away."

And who could doubt it?

Even as they gazed at the feather, it began to snow. It was Christmas Adam, the name the uncles gave to the day before Christmas Eve. By midafternoon they all felt ready for another adventure. True, there had been some anxious moments awaiting Pasquale's return, but in the end all had turned out well.

The third candle they chose was a green one, which they lit as the tea in their mugs was being replaced by evening shadows. The moment it flared to life they heard the sound of rushing water.

"More swimming!" shouted Harry.

"I'm not so sure," said John. "Hullo! What have we here?"

John was running his hands over what he thought were the arms of his rocking chair—only now they had a peculiar shape and feel. Then they all noticed that their chairs had been rearranged 1-2-3 in a row. And the chairs were really rocking now, bobbing up and down as in an earthquake. In truth it was no earthquake but a whitewater river along which the men were rushing in a large rowboat.

"Whee!" sang John Quagmire who loved boating.

But just then they were surprised by an odd, vaguely familiar sound, something like the crack of a buggy whip, and John's fedora flew off into the water. Then came another *crack!* and Pasquale felt a shudder through his entire body. Looking down, he was aghast to see a round, black pellet lodged in his wooden leg.

"A musket ball!" he cried. "Someone's firing at us, lads!"

"Oh, no!" they all groaned. Was this to be the adventure to end all their adventures?

Rowing like mad, more musket balls singing over their heads, somehow they managed to gain the shore and to hide themselves among the trees. But who was shooting at them? Trembling with fear, they gathered clubs and prepared to defend themselves against the unseen foe. Peering out from the branches, all at once they spotted him poking around their boat: a tall, swarthy pirate. He had a wooden leg, a black patch over one eye, and he wore a long royal blue coat with a tricorne hat.

"Quick, lads!" shouted Pasquale, who had been in many battles. And they all leapt from the bushes to pounce on their assailant and club him to death, when they heard him whistle to a band of his mates, still far down the river but speeding this way in a six-oared longboat.

"Hold your fire!" ordered Pasquale. And instead of

jumping the foe they jumped into their rowboat and shoved off into the rapids. In the process, they forgot their oars. And what was this? Somehow the pirate too had landed in the boat and sat smack in the middle beside HGF. He looked very distressed and made wild hand signals while barking out sounds in a strange language.

Everything had happened so fast that the uncles had no idea what to think. But soon they found out. For as they rounded a bend in the river, there, right before them, was a sudden drop-off, obviously the lip of a tremendous waterfall. What could they do? Nothing. The pirate hooted and hollered, the uncles backpaddled frantically with their hands, the lip of the falls flew towards them, and over they went.

Just then, as luck would have it, with a gurgling rush like that of water being sucked down a drain, the green candle spluttered out and the uncles found themselves bumping harmlessly onto the floor of their own cabin, just as if they had fallen off the couch.

"My goodness!" said HGF, tenderly feeling his bottom. "What an adventure that was!"

"I should say so!" said John Quagmire.

"And look, lads! It's not over yet!" cried Pasquale.

For there, beside them on the floor, sitting cross-legged and looking huge and very swarthy, was the pirate! What now? It was one thing to go off to some magical realm and have an adventure, but it was quite another to have adventure accompany you back to your own living room in the form of a big swashbuckling buccaneer. The fellow was still chattering away excitedly, and Pasquale, who had traveled widely and picked up scraps of many languages, managed to piece together his story after a great deal of yammering and jabbering and hand signals.

It seems that the pirate band had suffered a great famine, until finally their captain had hit upon a desperate plan. Sending out a party of his best men to search for food on land, he decreed that if any of them returned before finding enough to feed the whole ship, that man would immediately be eaten. Now, this captain was actually a very noble sort who really did not want his men eating each other. But he felt sure that at least one of them, driven not just by the need to eat but by the deeper need not to be eaten, must certainly return with food.

And so it happened that the pirate who landed in the living room of a cabin off the coast of British Columbia, half-crazed with hunger and despair, was in no mood to refuse the hospitality of three overweight uncles as they ran to their larder to fetch him some mixed nuts, pastrami, coffee-flavored ice cream, ketchup potato chips (Harry's favorite), and other delicacies of the Christmas season. Watching him eat, the uncles felt more certain than ever that Black Pete (which, as well as Pasquale could translate it, was his name) was real and no mere figment of fantasy. Indeed he and Pasquale hit it off famously, comparing their ligneous appendages and other battle scars. When Pete learned that Pasquale's apple wood leg was alive and continued to grow, he became quite jealous. As it happened, Pasquale's prosthesis was just that day in need of trimming, so he took the fresh cutting and grafted it into a knothole in the pirate's stump, whereupon it immediately began to grow.

The feast finished and the tea poured, they all set their minds to the problem of how to succor Black Pete's company of blackguards. Food was no problem for the uncles; they always had enough on hand for an army. But how to get it into the mouths of the starving sea dogs?

"Forks!" quipped Harry. But the others scowled at him so fiercely that he put on his thinking cap, an article he wore only on the most solemn occasions. And that was when he noticed a second green candle, the same shade as the first, still in the basket. With this clue John Quagmire, who of course was the best at thinking, came up with a plan.

"Here's what we do, lads. We pack every bag, box, and knapsack in the cabin with goodies and load it all into our rocking chairs. Then we hold tight to our seats and light the second green candle. And just to make sure we have enough time to complete our mission, I'll cut the candle in two and put the bottom half in my pocket. We'll light the top half first and save the rest for our return. If all goes well, we'll get Black Pete back to his mates in time to stuff every one of their hungry stockings for Christmas."

This plan struck everyone as so brilliant that they lifted John Quagmire high on their shoulders and trundled him back and forth through the cabin whooping and hollering the way pirates do. After John's harrowing boat ride, this wasn't exactly what he needed, but he bore it in good humor and then they all bustled around getting ready for their trip. Besides the aforementioned foodstuffs, they packed a great deal of popcorn, which they popped first (to make it lighter for carrying) and stuffed into large green garbage bags. As HGF reasoned, the starving pirates could not only eat the popcorn but string it into garlands for their Christmas tree.

Finally the moment came for cutting the second green candle in two and lighting the top half. Just as they hoped, all four of them and their heavy cargo were instantly transported back to the very scene of their last escapade. Black Pete led them on a trek to the top of a high cliff overlooking the open sea, from where they spotted the black, red-sailed, Jolly-Roger-flying pirate ship riding the main. Once onboard, what a welcome awaited this happy caravan! What a celebration they had, as gallons of eggnog and crates of ketchup potato chips were distributed to the famished freebooters. Of course it is not a good thing to feast on an empty stomach. But then, everything is different at the other end of a candle, and so all turned out well. In fact the uncles had such a good time that they stayed for weeks, feasting and merrymaking and learning all the underhanded ways of their pirate hosts.

But sooner or later they had to return. In a solemn ceremony with crossed cutlasses and much yo-ho-ho'ing (which the uncles felt was very Christmassy), the whole motley crew wept their farewells, especially Black Pete who was over the moon about his freshly-grown third leg. And so, holding hands, the three uncles lit the second half of the green candle.

(Not surprisingly, this led to further adventures, including a savage battle with an enemy pirate ship. But since Daddy only told me this rather grisly tale on summer evenings when it wasn't dark, I shall not relate it now.)

Eventually the uncles arrived safely back in their cabin, with chairs drawn up just as before in front of the big stone fireplace. Wondering what day it was, they switched on the radio to find it was still Christmas Adam, the same day they had left. And so they all turned in for a good night's sleep under the feather quilts.

They had now burned four candles, and three remained. On Christmas Eve their eye was drawn to a red one. Outside it was still snowing, and the red seemed a warm, cheery color that would surely lead to a warm and cheery adventure. Indeed, as they lit this candle it produced a glow very like the glow from their fireplace, only growing and growing so that soon the one small flame became many flames, all dancing and flickering and leaping up until the whole room was filled with warmth and cheer. Nothing caught fire, but everything glowed as if the cabin were encased in a great sac of friendly flame. And then this sac seemed to lift off the ground and to float up and up, until it became clear that this really was a big bag of hot air. In fact it was a large red hot air balloon and the three uncles were in a basket dangling beneath it.

"Oh, joy!" shouted John Quagmire, who had remained on the ground for the kite adventure. "I've always wanted a balloon ride!"

For a while they floated up through the falling snow, so that it seemed the flakes were racing by. Before long they broke through the clouds into a glorious sun-filled expanse, where a strong northerly wind picked them up and took them on a ride that was somehow both peaceful and rollicking, like being on a fast, slightly wobbling ferris wheel. They felt elated and free but not without a hint of peril, which after all is what one might expect from riding the wind.

All went well until John noticed that the snowflakes seemed to be falling upwards. They were losing altitude!

"Those clouds are getting awfully close," he observed.

"And darker by the second," added Pasquale.

"Unless I miss my guess," said Harry, "aren't we far out over the open sea by now?"

"And that water is mighty cold, I wager," said John.

"I've already had my bath today!" wailed Harry.

But all their talk, though it lifted their spirits some, could do nothing to lift the great red balloon that beyond doubt was sinking fast. Down through the clouds they dropped, and down through the snow that no longer drifted gently but swirled in a most squally sort of way, so that the icy flakes stung the worried faces of the three aeronauts. They seemed to fall forever through the flurries, yet all too soon they caught a glimpse of dark waves frothing and chopping below like the open jaws of sharks.

"Oh, no!" they all shrieked. "Is this the end?"

If only the beautiful red candle might choose this moment to burn itself out! But no, as they recalled the little old woman who had given them the candles, and who had last been seen rowing out to sea, for the first time the same thought crossed all of their minds: Kindly as she seemed, was it possible Granny was up to no good, and that all along she had connived to lure the three uncles to their deaths at the bottom of a frigid sea? Was the old lady really a witch?

On this bleak note, with the dark ocean speeding towards them like linoleum fired from a cannon, Pasquale Three-Legs reached into his pocket and drew out his pennywhistle. Many a bad scrape he'd been in, in many a foreign land, and many a time his trusty old pennywhistle had saved his bacon.

"How's about a little tune, lads?" he said with morbid merriment.

And he began to play. The whistle was a cheap thing, thin and tinny, but now amidst the billowing snow it took on the sweetest silvery tone, so much so that the music seemed to mix with the snowflakes and even to set them dancing. Here was music as it was meant to be, music to tame and to organize creation.

Little wonder, then, that Pasquale's tune had the power to call the birds. And the birds came! As if the very snowflakes clumped themselves into white, winged bodies, out of the squall appeared a great flock of seagulls which hovered all around the balloon's basket, now just inches from dumping its human cargo into the drink.

"Quick, lads!" shouted Pasquale. "Toss them the rope!"

Together they hefted the mammoth coil of rope from the bottom of the basket and pitched it over the side. Instantly the flock of gulls, in a fine display of airmanship, caught its loops one by one in their beaks, stretched it out to full length, and gave a mighty yank. Just in time they jerked the uncles up and away from a watery grave and proceeded to tow the great balloon back to shore. And just in time they arrived there, for the red candle had just enough wax left to lower the adventurers gently down through the top of their cabin and drop them bump, bump, bump on their living room floor. And there, too tired to move, they slept that whole night through, bathed in the soft reddish light from the coals of the fire.

They woke the next morning with a start, and with a vague feeling that they must be forgetting something. Something very important. And then they remembered.

It was Christmas Day!

"Oh, dear!" exclaimed Harry. "Here I've been too busy with all this candle business even to think of getting you fellows a present!"

And the other two said the same. What were they to do? They didn't even have a tree! Most troubling of all, as they inspected their basket they saw that it contained only two more candles, and white ones at that. A rather dull white they were, not nearly so enthralling as the other colors had been—which is no doubt why they had left these candles for last.

Well, there was nothing to do but to head out for a walk on the beach, where they picked up curious stones and pieces of driftwood, wrapped them in seaweed, and presented them to one another as gifts. Then they tromped through the snow into the woods and chopped down a tree. Chagrined to find no popcorn in the house, they decorated it with seashells, and then they made a big steaming pot of mulled apple cider and sat around singing Christmas carols and, just for the fun of it, all the other songs they knew, making up new verses suited to the season. In short, they did just the sort of things that three large, soft-hearted, avuncular uncles might be expected to do in a cabin on an island on Christmas Day. And a great deal of fun they had too.

Nevertheless they all knew that the real centerpiece of their celebration would be the lighting of the sixth candle, plain and white though it was. In the end they could not wait for teatime, nor for the onset of darkness as they had with the other candles. Instead, while daylight still burned at the frosty windows, they set the white candle on the table before the fire and drew up their rocking chairs around it. And touched a match to the wick, and waited.

And waited ...

And waited ...

This time, it seemed only too clear, nothing at all was going to happen. And why should it? After all, this was a very plain candle, quite unlike the others. And already the uncles had had more than their share of fun and excitement. Why be greedy for more? So without regrets they settled back in their chairs, resolved to enjoy basking in the delicate light of a very ordinary little candle, and in the much greater light of one another's beloved company.

Their talk came round, once again, to the question of gifts. It was all very well to exchange driftwood sculptures and stone jewelry, but they all felt that the occasion called for something more. Accordingly, they began to speak of the gifts they saw in each other, the unique gifts that each one, simply by being himself, had brought to their adventures.

"That pennywhistle of yours, Pasquale," said John, "saved all of our hides. The gifts I see in you are musicianship and resourcefulness."

"And courage," chimed in Harry. "Remember how he led us in that charge on Black Pete?"

And then they all spoke of the great gift they saw in their pirate friend, which was the gift of allowing them to be of service to him and his mates.

"As for you, John," said Pasquale, "your gift to us was that brilliant idea of cutting the second green candle in two. The gift I see in you is a keen mind."

"And balance," added Harry. "Pasquale and I would be in bad shape without your good sense."

Then John and Pasquale both looked at HGF, smiled broadly, and said together, "Harry, our dear friend and brother, the gift we see in you is a simply marvelous rubber whale."

Recalling their uproarious playtime in the water, they all began to laugh, until soon they were helpless with mirth, holding their sides and rolling on the floor in an agonized paroxysm somewhere between the pains of childbirth and being eaten alive by a hairy tickle monster. When it was all over and they lay breathless on the floor in that altered state induced by gargantuan merriment, through the big front window they noticed the giant disc of the sun resting on the horizon and casting the loveliest road of shimmering gold over the water. So inviting was the magic hour of sunset that it drew the uncles outside and down to the beach.

And that was when they realized the white candle was beginning to take effect. For so calm was the ocean that the golden road across it shone with such a pure and steady light that it appeared to be solid—solid enough for the three men to stand upon the water and begin to walk along the rays of the sun.

At first they moved slowly, testing each step. But soon they were strolling along as casually as on land, then striding and swinging their arms, then jumping and skipping like spring lambs. Breaking into a run, they ran faster and faster—even Pasquale—faster than they had ever run before and all without any effort or puffing, so light and lithe they felt. Such fresh vigor was coursing all through their bodies that with each step years seemed to fall away.

When finally they stopped, they knew that something about them was very, very different. Standing quite still, they looked intently at one another. The first thing John and Harry noticed was that Pasquale Three-Legs was no longer a three-legs but a two-legs! Gone was his forked stump of apple wood and in its place was a real, one-footed leg of flesh. Moreover the new leg was oddly shorter than the former had been, shorter by a good half. But then, so was his other leg shorter. In fact, *all* of their legs were shorter and all of their arms hung much closer to the ground. Their bodies were smaller and their little faces were fresh and shining and positively adorable.

And then it hit them: They were children! Their glorious run across the golden road had brought them to the land of youth. No more big baggy bodies of blowsy bachelors—no, they were boys again! Little boys full of beans, of vim and zip and vinegar. Needless to say, they didn't stand around long to meditate on this. It was playtime! Off they tore in all directions at once like puppies in search of their tails. They wrestled, they chased, they bounced like rubber balls and roared like fire engines. They found a forest of tall trees with twisty limbs perfect for building forts and tree houses, or for climbing to look for nests, or for pirates, or just to shout to the world. Along the water's edge were more trees with ropes to swing on, and big hollow logs readymade for rafts and canoes, and other sticks just right for paddles, poles, masts, or anything. In this place the only rule was that things could be whatever you wanted them to be and you did whatever you liked.

So they romped and played the whole night long—except in that country it was day. They played until the light began to fade and they saw the golden rays of the big sun stretching once again across the water, and they knew it was time to go back. Waiting for the moment when the wind completely died and the road of light was firm and steady, they set off across it, bounding at first, then slowing to a jog, then strolling, until finally they set foot, three grown-up uncles with five good legs and a peg, on the beach in front of their cabin.

Well, what an adventure that had been! And more than that, the uncles discovered that the white candle had one very unique property which set it apart from all the others. For now that they knew the secret of the golden road, whenever the sunset cast its rays over a body of water, they found that even without a candle they could travel back into the land on the other side, there to become little boys and play their hearts out all night long. And this is exactly what they did over and over for the rest of their lives without ever growing tired of it.

*   *   *

So that is the story my Daddy told me about the time his uncles came to stay in his house at Christmas. I know this story is true because when Daddy's family returned from Hawaii, they asked the uncles how things had gone.

"I suppose it's been pretty quiet?" said Daddy's father.

"Quiet?" replied John Quagmire, gazing up at the ceiling.

Pasquale Three-Legs chuckled. "Maybe quiet isn't quite the right word for it."

And then Harry Gooseface erupted in one of his famous laughs, leaving Daddy's family to shake their heads and say, "Those uncles... You never know what they're up to."

But Daddy remained curious about their reaction, especially when he saw Pasquale sitting beside the fire and working on a very interesting project. He had six exotically-colored strings that he was weaving together into a braid to be used for attaching his knife to his belt. Pasquale always wore a knife, which Daddy said he needed for paring his leg whenever it grew too long. Right away Daddy noticed that the colors of those strings were out of this world, colors he had never seen before.

"Uncle Pasquale?" he asked. "Where did you get those beautiful strings?"

And that was when the whole story came out. For these were the wicks from the candles in the old woman's basket. While the wax had burned, the wicks were inflammable, so that after each adventure a brightly-colored string was left behind. I myself have seen my great-uncle Pasquale's six-stranded braid many times, and still I marvel at those wondrous colors.

And one more thing: The first time I heard this story, that snowy Christmassy night when I was five and the power went off, I remember feeling at the end that something was missing. What was it?

"But Daddy," I said finally, "didn't you say there were seven candles in the basket? What happened to the last one?"

"Ah!" said Daddy. "I thought you'd never ask." He was gazing thoughtfully at the flickering candle beside my bed. "Remember you asked me to tell you a story about *that* candle? And I said that candle is a very special one. And so it is."

I studied it. It looked to me like any ordinary, plain white candle.

"You see, Emily," said Daddy, "the seventh candle was another white one. Since the uncles already knew the secret of the golden road, they had no need of a second white candle. So they passed it on to me."

I stared at this candle in great wonder.

"And we're burning that candle tonight?" I asked.

"We are," Daddy replied.

I had to think about this for a while.

Then I said, "But if that is so, why aren't I having an adventure right now?"

Daddy's voice became very, very quiet as he replied, "But Emily, you are."

"I am?"

"Of course. Tell me something: How old are you?"

"Five."

"Right. And how old did the uncles become in their final adventure?"

"About five?" I answered.

"So there you are. You are just the age the uncles became when they traveled to the end of the golden road. You are there right now."

At that, Daddy said good-night with one of his special snuffle-kisses, and put out the candle and tiptoed from my room. I didn't know what else to say. I had a thousand questions but I couldn't find any words for them.

At last, too puzzled to think anymore, I pulled up the feather quilt around my chin and snuggled down warm and happy into the mysterious adventure of being five.

(1996)

In the Stillness of the Night

Soon after Agnieszka Zajaczkowski started working at the Kan Yon, Paul and his buddies gathered over coffee and egg rolls to assess her AQ (attractiveness quotient).

"Those goofy braids with ribbons," said Dave. "Like a milkmaid."

"Too broad in the beam," said Carl.

"Fat legs," said Tom. "I hate that in a girl."

"*She's* not fat," offered Paul.

"And that accent," said Dave. "Where's she from?"

"Poland," said Carl. "Fresh off the boat."

"I wouldn't touch her with a ten foot pole," said Tom.

They all guffawed.

"You don't *have* a ten foot pole," said Dave.

Louder laughter.

"She's actually not half bad ..." mused Paul.

"Why don't you ask her out?" said Carl.

"Get serious," replied Paul.

"I am. She's perfect for you."

"C'mon, Paul," said Dave, "you're almost thirty and you haven't had a date in what—five years?"

"And you've always wanted to learn Polish, right?" said Tom.

They all ganged up on Paul until finally he said, "Okay, okay. I'll think about it."

He didn't know why he was giving this chick the time of day. She really wasn't that cute. For some reason he just felt like defending her.

*   *   *

He didn't act right away. It was early December and things were busy. For as long as he could he postponed the idea, until finally it just wouldn't go away. It wasn't like he had a lot of other options. And what if somebody else snatched up the new girl? That was the kind of thing you could regret all your life.

Besides, without even trying to arrange it, while having supper at the Kan Yon one evening after work, he found himself alone with her. Only for a few minutes, but it was long enough to obey the impulse to ask her to a movie. *The* movie; there was only one theater in Hope. Paul didn't even know what was playing.

It turned out to be a 70's film, *Black Christmas*, about serial killings in a sorority house. Pretty okay, thought Paul. But he had enough sense not to ask Agnieszka what she thought. The immediate problem afterwards was where to go. Obviously the Kan Yon was out. And Agnieszka surprised him by saying she didn't drink, so they couldn't do that either.

They ended up at Paul's place, perched on his floor cushions and sipping instant hot chocolate. Conversation came haltingly, and Paul began to think this whole thing had been a very bad idea. Dutifully he asked about her family and background, and how she had landed up, of all places, in the little town of Hope, British Columbia.

She'd come to Canada the year before, taking a job in Chilliwack as a nanny. It hadn't worked out; the family was "queer" (whatever that meant). But she'd fallen in love with the mountains and was thrilled to find a cheap place to rent in Hope.

"It must be the most beautiful place in world!" she enthused. "Don't you agree?"

For Paul, having grown up in Hope, beauty wasn't the first thing that came to his mind. But Agnieszka's voice was strangely pleasant to listen to and her English was quaint but pretty good. She'd studied the language all through school, then worked for three years at the Visitor Center in Krakow. She wanted to study music, but there was no money.

"Music?"

"I love to sing."

Paul didn't know what to say. He had no use for singing. To him it was as flakey as dancing.

Then, lowering the boom even further, she told him

her family were devout Catholics. In Krakow she had sung in the choir of the Wawel Cathedral, and she went on to speak passionately of her love for the new Polish pope, John Paul II, and how his visit to Poland three years before had sparked the formation of Solidarity, the first trade union in a Communist country.

Paul was at a total loss. Neither religion nor politics interested him—in fact he found these topics nauseating.

Agnieszka had questions for him, too. But what was there to say? He worked at Lordco, the automotive supply store. His mother had died; he'd lost touch with his father, who was an alcoholic. End of story.

* * *

Doing damage control with the boys after this fiasco, the only compensation was that Paul received ample sympathy.

"Just glad it wasn't me, bro," said Tom.

"Catholic?" said Dave. "Man, you don't wanna mess with those weirdos."

"Least you got to see a good flick," said Carl.

As far as Paul was concerned, that was the end of the matter. Until one evening two weeks before Christmas when he dropped into the Kan Yon and sat at a table by himself. He'd been avoiding the place, but he was hungry for Chinese and why should he give it up because of one lousy date?

"Howdy, stranger," she greeted him. "What brings you to these here parts?"

She was affecting a Texas drawl, and combined with her Polish accent, it almost made him laugh. Instead, noncommittally, he raised his coffee mug.

"What have you been up to?" she pressed.

"Oh, you know. Work's been busy. And Christmas and all ..." Why did she have to wear her hair in those stupid braids?

She nodded, then cocked her head to one side. "May I ask you something?"

Uh-oh, thought Paul. "Ask away," he said.

"Do you know about the Othello Tunnels?"

Everyone in Hope knew The Tunnels. It was a big tourist attraction. "Sure. What do you want to know?"

"I'd like to go," she said. "I'd like to see them. I was wondering ... Could you take me?"

Paul looked down. This was about the last thing on earth he would have expected. To be asked out by a girl ...

But beyond that, much deeper than that, she had no idea what she was asking of him. He didn't like The Tunnels. He'd gone several times as a child, but in the last ten years, only once. That was enough.

But he couldn't think fast enough.

"Sure," he heard himself say. "I'll take you."

*   *   *

At the age of twelve Paul had been sent to visit his cousin in Brockville, Ontario. Cory, fourteen, had come to Hope the previous summer and he and Paul got along famously. But in Brockville Paul found himself outclassed by Cory's pack of older friends.

One thing Hope and Brockville had in common was a celebrated railway tunnel. The one in Brockville was actually the oldest in Canada, completed in 1860. A third of a mile long, it began at the waterfront and burrowed directly under city hall to emerge at the north end of town. On Water Street it made such a hump that Cory's father, flying over it in his muscle car, could gain significant air.

One day Cory and two friends, Matt and Buzz, with Paul in tow, were messing around near Tunnel Bay when they got the brilliant idea of taking Paul through the tunnel. They'd done it lots of times, they said; it was perfectly safe; they knew when the trains came through and there wasn't one due for another hour.

Entering the dark opening, Paul noticed how narrow it was, not as large as The Tunnels at home. And the ones at home, of course, had been closed for years. The possibility, however remote, that a train might suddenly appear in the Brockville Tunnel gave Paul a not-unpleasant feeling of creepiness, especially considering there was no room to get out of the way.

"Even if you flattened yourself against the wall," observed Buzz, "the speed of the train would suck you in."

"You couldn't flatten yourself against these walls,"

countered Matt. "They're too curved."

"I'd lie right in the center of the track," said Paul.

The other boys sneered. "You'd be dead meat."

They were striding along the ties, skipping every other one. Water dripped from the ceiling into black, oily pools, making an amplified, almost electronic sound. Their voices were hollow, otherworldly. Up ahead, the tiny opening at the other end seemed very far away.

About half way through, Buzz suddenly called a halt.

"Listen!" he whispered. "Hear that?"

They all stood perfectly still.

Buzz crouched down and put his ear to the track.

A moment later he shot bolt upright.

"Vamoose, guys! Train's coming!"

Instantly they took to their heels, now jumping four ties at a time. That was the only way to do it, the flat shoulder being too narrow to run along. The older boys seemed used to this awkward sprint, but Paul couldn't get the hang of it and fell far behind. Panicking, he stumbled, nearly spraining his ankle, but bounced back up and surged ahead. The thought of a train bearing down so blinded him with fear that he saw nothing, heard nothing but roaring blackness.

By the time he burst into the light he was sobbing. Flinging himself far from the tracks into the tall grass, he lay there spluttering into the ground.

When finally he quieted down, all was still. No train, no voices. Peering cautiously out from his nest in the grass, he saw no sign of the other boys.

He was all alone.

* * *

When he arrived back at Cory's place about an hour later, Buzz, spying him from the front porch, called out, "Sucker! There was no train! You really fell for that one, didn't you!"

And they all hooted.

That night, and many other nights since then, Paul had nightmares. Terrified of the dark, he still had to sleep with a light on.

No, the thought of taking Agnieszka Zajaczkowski to the Othello Tunnels did not thrill him at all.

* * *

It was a cold, clear Saturday as Paul and Agnieszka drove out the Othello Road in his souped-up Ford pickup. On the way he kept them occupied by playing a tape recording on the history of The Tunnels, which were part of the Kettle Valley Railway. Built from 1913 to 1916, blasted through solid granite, at the time it was the most expensive mile of railway track in the country. And with continual mud, rock, and snow slides, it was the most difficult section to keep open.

After a run of bad weather, said the recorded voice, *The Tunnels were closed in 1959. But that wasn't the last time a train went through. In 1974 the CBC aired a television series, The National Dream, about building the Canadian Pacific Railway. For the opening scene a length of track was re-laid at the Othello Tunnels and they filmed a vintage locomotive steaming out of the first tunnel.*

"My heavens!" exclaimed Agnieszka.

Her phrase sounded so peculiar, thought Paul. Nobody in Hope said *my heavens.*

The name 'Othello' comes from Shakespeare, continued the voice. *The engineer, Andrew McCullough, was an avid reader of the bard. He used to sit around the campfire at night with his workers and recite his favorite lines. He named many of the Kettle Valley stations after other Shakespeare characters, such as Iago, Lear, Romeo and Juliet.*

As the tape finished, Agnieszka commented, "I love Shakespeare. Do you?"

Paul nearly laughed aloud. Struggling through all those plays in high school—one every blessed year—had nearly killed him. "Let me put it this way. The only line I remember is, 'Et tu, Brute,' and I don't even know what that means."

When they arrived at the parking lot, Paul grabbed a flashlight from under the seat.

"What's that for?" she asked.

"These are tunnels. It's dark in there."

"How dark?"

"Totally. I mean, there are five tunnels—or four, depending on how you count. A couple are short, and in the longest one you can still see light at the ends. But the last one, it's long, too, and it curves. In the middle it's so dark you can't see a thing."

"Nothing?"

"That's what I said."

"Oh."

For a few moments she was silent as their footsteps crunched on the gravel path. There was no snow, but on his advice they had both worn boots with good treads.

Then she said, "I like the dark."

He glanced at her but she did not look back; all he saw was the blink of her dark lashes.

After a few more steps she added, "We don't have to use the flashlight, do we? It's just in case?"

This time he didn't look at her.

"We'll use it. In the longer tunnels, anyway. There's ice in there. It's slippery."

They walked on in silence toward the dark mouth of the first tunnel. Beside them the bottle-green water of the Coquihalla River frothed and tumbled along toward the gorge ahead. Just before the tunnel entrance, Agnieszka spotted a large overhanging rock. Inspired, she got Paul to stand beneath it with one arm stretched high, palm flat against the rock's underside as if he were single-handedly holding it up. Then, producing a compact camera, she snapped his photo. Paul felt ridiculous, yet as he set foot in the tunnel, the remembered touch of the rock seemed to infuse him with strength.

Like banks of organ pipes, or like the jaws of a monster, the mouth of the tunnel was studded with icy stalactites and stalagmites. Agnieszka oohed and awed over them as Paul gazed down the dragon's throat. Penetrating deeper and deeper into the darkness, he tried to focus on recalling the touch of the rock. Even so, the flashlight beam jiggled wildly in his hand. To cover his fear, he made a show of pointing out places where dripping water had pooled and then frozen into treacherous patches.

"Careful here," he kept saying. But he sensed that Agnieszka, obviously entranced, was hardly listening.

The first tunnel, though the longest, was at least straight, so that the daylight at both ends remained visible. And it wasn't nearly as long as the Brockville Tunnel. Still, nearing the middle, Paul felt weak all over as the old terror overtook him. Indeed at this point the distant roar of the river, funneled through the dark tube, did eerily sound like an approaching train.

For some ungodly reason Agnieszka wanted to stop here, but Paul urged her on, and somehow he made it through to the far end. On finally emerging, needing time to catch his breath, he led Agnieszka to the railing where they stood peering down into the boiling torrent of the Coquihalla rapids. Between rocks the size of cars, worn smooth as marble sculptures, the pale greenish meltwater gushed, beautiful and terrible.

"Wow!" Agnieszka exclaimed.

The fresh air cleared Paul's whirling thoughts enough

for him to say, "In the early years the train only came through here at night, so the passengers wouldn't be scared looking down into the canyon."

"Wow!" Agnieszka repeated.

"Did you see the movie *First Blood*?"

She hadn't.

"It was filmed here just last year. At least, one scene." Paul pointed. "That's where the cop fell out of the helicopter and Rambo clung for his life to the cliff. Sylvester Stallone stood right there. Or his double."

Compared to being in a dark tunnel, the thought of clinging to a sheer cliff above raging waters didn't faze Paul at all.

Agnieszka turned away, and they continued on through the next two tunnels, which were mercifully short. But Paul knew the big one was coming up, the one with the bend in the middle.

Entering this one, instinctively he took Agnieszka's hand. The gesture was not in the least romantic; it was sheer survival. Thankfully, she did not resist. Otherwise he really didn't know how he could have gone any further. Scarcely had they taken a few steps before his eyes swam with inky spots, his heart pounding, his whole frame vibrating.

Did Agnieszka perceive what was happening? He had no idea. He knew nothing, nothing at all.

"Let's stop," she said.

Her voice, emerging from the darkness, startled him.

"What?"

"Stop. Right here. Please."

It was a command. Against his will, Paul stopped. They were in the middle of the tunnel, no light visible at either end. Without the flashlight, he knew, it would be pitch dark. His panic deepened.

"Now turn off the light," she said.

"What?"

"The flashlight. Turn it off."

"But ..."

"We're not going to slip on the ice if we stand still, are we?"

Plunged in turmoil, Paul could think of no response.

"What's wrong?" she asked him.

"Nothing."

He wouldn't meet her gaze.

"Are you okay?"

"I just ... don't like ... the dark," he managed to say. "It's not natural."

"Darkness is as natural as light," she replied. "Let's just try it. Please?"

Releasing a ragged sigh, he closed his eyes, and switched off the light.

He tried to imagine himself on a sun-drenched beach. Hearing Agnieszka breathing beside him, he tried focusing on that.

And suddenly the darkness and the stillness exploded— *blossomed*—into another sound—high, pure, clear as light itself.

He opened his eyes. He couldn't believe what was happening. It was so ... shocking.

Or was it the opposite of shocking? It seemed—as Agnieszka herself might have said—as natural as a summer's day.

She was singing.

He couldn't see her, couldn't see a thing, but the vibrato of her voice was in the air all around like a cloud of fireflies. And that voice— so utterly, indescribably beautiful, as though heaven itself, through a mountain of granite, had opened right over his head. Practically *in* his head. He felt that never in his life had he heard, or experienced, anything so ravishing. Eyes wide open, he forgot all about the dark and saw only, in the sound of that voice, a kind of light.

Before he knew it, it was over. Deeply, achingly, he longed for her to keep singing. But she was done.

"I needed to try that," she said. "It's like a cathedral! You can turn the light back on now. If you want."

"No," he heard himself say. "Let's just wait a minute."

He was still hearing it, her music, like the very sound of her soul. He wanted it to go on and on. But after a while he grew embarrassed.

"Let's go," he said. "We can pick our way along in the dark."

Soon the other end of the tunnel loomed into view, and minutes later they emerged into daylight. The moment he could comfortably do so he turned to her and said, "What *was* that? That song?"

"A Polish Christmas carol," she replied. "We have our own carols, called *koledy*, different from yours. That's one of my favorites—*Wsrod Nocnej Ciszy*."

"Huh?"

Agnieszka thought for a moment. "It means *In the Stillness of the Night*. It seemed perfect for inside the tunnel. I just had to do it."

"In the stillness ..." Paul repeated, lost in the words.

"*In the stillness of the night, a voice radiates,*" Agnieszka translated, "*Stand up shepherds, God is born for you!*"

"God is born ..." muttered Paul.

*   *   *

That night as he went to bed, he tried an experiment. Deliberately leaving the light off, he lay in the dark, thinking over the day's events, replaying everything in his mind. Seeing Agnieszka's face, her lively expressions, her bright eyes, and then not seeing her at all in the middle of the tunnel. Only hearing. And once again he could, almost, hear that voice. Rising and falling, lilting, hovering like a winged thing, coloring the darkness—even the darkness *in him*— and piercing it with pure loveliness.

At that moment he had fallen in love. He had fallen in love with a voice. And now, thinking of her there in the darkness, he fell all the way in love, with all of her.

He never got up to turn on the light. All night long he slept in perfect peace in the dark.

*   *   *

The next day they cut down a tree together and set it up at his place. Neither of them had any decorations, so they made paper chains, foil stars, popcorn balls. It couldn't have been more old fashioned or more fun. Agnieszka had taken her hair out of braids and it cascaded around her, darkly luxuriant with gleaming highlights, like the river of her voice.

As they worked, she sang more carols and regaled him with stories of Christmas traditions in Poland. Throughout the season, she said, from Advent to Epiphany, the *gwiazdory*, or star carriers, wandered through towns and villages. Some put on *szopki* (puppet shows) or *herody* (nativity scenes), while others sang the *koledy*, which were religious carols, or *pastoralki*, secular shepherds' songs. Many of these dated back hundreds of years and all Poles knew them.

She gave him a record of a Polish soprano, Teresa Zylis-Gara, singing *koledy*. Recorded in a church at Christmas with an orchestra and choir, Paul thought it had an extraordinary sound. Deep, shining, otherworldly, holy. He wondered about the words.

"This one," he asked her. "What does it mean?"

"*Gdy sie Chrystus rodzi?*" She made lovely shapes with her lips when speaking Polish, and her eyes sparkled in thought. Finally she translated:

> *When Christ is born*
> *And He's coming into the world*
> *The dark night drowns*
> *In radial brightness.*

"Drowns in brightness ..." he repeated. "I love that."

He also loved the sound of her name, Agnieszka, which she told him meant *pure* or *holy*. Just like her voice, he thought.

*   *   *

In the days before Christmas Paul played the record over and over, especially the first song, *Wsrod Nocnej Ciszy*, and the last one, a haunting lullaby. How strange that another country could have a whole different set of carols—like a parallel universe.

On Christmas Eve Agnieszka cooked *wigilia*, the traditional Polish vigil supper. According to custom they waited to eat until the first star appeared, then began with the *oplatek*, the Christmas wafer. They were joined by Carl who had nothing else to do.

"If only it would snow," said Carl, who worked at a stable, "I could take you lovebirds on a sleigh ride tomorrow, in a real cutter with Clydesdales and bells."

By next morning the snow was drifting down like angel feathers. In the pewtery light of afternoon they went sleighing and the whole thing was as perfect as a Christmas could be.

*   *   *

Paul and Agnieszka were married the following summer at Our Lady of Good Hope Catholic church. Agnieszka designed a white wedding—to remind them of falling in love at Christmas. Even the boys—Carl, Dave, and Tom—were decked out in ice-cream suits with white satin ties. At the reception people said it was amazing the church hall was left standing, so many polkas were stomped out that night.

Paul fell in love for a second time that week—with Agnieszka's parents, who'd arrived from Poland and who spoke passable English. Taking them on day trips around Hope, it was as if Paul were seeing these spectacular sights for the first time. And it so happened that Mr. Zajaczkowski owned an auto supply store in Krakow, so there was much shop talked over coffee at the Kan Yon. Nor did they speak only of cars. As a result of Paul's "miracle," during the previous months he had warmed to Agnieszka's frequent references to her faith. And once Mr. Zajaczkowski got hold of him, there was no looking back.

Of course Agnieszka sang at the wedding, joined by

her new friends in the small Catholic choir, who had lost no time pushing her forward as the church cantor. Every Sunday she led the psalms, sang the solo parts, and generally elevated the quality of the whole group. As the following Christmas rolled around, she urged Paul to join them in a caroling party.

"What? Me?! I don't sing."

"But you could."

"No, I can't."

"How do you know?"

"I know. It's just not in me. It's a girl's thing."

"There are men in the choir."

"Yeah, and they can't sing either."

With a toss of her gleaming hair Agnieszka concluded, "Which is exactly why we need you."

And that was when the next miracle happened. Practicing with his wife before the big event, Paul realized that he did have a voice. "Try closing your eyes," she told him. "With your eyes closed no one can hear you." He did so—and out it came. Not a great voice, nothing like Agnieszka's, and certainly not a solo voice. But somehow it blended very nicely with hers, as if he had the darkness and she had the light, and they belonged together.

Standing on doorsteps on the longest night of the year, filling the crisp air with beautiful old English carols, and a few Polish ones too, as the star-bright sky and the dark shapes of the mountains crowded near to listen, Paul felt centered in the universe, and in himself. Located, found.

*   *   *

He joined the choir, and the next spring they all trooped out to The Tunnels, stopped in the middle of the longest one, and lifted their voices in hymns and anthems or, best of all, simple canons such as *Jubilate Deo*. The sound was sublime.

In all their ensuing years together Paul never tired of hearing his wife's voice. It seemed a continual miracle to him, an inexhaustible well of joy and amazement. Moreover they had five children, all of whom, almost before they could walk, both sang and played instruments. Their home was always full of music.

In the thirteenth year of their marriage, the music turned somber, as Agnieszka was struck with breast cancer. Surgery, chemo, radiation, and endless trips to doctors and clinics in Vancouver filled the following year. She lost her glorious hair, and Paul shaved his. She was the Bald Soprano and he was the Bald Bass. They joked, even half-believed, that it improved the resonant quality of their voices. And that Christmas they cried as they read aloud O. Henry's *The Gift of the Magi*.

Somehow they made it through, and five years later she was cancer free. But five years after that, the dark ghost came calling again, this time to stay. With locomotive speed and power, metastases to the brain cut her down, and in two months she was gone.

There was just time to have the funeral before Christmas. With all the family gathered, for the next week there was life enough around the place. New Year's Eve Paul spent with Carl, and the following day they all collected again for the big dinner.

After that, despite having two teenagers still at home, Paul felt loneliness close over him like a cave. Since coming to faith he had begun to believe that if someone close to him died, he would have a sense of being prepared. There would be some advance warning.

There was none. The same way he had fallen in love—suddenly, utterly—death, like an axe, fell and clove his heart.

*   *   *

For a couple of months he stayed away from choir. When he did return in March, he found he couldn't sing. He could open his mouth but not his throat. Though it felt like some strange physical impediment, he knew it must be due to grief. He wouldn't have believed the human breast could hold so much sadness. He wanted to sing, just as he wanted to get back into the swing of so many other things. But he couldn't. Neither at home nor in the choir had he ever sung without Agnieszka. Without her, he had no voice.

And without music to soothe him, and to keep him connected to Agnieszka, little by little his nighttime fear returned. He hardly noticed at first; he'd all but forgotten it. But with no Agnieszka at his side as he went to sleep, it seemed natural to leave a light on. It was some comfort.

But he couldn't sleep, even with the light. And sleeplessness led to fear of not sleeping, and thence to fear of night itself, of the dark.

His old enemy.

*   *   *

For his birthday in April, one of his daughters gave him a penny whistle.

"What's this for?" he said, rolling the polished wooden tube in his hands, feeling its silken lightness, fingering the holes. There were no woodwinds in the family. Brass, stings, piano, percussion—but no winds. Besides, Paul had never played an instrument of any kind.

He shrugged. "I can't play this. My hands are too big. Look at them."

All his life he'd worked on cars. Having retired from Lordco a few years before, he now did part-time mechanical repairs. His fingers were stubby, the skin calloused and scarred.

"Perfect for blocking the holes," said his daughter. "Try it."

For her sake he tried, and after a few toots he set it aside. He didn't like the shrill tone.

But the thing came with an instruction book, and later that evening, as darkness closed in, he took it up again. In no time he was playing *Michael Rowed the Boat Ashore* not too badly. He was surprised at the pleasure it brought him.

After that, he set himself the goal of learning a new tune each night—everything from *Amazing Grace* to *Black Velvet Band*. He played haltingly at first, but dexterity came as he practiced one bar a time. Before he knew it, eight bars would make a tune. An hour of playing and he was ready for sleep.

The little penny whistle became his sword against the darkness.

*   *   *

Over the next few months he bought half a dozen more whistles. There was a vast range of choices, he discovered, in various sizes for different keys, and in materials from wood to plastic to metal. Each whistle had its own unique voice.

One day in August he was going through old photographs, when he came across the one Agnieszka had taken on their second date, of him single-handedly holding up the big rock at The Tunnels. He studied it for a long time, recalling the mysterious strength that had flowed into him through the stone.

The next day he packed up his music and whistles and rode one of the kids' bicycles out to The Tunnels. He hadn't been on a bike in years, but somehow a bicycle and a whistle seemed to go together. This time, to avoid the big hill on the Othello Road, he approached The Tunnels from the opposite direction, riding north along the old railroad grade. It was a bright, breezy day as he pedaled by the river, letting its effervescent roar fill him like a great shell pressed to his ear. Before long he arrived at the southernmost tunnel, the curved one, where he dismounted. For a fleeting moment he could almost see Agnieszka, standing in the dark opening, smiling. The image stabbed him, and he had to sit down to compose himself.

After a while he pulled out a whistle and tried a tune, but the breeze swallowed it. Whistles were no good against the wind.

Rising, he locked his bicycle and proceeded with his plan: to stand in the middle of the tunnel, in the very place where he had first heard Agnieszka sing, and there to play his music. The old fear was with him, doubled now by loneliness. But he pressed on into the tunnel until he was in the great bend, where even on such a bright day the darkness was like the sable pelt of a giant breathing animal. By now he was in a panic; he wasn't sure if his trembling hands could stop the holes of a whistle. And another problem: Where to place the music? Then he dropped the whistle and had to go on hands and knees to find it. For a minute he wondered if he would ever get up again. Couldn't he just die right now?

Finally he rose and moved unsteadily back down the tunnel to a point where he could at least see the light at the end. Then, from memory, he played *You Are My Sunshine*.

It was no good. He had hoped for the splendid acoustics he'd always experienced with the choir. But his lone whistle was no match for the monstrous black beast. The sound was muddy, too complex, oppressive. Even his simple tune seemed as threatening as the darkness itself.

Ceasing abruptly, he retraced his steps back to his bicycle. He was just about to depart when he had another thought. Wheeling his bike into the tunnel's mouth, he set the kickstand, and devised a way to prop his music on the handlebars. Here, just a few feet from the entrance, he was in the tunnel, protected from the wind, yet still in sunlight. And taking out his finest, handmade whistle, he played *Amazing Grace.*

The sound was unbelievable: pure, clean, divine. Hardly had he finished one verse before his fear was deflating. He almost felt he was playing *to* his fear, taming it, as if it were a cobra rising slowly from a basket, languidly waving. Turning the pages of his music book, he played tune after tune: *Loch Lomond, Black Thorn Stick, MacPherson's Lament, The Holy Ground.* He couldn't get over the quality of the sound. As Agnieszka would have said, it was like playing in a cathedral, the tunnel acting as an enormous gourd to deepen and enrich the whistle's thin timbre. Each note had an exquisite decay, but without being echoey, and the breathiness that shadowed all wind instruments was somehow diminished, leaving the sound cleaner and mellower. It was as though Paul himself were in the audience, hearing his own music from afar.

And audience there was. If he'd rented a hall and sold tickets, no one would have come. But the Othello Tunnels drew a stream of visitors, many of whom stopped to listen to the lone piper. A few even threw him coins. But Paul was oblivious, as possessed by the music as he'd formerly been by fear.

*   *   *

All that fall, weather permitting, two or three times a week he rode his bike to The Tunnels. He tried different spots, but the mouth of the curved tunnel was best, both for sound and for light, as it caught the afternoon sun. And more and more, instead of ignoring the tourists who paused to listen, he took time to chat. Otherwise shy, he enjoyed this opportunity to meet people, as it brought some comfort to his loneliness. His favorites were the children, some of whom acted as if they had never seen a live musician. And once, while playing the Irish tune *Carrickfergus*, he was surprised to hear a choir of voices in the distance, singing the lyrics:

> *I wish I was in Carrickfergus*
> *Only for nights in Ballygrand*
> *I would swim over the deepest ocean*
> *Only for nights in Ballygrand*
> *But the sea is wide and I cannot swim over*
> *And neither have I the wings to fly...*

Paul almost stopped his playing to hearken to the singers. Who were they? But he kept on, finally spotting them out of the corner of his eye, approaching from the far end of the tunnel: half a dozen young women, all as fresh and pretty as this October day. Coming right up to him, they continued singing until his tune was done.

Lowering his whistle, he exclaimed, "You know *Carrickfergus!*"

"We're Irish!" they replied. "You're very gu-u-ud."

And then, of course, he played all the Irish tunes he knew.

*   *   *

Throughout December, with the weather mild and no snow, Paul kept biking out to The Tunnels. His singing voice had returned, but his love for the penny whistle was undiminished. As much as the human voice, he felt, it delivered such an intimate sound, so little interposing between the breath and the music. On most of these days he had the Cathedral, as he'd come to call his venue, to himself. By now his playing was much more fluid and he had many tunes by heart. He played the way birds sang, his only audience the rocks, the river, the trees, the sky, the light and the darkness.

As Christmas approached he turned to the carols, first to the common English and American ones, and later, as the days grew holier, to the Polish tunes. One afternoon, without thinking about it, he began playing *In the Stillness of the Night*. Hardly had he begun when he heard the voice—*her* voice—the one he knew so well but had almost forgotten, or at least could never call to mind at will. She was singing with him:

> *In the stillness of the night, a voice radiates—*
> *'Stand up, shepherds, God is born for you!'*
> *Go as quick as you can,*
> *To Bethlehem, hurry*
> *To greet the Lord.*

The sound of her voice—it was so real! She was right there with him, in the mouth of the tunnel, as though she had come through the great darkness to be with him, and sang in a tone purer, more sacred, more ravishing than he had ever known, yet still utterly herself. He played all the verses, and she sang all the words, and when he was done and stood in the stillness, listening, the uncanny sense of her presence lingered.

He tried another Polish carol, but she did not sing that one, so he put away his whistle and remained there a long time in the silence and the gathering dark.

*   *   *

In the ensuing years with his children and grandchildren and friends, Paul lived a life rich with love, laughter, music, and some sadnesses. Yet hardly had he passed his sixtieth birthday when there came his own turn to encounter the dark ghost. By mid-December, as happens with so many, the great light of winter's feast fell on his ebbing soul like a shadow, and he could not abide for one more Christmas.

In the evening of his final day, the daughter who sat with him, thinking he had moved his lips, leaned close to listen.

"What is it, Dad?"

"Hear them?" he whispered.

"Who, Dad? Who do you hear?"

For a long time he gave no response, but his face was radiant.

"Hear ... them ..." he muttered.

"Who, Dad? What are they saying?"

"Singing ..."

Another long silence; then he breathed—

"*Wsrod nocnej ciszy...*"

(2014)

Bound for Glory

A light rain was falling as I set off across the platform. The weight of my bag felt good, and I had that feeling of self-importance that sometimes accompanies a solitary journey. I was certain no one on this train would know me. Dressed as I was in my best suit and a brand new trench coat, I would likely be taken for a person of distinction. A man of mystery, even to myself.

It was Christmas Eve, close to midnight, and the station was unusually busy, though not with the bustle of a daylight rush hour but with the trance-like commotion of darkness. Everywhere hunched bodies, shadowy but also shiny with the black gloss of the rain, seemed to scud along like ghostly sailboats, gliding as in a dream. All the lights on the platform bloomed with haloes of mist, softly rainbow tinted, and the pavement was black and slick like a sheet of ice in moonlight. As I fell in with the movement of the throng I saw another man, one even more mysterious than I, walking directly beneath me, at each step planting the soles of his feet against mine, his head thrust far away into the dark glimmering sky of another world.

The train waited, steaming and spirited like a high-mettled horse. I found my car, mounted the steps, and upon opening the door I felt a soft rush of wind. The lights and warmth from inside were most inviting, and I looked forward to finding a seat by myself and relaxing. But a surprise awaited me, for not only were there no empty seats, but the passengers were jammed in so tightly that even many of the windows were entirely hidden behind precarious piles of coats and luggage. People held large boxes and baskets on their laps. Trunks and bedrolls and canvas packs filled the overhead racks and plugged even the center aisle. Never before had I seen a train car so crowded.

Quickly I turned to go. But while crossing over the coupling into the next car I met a porter who told me abruptly, "There's no use looking for another spot, sir. The whole train's like this." On questioning him further I learned of an astonishing announcement by the authorities that all the checkpoints would be opened for emigration on Christmas Day. No one knew why, nor exactly what was happening, but thousands of people had packed up all they could carry and were rushing toward the borders. It was an unprecedented event and the whole country was astir with it. For my part, having spent all that day and evening poring over my research in the state library, naturally I'd heard no news. In any case, since I was a foreigner, this was not something that touched me directly.

After glancing into the next car and finding it no less crowded, I turned back to the first car and sat down on my suitcase, with knees to chest and my back against one of the metal seat braces. There were so many passengers that it was impossible to sit anywhere without being scrunched up against another body. I felt slightly panicky, claustrophobic, but decided to make the best of things, and slowly it dawned on me what an extraordinary event I had been caught up in. A Ph.D. candidate in history, I experienced the ambivalent thrill of suddenly finding myself a participant in the living drama of history in the making. What great political upheaval had taken place? In my own country the reports were no doubt being broadcast this moment on special news bulletins.

Glancing around at the packed trainload of human flesh, I couldn't help but be reminded of the Jews in World War II being shipped off in boxcars to concentration camps. In this case, however, the apparent destination was freedom. These people had left nearly everything behind them to travel through the darkness of Christmas Eve into a totally unknown future, with the sole hope of gaining their liberty. I began to feel an admiration for them and an interest in who they were.

Bunched up against me was a bearded young man in a striped overcoat, and directly above me, so that I sat at her feet, was a girl wearing a sky-blue cape that came right to the floor. With dark radiant hair and almond eyes that gazed wonderingly out from the blue loop of her hood, she looked hardly old enough to be a mother. Yet in her lap she cradled a tiny baby, nearly invisible within a bundle of blankets. This was the only infant I'd noticed, though about a dozen older children were present, all sitting on laps or tucked away in the narrowest of corners. The bulk of the passengers were men and women in their thirties and forties, most wearing the drab, heavy clothing of the lower classes. There were men with bushy moustaches and large women with kerchiefs encircling round, oily faces. Their features were plain, yet etched with a peculiar determination. They were faces not used to much laughter, faces made, it occurred to me, for the bearing of hardship and pain.

All of us were anxious for the train to move. But it didn't budge. Though it was now well past midnight, no one slept, not even the children. The latter squirmed and chattered and the adults too engaged in animated conversation. Waves of excitement ran through the car like wind over a wheat field. It was as though these people were one single body, charged with the same blood. There were periodic shouts of "The best Christmas present ever!" and "Let's get this machine out of here!" Even the silent heaps of baggage bespoke movement and anticipation.

Still the train did not stir. The night was very dark; black beads of rain bled against the gray windows. From where I sat I glimpsed a few strings of Christmas lights winking in the distance. Chatting to the man beside me, I learned that he was from a rural area and had already traveled several hundred kilometers that evening. They had left everything, he said—friends, family, a good job, many possessions. But he had no regrets.

"This is the very thing we have been waiting for all our lives," he said. His beard was close-cropped and he spoke quietly and seriously. He had the rough hands of a worker and his face, though young, was deeply lined, with a quality of such gentleness that it gave me an awkward feeling just to look at him. Glancing up at the girl with the baby, I asked him if she were his wife. No, he replied, they were only engaged, and this surprised me. Unwed pregnancies were still a thing of scandal in that country, and besides, this man impressed me more as a husband than as a boyfriend or fiancé. He had an air of responsibility, and though shy he seemed not at all ashamed of his baby—a son—and spoke candidly of wedding plans.

One o'clock came, then two o'clock, and the mood of buoyant expectancy gave way gradually to agitation. "Something must have gone wrong," people were muttering. Either something was mechanically wrong with the train, or else, more seriously, we had run into some bureaucratic snag. As time wore on the latter eventuality seemed more and more likely. No railroad officials were to be found. It was a fair trek back to the station house, and none of us wanted to get off to enquire, for fear the train might leave without us. Knowing well the ways of the authorities and the capriciousness of the system, we all knew there was nothing to do but stay put and wait it out patiently.

The boisterous cries of "Let's get this train rolling!" died away. A group toward the back who had struck up a chorus of Christmas carols, stopped singing. The night grew colder and blankets were brought out. The rain had turned freezing and all the windows were hung with black curtains of ice. Fear grew in the car like crystallized fingers of frost. There was every reason to suppose that the government might change its mind or that this entire affair would turn out to be a cruel hoax.

Toward three o'clock the door of the compartment opened and a tall man stepped in. He wore a gray floor-length cape sparkling with beads of ice, and in concealed arms he cradled an automatic rifle. From his officer's cap with its crest of gold wings, I recognized him as a state soldier. He stood squarely in the open doorway in a position to command the whole car, and I saw that two other soldiers, also with rifles, were directly behind him. They were all very tall, as though of a different race from the passengers, and their bell-shaped, ice-spangled ponchos made them appear even larger.

When the first officer spoke, I was surprised at the quietness of his voice. He had a thick dialect that I found hard to understand, but his message was perfectly clear from the actions that followed. He began to walk through the car, poking the barrel of his weapon into the chest of one child after another. Softly he would enquire who the parents were, then swing the rifle in their direction, and with gentle insistence instruct the child to go and stand by the back door where two more soldiers stood guard. These two, along with the pair at the front, held their rifles level at their shoulders and swept them slowly over the passengers while the first man, stepping over bodies and luggage, passed methodically through the car. It was a very quiet process. Everyone was terrified. No one uttered a word of protest, and each child was unhesitatingly obedient. There was no crying. Their small faces were firmly set, darkly brave, each as serious as any adult's. They looked like little soldiers themselves.

Not until the officer reached me did I suddenly recall the baby. How would the young mother ever bring herself to surrender him? Briefly I entertained a wild fantasy of saving the infant myself, somehow using the leverage of my foreign citizenship to protect him, or perhaps even putting up a struggle. But then I thought of the four automatic weapons trained upon us, and knew how dangerous it would be to make any move whatsoever. Besides, we did not yet have any clear idea of what the soldiers' intent was. The commander spoke so quietly and was so strangely gentle in his actions. Perhaps there was simply such a crush of emigrants heading for the borders that they had somehow to be separated and sent on in stages. Such a possibility seemed most unlikely, but we all held our breath and hoped against hope.

Miraculously, the baby was passed over, and the grim operation of selection continued on into the back of the car. As I glanced up at the young mother, a chill passed through me when I realized that she had concealed the infant beneath her blue cape. The slight bulge at her stomach might have been pregnancy. Her face was serene but very pale. I looked quickly away.

One by one a dozen frail and silent children were gathered at the back of the train. The head soldier had threaded his way down the whole length of the car like some terrible harvester picking off the tenderest shoots. Finally he stood in the midst of the children and issued a curt statement, his voice so hushed now that it was difficult to hear him at all. From what I made out, he said we were all traitors to the state and deserved to be shot on the spot. But instead, only the children would be sacrificed, while the rest of us were allowed to proceed on that basis. If it was freedom we wanted, then freedom we would get. It was our own choice.

And with that he turned and disappeared, herding the children out through the open door so swiftly and efficiently that not a word of protest was raised. Only after came cries of alarm, screams, weeping. Cold terror gripped everyone. Even I shuddered to think what the parents must be feeling. A couple of the men jumped to their feet as if to do something, but the two rifles at the front swung toward them, and the men froze. At any moment we half expected to hear shots from the platform, but none came. Finally all the soldiers left, from both front and back, and stood on the couplings just outside the doors. In the wake of such great loss, the whole weight of the dark icy Christmas sky seemed to cave in upon all of us.

Only minutes later our car began to roll, at first gently, almost imperceptibly, and then with loud creaks and groans of the steel couplings and wheels. Shudders rang like shots down the length of the train. We picked up speed, and soon we were separated from the group of children as completely as if they were on the other side of the world. We could only guess at what their fate might be. The soldier had spoken of "sacrifice." Were they sure to be killed, then? Or was it, rather, that the state wished to retain its children? All we knew was that the opening of the borders appeared now as some diabolical scheme, perhaps intended to single out those citizens who were secretly disloyal to the state, and with one terrible blow both to punish and eliminate them.

And so we rolled on through the night, the soft clacking of the wheels like the sound of the pins and bars of fate falling into place. There was scant talk now. Heads hung low, bodies were motionless, stunned with remorse. A few women quietly wept. I imagined all the parents going over and over how things might have been different, wishing they had stayed at home, reproaching themselves bitterly for having grasped at such foolish dreams of liberty. Condemned to live with the loss of their most precious possession, they would carry forever the wound of their own rashness.

Among those who were not parents, however, I noticed some whose mood seemed mostly one of relief. "At least now," I heard a woman remark, "they ought to let the rest of us go in peace. Surely the sacrifice of all those inno-

cent lives will be enough to buy freedom for the rest of us."
And I must confess I had mixed feelings myself. Naturally I
had been impatient about the delay. I was looking forward
to spending the holidays with my girlfriend and her family.
Even as a student of history, I had no desire for history itself
to interrupt my personal plans. And yet I could not escape
the sense of my lot being thrown in with my fellow passengers. It is something that happens on a journey, even in the
most ordinary of circumstances. On this holiday night,
especially, I could hardly help but be filled with an unusual
compassion for my companions. I knew that a deep scar
would be left in all of our memories for every Christmas
hereafter. I thought again of the young man and woman
nearest to me and of their tiny baby. Would they be able
to smuggle him across the border? The man, I noticed, had
reached up and was holding the girl's hand. Their heads
were bowed, and there was the slightest quivering of their
lips. I realized they must be praying.

It was over an hour before we came to the next station.
There was a screeching of steel as the train ground to a halt.
We were all startled when the compartment door opened
and the same tall soldier entered and stood in the doorway,
his wet rain cape like a great dazzling pair of wings folded
about his body. A single cold shudder ran through all of
us. Hate permeated the air like an incense. This time the
dreaded officer did not make his way through the car but
simply announced that all the male passengers were to rise
in an orderly fashion and leave by the rear door. There was

a stunned silence; for a moment no one moved. But these were people long used to taking orders from the authorities. And now, as before, two pairs of rifles were trained directly upon them. Accordingly, after a moment of embracing, kissing, squeezing hands, in surprisingly quick order the car was completely emptied of all its men.

All, that is, but myself. As the last of the men were filing out, I got to my feet, trembling, and begged a word with the man in charge. I was terrified he would mow me down, no questions asked. But waving my passport and papers in the air, I hurriedly explained that I was a foreign citizen. He made his way toward me, leafed through the documents, and appeared satisfied that they were in order. Without a word, then, he turned away, and he and the other soldiers departed, their great capes swishing like the rain itself. The train started up without delay, and soon we were buried again in motion and in night.

The car seemed monstrously empty now, as empty as if a thousand people had left. The raw shock was, if possible, even bitterer than before. It seemed clear now that there would be no emigration at all. What appeared to be happening was that men, women, and children were being split up, perhaps to be shipped off to separate camps. It occurred to me that I might soon have the train all to myself—a strange irony as I recalled my initial disappointment upon seeing the crowded seats. By this point I would gladly have ridden on top of the baggage rack if only that car could have been filled once again and all of us pass safely over the border together.

But it was not to be. A lump of guilt clotted in my breast as I pondered my sterile immunity to the evil rampant all around me. My good suit of clothes, my new coat, my Ph.D. thesis, my citizenship papers: all appeared suddenly detestable, standing as they did like rolls of barbed wire between me and these persecuted folk. Was there no way I could help them, nor even express solidarity with their plight? Nothing in the world so demanded to be shared as suffering.

All the women now were silent, save one who prattled incessantly in a strident, nerve-wracking voice that put us all more on edge than ever. As there was no longer any shortage of seats, I moved up and took the spot next to the girl in blue. As horrible as was the predicament for all these women, how much worse for a woman with a child! So far the little one had not made a sound the whole night. Through an opening in the blue cape I could just see his face, tiny as a fist, pink as apple petals, calm and radiant as a sunrise. I felt more peaceful myself just being beside him, having him to look at. It struck me that children could be far better at comforting adults than the other way around.

It was sometime after five o'clock when the train slowed down once again. I could see nothing outside. Not a single light gleamed in all the countryside. We appeared to be in the middle of nowhere. When the train came to a full stop there was no sound but the distant hum of its engine and the dry rattle of splinters of freezing rain against the windows. So once again it came as a surprise when the tall soldier appeared at the front of the car, his cape white and shining with its veneer of ice, but no surprise when he said, in a voice more hushed than the night itself, that this was where the women must get off.

As there was no one left now for the women to be separated from, without hesitation they rose from their seats and moved like a company of ghosts down the aisle toward the exit. And as they did so, I felt something that was like a spatter of freezing rain throughout my body, as though the hand of death had brushed against me. For the girl in the blue cape, even as she rose to go, quickly and stealthily as a thief slipped her baby into my lap. She put him right against my stomach and deftly covered him with the open flap of my coat. And then she was gone.

Instantly my stomach twisted into a hard fist of rejection. I wanted to jump up, cry out, make some desperate gesture, but my arms and legs felt shackled to the seat. How I wished that I too could have left the train! But I was paralyzed, rigid with alarm. Everything had happened so quickly that there was no time to think, no time for anything but to watch helplessly as the beautiful girl in the long blue cape passed between the soldiers at the rear of the car and vanished like a vision into the black, raining night.

And suddenly I was all alone. More alone, it seemed, than I had ever been in my life. Alone except for a strange tiny bundle of breathing pink flesh that I concealed involuntarily beneath my coat. The train began to move, and panic swept through me like fire. I wanted to run to the exit and heave the infant out into the ditch. Anything to get rid of it. Who would know? The soldiers were gone now from the platform. The drama of this night, for me, ought to have been all over, but instead things had taken an unimaginable twist.

Still I sat motionless. I dared not even look at the baby. What in the world had possessed the mother to do such a thing? Perhaps she had never wanted a child in the first place? After all, she wasn't even married. But no, hadn't she already gone to extraordinary lengths to protect the baby? For some time I rummaged among wild conjectures, until suddenly I hit upon what seemed almost certain to be the truth.

Knowing that the soldiers would eventually discover her secret and take the baby from her anyway, the mother had opted for the only other course open to her: to entrust him to a stranger, a foreigner, to smuggle him across the border to freedom. So desperate was this woman to keep her child alive that she was even willing to be separated from him herself—forever! I further surmised that she had probably been planning for this possibility ever since the previous fateful stop. How excruciating it must have been for her to contemplate! Had she detected something in me, perhaps in the way I looked at the baby, that caused her to trust me? God knows I had not looked upon him with any real love, but only with that grotesque mask of innocence that adults learn to put on automatically for children. I felt mysteriously that if anyone at all had loved and could be trusted, it was not I, but he, this tiny hidden one.

As there was no more need to leave him concealed, I took him out from under my coat to have a good look at him. He was still fast asleep. He wore a light blue knitted bonnet, from which his face shone out like a rosy patch of dawn sky. Is anything in the world so beautiful as the sleeping face of a baby? Such a contrast it made with the night's evil, with the vast web of peril and tragedy in which I myself was now implicated. I recalled the parents, during their last hour together, clasping hands and praying. Not one to pray myself, now all at once I did find my lips moving in the stillness. The words came haltingly, uneasily, and I suppose they were addressed more to the little baby than to anyone else—as a man will converse even with an animal for reassurance—yet gradually I did experience a sense of greater peace and comfort. I began to feel the child's warmth, and I noticed how astonishingly light he was. The long journey with its tense succession of events fell away into unreality as the baby glowed in my arms like one bright candle lit in the night, making a complete world of all it illumines while turning everything else to darkness.

Right then, I suppose, I resolved to do everything in my power to defend the child, whatever the cost. But even as I formed this proposition I saw my courage failing. Wouldn't it be better for all concerned just to leave him behind in his own native country? What if he should start crying at the crucial moment of passing through customs? Or what if I should be searched? The one thing that had kept me from any personal sense of danger—my passport—suddenly seemed the flimsiest of trifles, a mere worthless scrap of paper. What good was that in a country where families were being wrenched apart and the whole political structure had caved in overnight? The longer I gazed down at this helpless bit of life in my lap, the more acutely was I aware of my own vulnerability, my own utter helplessness. The great wide world held onto me, I realized, even more precariously than I held onto this infant, and with less willingness, still less love. Had anyone ever looked down on me, I wondered, and debated whether to hand me over to the authorities, toss me into a ditch, or else risk their own life to save me?

From then on my plight worsened. It was the hour before dawn and I had had no sleep. My mind played tricks and my nerves quivered with fear and exhaustion. I was intensely lonely, especially amidst the heaps of baggage that weirdly evoked the ghostly presence of the departed passengers. I tried to form some plan of action for getting through customs, but I could not steady my thoughts. Moreover, just as I had feared, the baby woke up and began to cry.

What to do? How to comfort him? I was no mother, and no longer was he a beautiful, sleeping abstraction, the ideal of innocence, but rather a live, squirming person, making demands. I had wanted a nice quiet trip, not this. But he wailed and wailed, enough to wake the dead, almost as if he sensed, even more acutely than I, all that lay ahead.

My panic deepened as clusters of lights and then lighted buildings and streets appeared in the windows, and I realized we must already be entering the border city. The train slowed, and for the longest time crawled at an agonizing pace, clacking ominously like something being bumped along over stone. I knew we would soon arrive at the central station, and desperately I tried everything I could think of to silence the baby's crying. I tried to will myself into composure, hoping that that in itself might comfort him. I even thought, if worse came to worst, I might knock him unconscious. That is how totally resolved I was that he should not fall into the hands of the authorities. But finally, as the station house came in sight, I simply prayed with all my heart that something would silence this confounded kid.

The train stopped. We were under the dark dome of the station. I tucked the child under my coat and did up the buttons. The darkness within did seem to quiet him some. To muffle the sound more, I could pretend I had a bad cough. I would leave my suitcase behind, as too awkward to carry. I was just trying to calm myself, to go over things once more in my mind, when the door of the compartment opened and in walked the tall state soldier, bigger than any man I had ever seen. He strode straight up to me and stood there, towering. I thanked God that the baby was now perfectly quiet. At the same time, I feared I could not possibly rise from my seat with the man watching. I might as well have been nailed down.

"It's time now, sir," said the officer in English. "I'll have to ask you to come with me."

Though his accent was perfect, I thought perhaps I had misunderstood him. I stared.

He added, "You're under arrest, sir. You cannot go any further. You'll have to leave the train now."

"But you can't ..." I protested, almost under my breath. "You can't ... take me. Not now!" I could barely find my voice. "I'm a citizen of ..." I would have reached for my papers but they were inside my buttoned coat.

As before, other soldiers stood at the back of the car, rifles at the ready. The commander angled his head meaningfully toward them and then looked back at me.

"I'm under orders, sir. I think you'd better come."

Motioning me to follow, he walked away down the aisle. I experienced a moment of total dismay and confusion. What could I do? Rising slowly to my feet, I let the baby slide down gently between my legs, still inside the coat, all the way to the floor. I pretended to be gathering luggage together, checking things over.

"You won't be needing your baggage, sir," said the officer.

Glancing down once, quickly, I saw the little bundle of blankets there, almost hidden beneath the seat. He was so good and quiet: I really loved him then. This, I felt, was our only chance. The train might still be searched and unloaded, but it might also pass through unchecked. At least there remained one slim hope that someone other than a soldier might discover him. Like his own mother, I thought it better to leave him to providence than to see him fall into the hands of the authorities.

At least, that is what I told myself. But was the truth, perhaps, that I simply abandoned him?

In any case, I left, following the soldiers out into the early dawn. It was still dark on the platform, but at the end of the long tunnel that arched over the tracks I saw a glimmering patch of eggshell-white sky. We walked towards it. It was Christmas morning, I remembered. It felt good to stretch my legs. The air was cool and fresh. My responsibility was over, and a great weight passed from my shoulders. I had not a care in the world for my own safety.

The soldiers, three of them, escorted me into the station house, marched me down a long hallway with beautiful old marble arches and then underneath a gigantic dome and on into another hallway. Our footsteps rang like gavels. I felt an absurd sense of importance at being given such special treatment. Finally we arrived at a plain wooden doorway and I was shown into a small room, all white, high-ceilinged, with nothing in it but a desk and chair. Two of the soldiers took up positions at the door while the man in charge seated himself at the desk and gestured for me to stand before him. He had removed his hat and rain cape and was dressed in an ordinary blue suit much like my own. I was surprised to see that he was not wearing the state military uniform.

He began by informing me that I had been found guilty of a great number of crimes. He had a thick sheaf of papers which I soon gathered to be a dossier on me. As he listed the charges I grew more and more astounded. They were things that concerned not only my movements in this country but activities at home as well. In fact there were things that went right back to my childhood. Who could this man be who seemed to know everything there was to know about me, even the things that were most unutterable?

I was so bewildered that I fell into a sort of trance while his deep voice droned on and on and my whole life was paraded before me. Wrongs and hurts that I had completely forgotten or suppressed became as vivid as if they were happening again that very moment. It seemed that not a single transgression, not so much as a ghost of a thought, had been overlooked. Everything was meticulously recorded, and all of it was now laid matter-of-factly, officially, before me.

But the strangest thing of all was this: I felt no guilt or condemnation, but only a numbed and amazed relief at having all my shameful secrets finally exposed, spoken aloud by one who did not flinch before their horror. How can I describe this sensation? It was like standing in a waterfall, a torrent that carried all these horrors away. A waterfall of utterly unfathomable amnesty.

Emerging from this reverie (how long it went on I have no idea), I looked in front of me and saw a wall of fire. The desk and its great sheaf of papers were consumed in a blaze so hot and suffocating that I had to shield my face and back away. And there at the door was the tall soldier, beckoning me. I saw that he had donned his rain cape again, but now it was a brilliant white, like a robe made of light itself, and his rifle had become a sword that he carried upright before him. I followed him down another long hallway that eventually brought us outside into a dazzling new morning where the sun shone with a brightness like the sound of thousands of crashing cymbals in the sparkling air. The freezing rain from the previous night had left a glistening patina over everything, so that the whole world looked white and pure and beautiful, full of lustrous cool fire with the perfect clarity of diamonds. I could not restrain a gasp of wonder.

But there was more—for the man in white pointed with his sword, and there stood a brand new train, one not made of iron and steel but of resplendent silver, waiting on tracks of pure gold that stretched away into infinity, and with an engine like a magnificent white horse with a smoke of stars and galaxies steaming from its nostrils. Approaching it, we soon stood beside a coach decorated as though for royalty, trimmed with bunting and adorned with all the colors of the rainbow. As I climbed inside I saw that it was packed with men and women and children who were all dressed in the same brilliant white raiment worn by the tall man. It looked as if they were on their way to some great festival of choirs. The train seemed full of snowy white wings, dancing and shimmering like the clear foaming waters of a mountain stream. Everyone mingled, laughing, singing, celebrating, drinking purple wine from a great crystal bowl.

And once again I thought: *It's Christmas morning!*

Then I had another surprise—for I looked into the beaming faces of my fellow travelers and recognized many of them from the carload of drab emigrants, the men, women, and children who had been with me on the fearful train ride of the night before. Gone now was any hint of the night's tragedy; all was light and joy and every face shone like a star. And happiest of all, I thought, were the young parents of the poor little baby I had been so powerless to help. Though he appeared absent from our company, the young mother showed no signs of grief, and it was she who met me at the door, took my coat, and replaced it with one of the radiant white garments. And so I joined the others and soon was singing and dancing and rejoicing just as if there never had been any dark train ride in the night, nor any threatening soldiers, nor any such thing as danger or separation or sorrow, nor any tiny baby abandoned under the seat of a railway car.

Nevertheless, as complete as our joy was, we could not entirely forget him, the little helpless bundle left behind in that other world. Indeed I was sure he was uppermost in all of our minds, a more vibrant presence than any other on the train. Who could conceive what tortures he would even now be undergoing, encumbered with all the old use-less baggage the rest of us had shed while his train rolled on into some deeper night? For the country to which he was headed, I knew all too well, was not truly free, not free at all compared to this one. Everything in that old life was unmitigated suffering compared to this. And we all understood now that that innocent infant was the one the soldiers had sought to isolate all along, singling him out for a destiny more terrible than any of the rest of us could bear.

Even as I had these thoughts, however, I caught a glimpse through one of the windows of the tall brilliant man in his refulgent robe climbing astride the great white steed at the head of the train. And pointing his sword at the summit of the sky, he whispered a command in a voice so small, so still, it seemed that eternity stopped to listen.

And then our train began to move.

(1984)

Acknowledgments

This book encountered considerable struggle finding its way into print. One publisher after another said that, as much as they liked it, there was no market for short stories—and this in the same year that a Canadian short story writer won the Nobel Prize! Finally, after consigning my manuscript to a drawer, a publisher appeared just three blocks from my home. Many thanks to Tim Anderson of Alphabet Imprints for launching his publishing venture on the sea (pond?) of a book by a Canadian short story writer.

Thanks also to my incomparable editor, Karen Cooper. A few years ago Karen told someone that one of her dreams was to edit a book by Mike Mason. A few months later, without her mentioning a word of that to me, we were working together. My dream has been to have an editor like Karen Cooper.

I'm grateful to Ron Reed for his Foreword, and for

giving some of these stories their first public airing on the stage of Pacific Theatre's annual *Christmas Presence* show. And thanks, as always, to my writers group, faithful friends and critics for a quarter of a century. And a tip of the hat to John Anonby, a former professor of mine at the University of Manitoba, who has made a family tradition of reading aloud "The Anteroom of the Royal Palace" every year since 1989 when it was first published.

I'm especially indebted to all those who have served as the inspiration for these tales, either by telling me their stories or by living them. I've mentioned some of these names in the Preface, but here are a few more: Dan Adair for "Crack;" Alan and Susan DeLong for "In the Stillness of the Night;" Chris and Alix Harvey for "The Christmas Letter;" Miles for "Miles;" W.R. Morrison for "The Ghost of Christmas;" Vern and Lu Peters for "Born With Wings;" Chris Walton for "Yabba-ka-doodles!"; Marilyn Wiebe for help with understanding Alzheimer's; Clancy Wolpert for "Festival of Lights;" Choices Unlimited for "The Three Fools;" and our Home Group at Pacific Community Church for "A Subtle Change." (By the way, I don't mean to imply that any of the stories these people inspired are true; most have been fictionalized.)

I'd like to give special mention to Bob Rose, a particular friend of these stories, who would have loved to hold this book in his hands, had he lived.

Thank you, Heather, my daughter, for being (along with Karen) my first audience, and for your comment on first seeing this collection: "I'm so excited to have this book in the family for generations to come!"

Finally, Karen, my love—what can I say? You get the Noble [sic] Prize for constant encouragement and love.

Previous Publication

Some of the stories in this book have appeared previously, in a different form, in the following publications:

"The Changeling," "The Ghost of Christmas," and "Bound for Glory" were published in *The Mystery of the Word: Parables of Everyday Faith*, Harper & Row, San Francisco, 1988.

"The Anteroom of the Royal Palace" and "Yes, Mr. Church, There Is a Jesus" were published in *The Furniture of Heaven & Other Parables for Pilgrims*, Harold Shaw Publishers, Wheaton, Ill, 1989.

"The Three Fools" and "The Giver" (under the title "A Christmas Story") were published in *The Mystery of Children: What Our Kids Teach Us About Childlike Faith*, WaterBrook Press, Colorado Springs, CO, 2001.

"Yabba-ka-doodles" first appeared in *Christianity Today*, Dec 3, 2001, and was later published in *Champagne for the Soul: Celebrating God's Gift of Joy*, WaterBrook Press, Colorado Springs, CO, 2003.

All the above books are © Mike Mason

For more Mike Mason writing and links, please visit

www.mikemasonbooks.com

CPSIA information can be obtained at www.ICGtesting.com
Printed in the USA
BVOW02s0221120116

432466BV00002B/8/P